GOLDEN ONE

AN OMEGA FILES ADVENTURE

RICK CHESLER

PROLOGUE

October 29, 1618
London, England

The end had finally come for Sir Walter Raleigh. At the age of sixty-five, after a rich and full career served in the military, politics and exploration, it had all come down to this.

He knelt on the unforgiving wooden planks of a raised platform in the Old Palace Yard at the Palace of Westminster, the site of many executions before his, and of many after. In front of him, a stout wooden block was fixed to the platform. Next to that towered above him a man wielding a formidable axe—robust metal blade, long wooden handle. All around the platform stood a gathering of onlookers, some supportive of Raleigh despite the state's accusations against him, others less so.

Hands bound behind his back, Raleigh looked up at his executioner and said, "Let us dispatch. At this hour my ague comes upon me. I would not have my enemies think I quaked from fear."

Wordlessly, the executioner held out a black piece of cloth so that Raleigh could see it, before pulling it taut with both hands and leaning in towards his face.

"No blindfold," the explorer said. "This ax, it is a sharp medicine, but it is a physician for all diseases and miseries." Raleigh's eyes grew distant as he reminisced on exotic oceans and faraway lands, on sailors perishing in the dingy holds of ships due to scurvy, loyal men bleeding out from wounds of war while conquering and vanquishing new lands.

The crowd huddled closer around the platform, sensing the event was at hand. The executioner pocketed the blindfold and straightened. Raising his voice, he commanded, "Your last words, Sir Raleigh!"

Raleigh felt a swelling of pride at the use of his formal title, bestowed upon him by the former Queen of the government that was now putting him to death. He spoke his prepared and rehearsed statement before his emotions could get the better of him. "For a long time my course was a course of vanity. I have been a seafaring man, a soldier, and a courtier, and in the temptation of the least of these there is enough to overthrow a good mind and a good man. So I take my leave of you all, making my peace with God. I have a long journey to make and must bid the company farewell."

The executioner's stern gaze never left Raleigh's kneeling form as he waited a moment to see if he had anything to add. In a low voice, much lower than the words he had just spoken, Raleigh said to the man whose job it was to kill him, "Make it quick, one solid blow. I will even give you a gift if you promise to do it swiftly and clean."

Raleigh had not only heard, but actually seen with his own eyes the nightmarish spectacle of beheadings gone wrong—some said deliberately so, whether for reasons of revenge or for sheer entertainment value—where blunt instruments were used on purpose, where blows were intentionally weak or perhaps deliberately misplaced so as to result in agonizing gore rather than instant death. These were simply chalked up to an accident, a physical miscalculation on the part of the executioner who would be sure to try harder the next time. Wanting to suffer no such indignities or anguish, Raleigh made pleading eye contact with the man who would shortly take his life. Around them the crowd still gathered, and a few cried out for the axman to get on with it.

Raleigh looked out on the people in the crowd while he waited for the executioner to respond. He scanned the faces of the few women in attendance. One of them reminded him of the late Queen Elizabeth I, and he flashed on his knighting ceremony, presided over by Her Majesty more than a quarter-century earlier for his service in the battles against Ireland. How far he had fallen, he reflected while kneeling in front of the chopping block. Where had it all gone so wrong? He knew the answer lay in the New World, somewhere between the island of Trinidad and what would centuries later become a country called Colombia.

In his travels he had found it necessary to leave one of his ships behind, entrusting its captain to carry out Raleigh's orders. One of these orders, issued to him directly from the English Crown, was not to engage in conflict with the Spanish, who were also exploring and seeking to colonize the New World. Raleigh's charge did not obey these orders, instead attacking a Spanish expedition competing for resources and treasures, a move that resulted in casualties on both sides and the real threat of war with England. Raleigh was found guilty of treason, and without Queen Elizabeth to protect him, he had ended up here, quite literally on the chopping block.

All of his exploring hadn't been for nothing, however. Although he had heard the rumors, the whispered tales, and even seen the supposed maps, Raleigh early in his career had thought the legend of *El Dorado*—the famed city of gold, where the buildings, and even the roads, were constructed entirely out of gold—to be either wishful thinking on the part of explorers, or else a deliberately invented fable meant to keep rivals away from the real treasures. Indeed, the known gold and silver mines of the southern New World were the reason for the state-sponsored expeditions. These treasures were real and palpable, metal ores mined from the Earth by the forced labor of godless Indians with no greater purpose in life. And yet, throughout his travels in the New World, particularly in the densest of jungles rife with the greenest of Hells, he could not deny the clues and intimations that trickled into his intellect like a steady drip of the purest water falling from the roof of a subterranean cave.

And now Raleigh's only card left to play was to offer up the location of what he knew to be the greatest treasure in the world—New World or Old-

- in return for a quick and merciful death.

"And what sort of gift might you have for me?" The executioner leaned into Raleigh, speaking softly while holding eye contact.

It took the explorer a moment to realize he had taken the bait before he was able to tear himself from his remembrances. "In my cell, you will find my tobacco pouch under a loose brick in the leftmost corner when facing the window."

The executioner guffawed. "Tobacco? If that is the best you can do...."

"Beneath the tobacco in the pouch, you will find something of great value, incalculable worth," Raleigh persisted. "I speak only truth." Raleigh made sure that his gaze was as earnest as he could make it.

The executioner backed away from the condemned man and straightened. "Very well. I had every intention of killing you swiftly anyhow, and I will now do my utmost to ensure the deed is carried out."

Raleigh braced himself for his final moment as the executioner straightened, backed up a couple of steps, and hefted the tool of his trade. He heard the man's voice behind him, deliberately loud enough to be heard by those in attendance, who had hushed upon seeing the axe raised.

"The last words of the condemned have been spoken. The sentence of death will now be carried out."

Raleigh placed his head on the chopping block and closed his eyes for the last time as he spoke his actual last words.

"Strike, man, strike!"

The executioner gave his axe a test swing, knowing Raleigh couldn't see it, but the crowd roared just the same, causing Raleigh to press his head on the block even harder. Then the axman adjusted his stance slightly and made brief eye contact with Raleigh's wife, whose pleading eyes begged him to make it quick, make it clean. He disliked this part of the job the most— loved ones of the soon-to-be-deceased who must witness their family members' demise, but it was all in a day's work. He swung for real, a perfect motion, the metal blade connecting smoothly with the flesh and bone of the explorer's neck.

The sound of what for most people would be a sickening thud—that of the head of the deceased striking the wooden platform as it tumbled from the chopping block—elicited no such reaction from the executioner. To him, it represented only the successful conclusion of yet another sworn duty. To those in the audience, along with the ghastly sight of the decapitated head rolling briefly before coming to a stop, it triggered a brief frenzy of raucous applause, jeering and celebratory commotion.

Raleigh's wife rushed forward and scooped her dead husband's head into a velvet bag, denying onlookers their grisly thrill.

The executioner stepped down from the platform, carrying his trusty axe, walking briskly toward the jail. As usual, he very briefly acknowledged those who congratulated him on a job well done with a curt nod, but did not linger. He reached the old brick façade and entered through an arched doorway with an iron gate that was swung open for him by a guard, then immediately shut behind him.

He strode purposely toward where he knew the late Sir Raleigh's cell to be. Normally he would have to inquire as to a prisoner's precise holding quarters, but in this case Raleigh was somewhat of a nobleman, a statesman gone bad, a celebrity with notoriety, and thus his cell location was familiar enough. The executioner nodded to another guard and turned down a dim hallway. Prisoners called out to him as he passed their cells, some heckling him nonsensically, others asking for help or information. He ignored them all equally and continued down the hall to the last cell on the left.

The door was open since the space was currently unoccupied. The executioner paused in the doorway, glancing around the cell to make certain no sort of booby-trap awaited him. Seeing or sensing nothing but the utilitarian, Draconian space it was designed to be, he entered the cell.

Recalling Raleigh's private words, he moved to the leftmost corner while facing the window. Eyeing the corner near the floor, none of the bricks there looked loose to him, but he also knew that prisoners with lots of time on their hands were masters of deception. The executioner knelt with a heavy exhalation, convinced he was wasting his time on the word of a desperate man. Nevertheless, he had upheld his end of the bargain, and he had to admit that his curiosity was piqued, given Raleigh's exalted reputation as an explorer and treasure hunter.

The executioner's fingers explored the corner bricks, seeking purchase around their edges. Shortly he felt a brick wobble ever so slightly as he pressed on it. He shifted his weight and then tried moving it again, and this time he was able to jar it free. He pulled the squarish brick away and set it aside, eyeing the cavity in the floor. A small leather pouch lay at its bottom. He picked it up, noting it was drawn to a close at its top with a cord of leather. He shook the pouch, hoping to hear the jingle of gold coins or some sort of metal, but whatever was inside made no noise. Probably is just tobacco, he thought, as his fingers loosened the drawstring.

Peering into the pouch, he saw a bunch of tobacco leaves. Shaking his head, he removed them, noting they were of high quality but dropping them on the floor nonetheless. At the bottom of the pouch he could see a piece of folded paper. He plucked it from the bag and carefully unfolded it, noting the yellowed wear and creases.

The executioner's brow furrowed as he took in the numerous lines and drawings on what was obviously some kind of map. The sound of footsteps approaching from down the hall toward Raleigh's cell interrupted his examination of the map, but not before he read two words at its center: *El Dorado.*

Hurriedly, the executioner folded up the map and put it back into the pouch, which he pocketed before exiting the cell.

CHAPTER 1

Carter Hunt was not surprised to see the auction house at half capacity as the auctioneer banged his gavel to signify another item sold. A treasure trove of pre-Columbian artifacts was up for sale this afternoon, and though their cultural and archaeological value was for all intents and purposes priceless, the draw was simply not there compared to say, certain pop-culture items. Carter knew that a pair of shoes worn by a famous actress in a movie would easily fetch as much if not more than the jade figurine that had just been sold to the highest bidder, an anonymous buyer participating remotely from Singapore.

But Hunt was here because he did know the true worth of these items. For him they represented nothing less than humanity itself, and the fact that he felt they belonged to *all* of humanity rather than some rich collector was his reason for being here today. He scanned the crowd from his position near the back of the auction hall. Like most of the other attendees, he was seated in one of the chairs arranged in rows, a smartphone in his hand, wearing an expensive designer suit. He looked like he was one of those rich collectors, but in fact he was anything but.

Now two years out of the military, where he had served as a Naval officer for ten years after earning a degree in History, Hunt ran his own business specializing in the recovery and preservation of cultural and archaeological treasures. He had named his company OMEGA, an unofficial acronym he had coined after thinking about the disillusionment he had experienced while serving in the war-torn middle east. He had witnessed the looting, destruction, and theft of hundreds of irreplaceable artifacts from Iraqi museums and cultural centers, and it angered him to no end that ultimately it was the Iraqi people who suffered the most. He had thought about it until the letters of the word OMEGA swirled in his mind's eye into words, and in time, the words into a phrase: Objects Meant to Endure for Generations to Admire. With the acronym of his new venture succinctly encapsulating his views on the subject of recovered artifacts and treasures, and with the very word Omega meaning a unit of resistance, Hunt had enlisted the help of his former Naval buddy and long-time friend, Jayden Takada. Although not with him today, his OMEGA associate was aware of Hunt's trip to New York and on standby should Hunt be able to acquire the object he sought.

Now, as the auctioneer returned to the podium and banged his gavel, Hunt was about to find out if he would be able to.

"Ladies and gentlemen," the auctioneer, a lanky bald man wearing a tuxedo and rimmed spectacles began, "presenting our next item up for bidding...." He extended an arm to the left, where an employee lifted a black sheet from a cart. A spotlight in the ceiling illuminated the object on the cart, which immediately elicited gasps from the audience.

"Presenting an authentic gold piece recovered from Colombia, dated by experts to have been made somewhere between 600 – 1600 C.E., or A.D. if you prefer. Constructed from an alloy analyzed to be gold-silver and copper, this piece, while authentic in its own right, has been described by archaeologists as being an exact replica—probably an independently created piece—of a known artwork from the same period and locale known as the Muisca Raft, named after the Muisca tribe, which was one of the big four early civilizations in Central and South America: Aztec, Maya, Inca, and

Muisca. The artifact is currently under the esteemed auspices of the Gold Museum in Bogota. This one, however, could be yours. I reiterate that the materials, chemical composition and construction are identical to the museum piece, and that this piece was recovered from a cave in Colombia, the same country where the other piece was also found."

The auctioneer paused to let this sink in while gazing lovingly at the golden statuette, which continued to gleam in the bright artificial light. The exquisite work of art, replete with detail and style, depicted a man wearing an elaborate headdress and tribal garb standing on a raft. Around him stood a number of smaller tribal figures, facing the same direction. The entire structure was roughly oval shaped, and about ten by five inches.

"Behold, the Golden Raft of El Dorado," the auctioneer continued. "This masterful work of the highest level of metal craftsmanship is a moving portrayal of what scholars generally believe to be a religious ceremony. The raft was rowed out onto a lake, some say Lake Guatavita in modern-day Colombia, where the central figure, the Chief of the Muisca people, was showered with gold dust from head to toe. Thusly glittering, the chief would commence to jump into the lake along with a shower of gold and emeralds thrown in by his assistants as an offering to the Gods. "

Carter Hunt nodded silently as he listened to the auctioneer and gawked at the artifact. From this distance he still couldn't be sure himself it was genuine—even high society auction houses fell victim to fakes now and again—but his hunch was that it was the real thing. He continued to watch with interest as the auction played out.

"This is *your* chance, ladies and gentlemen, to own a piece of some of the most exciting history in the last 2500 years! Imagine holding this metallurgical masterpiece in your hands and knowing that perhaps it once resided in the legendary city of El Dorado! The bidding will open now at one hundred thousand U.S. dollars…"

The auctioneer banged his hammer to signify that the auction was now underway, and his role transitioned to that of bid caller. He pointed to a participant in the audience who had raised a sign with a number on it. "One hundred and twenty-five thousand," the bidder said confidently.

Another sign was held up and the bid caller spat again. "One hundred and fifty thousand for this inspiring Muisca Raft golden figure. Do I hear one-seventy-five?"

Hunt tested the weight of his own sign, as if to make certain he would be able to raise it swiftly when he needed to. He was here to bid on this very object, the highlight of the pre-Columbian treasure trove that had been put up for auction due to an unusual set of circumstances. Hunt's hand wavered for a moment, and he caught a man next to him eyeing his sign. But Hunt did not bid. The man next to him raised his own sign and said, "One hundred and seventy-five thousand."

The bidding continued fast and furious for the next several minutes with multiple bidders escalating the cost of the golden work of art while Carter Hunt kept his bidding sign in his lap. He cautioned himself against having an itchy trigger finger. He didn't need to bid up the price of the artifact any higher than it was going to go already. For many of these people, Hunt knew, money was no object. The only thing keeping the artwork out of a runaway price range whatsoever was that its history was relatively unknown, and that it was made by an unknown artist or artists. But the El Dorado tie-in was seductive, and he had no doubt that was the primary force driving the bidding now, as the auctioneer's gavel slammed down yet again.

"Five hundred thousand, we have half a million dollars for the Muisca Raft! Ladies and gentlemen, do I hear five fifty, five fifty?..."

Hunt shook his head at the madness of it all, and the woman seated next to him gave him a knowing look, one that said, *Too rich for my blood also*, as she lowered her sign. But that wasn't the source of Hunt's disbelief. He was reflecting on the circumstances that had created this auction in the first place, that had made this cache of artifacts available for the public to purchase. He thought back to the news headlines a few months earlier, when Tyler Harding, the founder of an alternative digital currency, had suddenly died in a hang-gliding accident. Besides his company, he left behind an encrypted laptop with billions in investor funds locked away inside.

Despite expert attempts at decryption, and even a ten million dollar cash reward for anyone who could unlock it, the laptop could not be accessed and so as a way to mitigate investor losses, the e-currency magnate's estate was auctioned off, including his extensive art collections, a small subset of which were the South American artworks on the block today. When Hunt's attention had been alerted to the fact that some of those items were of archaeological value, especially the Muisca raft, he had arranged to be at the auction.

"…at nine hundred thousand dollars." A small collective gasp erupted in the audience and Hunt's attention was drawn back to the auction. "Do I hear 950, that's nine hundred and fifty thousand?" This time there was a prolonged silence as the bidders realized they were near the top of the range for this item, as enticing as it was. "Going once…." The auctioneer began. And then another sign went up, from an African American man seated in the front row.

"One million dollars!" the auctioneer exclaimed. "Bidding has now reached one million U.S. dollars for the exquisite golden Muisca raft. Bidding increments will now shift to one hundred thousand dollars. Do we have one point one million, that is one million one hundred thousand dollars?"

To Hunt, although the air conditioner cooled the room more than adequately, the space suddenly seemed stuffy.

Hunt raised his sign. "One point one million," the auctioneer stated.

Inwardly, Hunt cringed at the enormous sum of money he had just pledged to spend on a small piece of art. But he did have the funds, thanks to a multi-million dollar inheritance left to him by his grandfather. It was the reason he had been able to leave the service early and start his own business recovering artifacts. The exact sum of money Hunt had was the subject of speculation among his friends, but he would never disclose the actual amount. "Enough to do some good for the world," is all he would say. He was confident that he was doing the right thing in acquiring this piece and then donating it to a museum for the world to appreciate. But would one-point-one million be enough? He knew that good intentions or not, he really could not afford to go much higher than that.

The auctioneer straightened at his podium, gavel paused. "Do I hear one-point-two million?" His question was greeted with silence. "One-point-two million? Going once....."

The African-American man in the front row thrust his sign high. "One-point two!"

All heads in the room turned. The bid-caller didn't miss a beat. "One-point two million U.S. dollars for the golden Muisca tribe artwork. Do we have one million, three hundred thousand, one-point three million?"

The black man turned around in his chair and made eye contact with Carter Hunt, who slowly and deliberately put his sign hand into the air. "One million, three hundred thousand," he said, voice flat.

"The bidding now stands at one-point-three million for the Muisca Raft. Do we have an offer of one-point four million dollars?" The auctioneer's gaze travelled around the room, gauging the interest level of the audience. Most of those in attendance had lay their signs in their laps. The bid-caller eyed the black man in the front row, who lowered his bid sign and shook his head.

"Going once...going twice.....sold, for one-point three million U.S. dollars!" The runner-up bidder turned around to glare ever-so-subtly at Hunt, who ignored the eye contact. He shook hands with the attendees on either side of him who congratulated him on his win, and then rose from his chair. He walked to the podium, accepting the congratulations, and "Enjoy the piece!" from others, though he was secretly disgusted with it all.

"I plan to donate the piece to a museum," he said as he reached the auctioneer. The cart with the Muisca Raft was wheeled out by an auction employee through a side door, and then Hunt was ushered through the same door by the auctioneer and two armed security guards.

Hunt wired the funds for his win to the auction company, and when the receipt of funds was confirmed, he was told he was free to take the artifact. "If you like we can hold it for you securely in our safe room until you depart your hotel, sir," the auctioneer informed him. But Hunt shook his head.

"No thank you, I'll be taking the piece with me now. An escort to my vehicle would be appreciated."

"Of course, sir. And your vehicle is parked with our valet service?" Hunt informed them that it was.

"Very well, we will make the arrangements to have your vehicle brought to the entrance, and you will be escorted by our security team as soon as it is ready. It will be just a few minutes. Until then, please feel free to mingle in the auction room or to enjoy a complimentary beverage."

Hunt nodded and walked over to the Muisca Raft, where an auction employee wearing rubber gloves carefully placed it into a small padded crate. No sooner was he done packing the item than another auction employee came over to inform Hunt that his wire had been received and cleared. "Thank you for your business, sir, and enjoy!"

Hunt thanked the man and took the crate handed to him from the employee. He moved to a small couch that was set up against a wall and sat there to wait. He opened the lid on the crate and peered in on the lustrous piece as he considered how he had come to possess it. For such an astounding relic, he knew remarkably little about exactly how it had been obtained. Whomever had originally found it decided to sell it to the cryptocurrency magnate, who had it in his possession for no more than six years, by Hunt's estimation, since his currency and online transaction company did not exist before that. Probably four to five years, Hunt guessed, since that's when the company went public with the IPO that made him a multi-millionaire overnight.

He had researched Tyler Harding prior to coming to the auction, but still knew little about him, as he was a notoriously private person, right up to his untimely death. What he did know, however, troubled him, since he had a penchant for collecting rare antiquities, artifacts, and relics. And there was a decent chance some of those relics, Hunt knew, came from the black market. And if they came from the black market, there existed a better than average possibility that Harding had done business with none other than Hunt's archnemesis, Treasure, Inc., a multinational shell company specializing in unauthorized acquisition of artifacts, treasures, and ruins, usually with cultural association and value. Treasure, Inc. had notoriously sold a stolen chunk of the Berlin Wall for a princely sum, although most of their trade objects skewed significantly older, and often more expensive.

Hunt put a hand on the golden artwork in the crate, connecting with it while he pondered its significance. All this assumed the Muisca Raft was in fact genuine, Hunt thought, gazing into the crate. He would, of course, have to have it authenticated by one of his trusted labs, the auction authentication notwithstanding. His own labs could tell him even more about the piece's origins. But assuming it was legitimate, it made an even stronger case for the legend of El Dorado, the same one that the auctioneer had given a spiel on during his sales pitch. He allowed himself to consider for a moment whether the rumors could have any truth to them. There were still parts of the South American rain forest that were unexplored, after all….

"Mr. Hunt. Sir?"

Hunt was torn from his contemplation by an auction house employee approaching him, and two burly men in suits trailing a couple of steps behind.

"Your security detail is now ready to escort you to your vehicle."

He looked up from the crate and nodded. Then he glanced back down at the golden figure as he put the lid on it. The chieftain's golden head gleamed under the fluorescent lights and he caught one of his guards eyeballing it. The chieftain commanded attention, Hunt thought. He was, in fact, the Golden One. Hunt knew that for all the expeditions in search of the famed golden city, one of the reasons it had never been found was because, he thought, *El Dorado is a person, not a place.*

Hunt stood up with the crate under his arm, signifying he was ready to go.

"Follow me, Mr. Hunt." The slightly taller of the two guards said. "My associate is going to walk behind you until we reach your vehicle. I'll lead the way, and he's got your back. Okay?"

"Got it." Hunt nodded and the lead guard wasted no time. "This way then. Through this door, then we'll take the elevator to the valet parking garage."

"After you..." Hunt fell into step behind the lead guard. He was pretty sure he could see the outline of a pistol concealed beneath his suit jacket. Behind him, he sensed the presence of the second guard falling into place. Although he was certain part of it was showy pomp and circumstance meant to fuel the spectacle of a high net worth affair, Hunt had to admit that he was glad for the security. Walking around alone in New York City with a highly publicized purchase worth over a million dollars wasn't the safest thing. He stepped into the empty elevator with the two guards, and they rode it down several floors to the garage.

Hunt was pleased to see his vehicle, a brand new Chevy Camaro he had rented upon flying into the city from his hometown near Los Angeles, idling in front of the elevator as soon as the doors opened. The driver side door was being held open by the valet. The two guards took up position at the front and back of the car while Hunt placed the crate on the passenger seat and slid behind the wheel.

The valet pointed to the garage exit and Hunt thanked him and his security detail before putting the Camaro into gear. Hunt drove up to the gate house, where the arm lifted immediately. He drove through and up a steep incline out to a narrow but busy New York City street. It was customary in NYC to take a cab or Uber, but Hunt knew there was a chance he'd be leaving with a valuable item and so he had made sure to have his own private transportation. He was glad for it now as he drove onto the street, eyed the crate on the seat next to him and hit the switches to roll up his windows and lock his doors.

He considered his next steps as he negotiated the heavy traffic down the one-way street. He hadn't anticipated spending this much money on an artifact. He wasn't sure if he should cancel his reservation to fly home and drive the rental car back to California, or if he should try to carry it on the plane and simply hold it in his lap and never let it out of his sight. Both options had pitfalls. Or he could entrust it to a commercial carrier and fully insure it. He would likely need to ship it anyway when it came time to have it authenticated and tested by the labs he used. He wanted every clue he could get that might tell him exactly where this artifact came from. He had researched it on the Internet to the extent he could and had run into a dead end. Right now, he just needed to decide how to get it safely back home.

He was still mulling that over as he made the left turn onto a wider, busier two-lane street. A white sedan also made the same turn he did, three cars back. Something about the precision and urgency of the driving caught Hunt's attention. Telling himself he probably just had a case of the heebie-jeebies, the treasure hunter took the next right even though he needed to go straight. The light was green and he didn't need to wait. As he straightened out onto the new road, about the same size and traffic level as the last, he glanced in his rear view mirror. Sure enough, the white sedan pulled into view, now only two cars behind him.

CHAPTER 2

Carter Hunt stepped on the accelerator, eking out as much additional speed as possible on the packed New York City street. *Someone's after the Musica raft already.* He thought about who it could be as he weaved through traffic in a responsible manner, not wanting to make an out-and-out break for it yet. It could still be a coincidence, or if not, his pursuers could change their mind, deciding a car chase was not worth it.

Did high-priced auctions attract brazen thieves who lurked just outside the doors waiting to accost those who leave with their valuable won items? He doubted it was a regular occurrence. Security at the event he had just attended was good, with both visible and behind-the-scenes measures in place. Glancing at the crate on the passenger seat, he thought it more likely it was someone who understood the archaeological relevance of what it was he now had. Someone with close knowledge of the specific auction itself. Likely someone who was in the very auction room with him today, he thought as he glanced in his rear-view mirror in time to see the white sedan pull to within two car lengths behind him.

A yellow taxi pulled right in front of Hunt and he had to slam on the brakes. Then the cab switched lanes and pulled ahead, avoiding collision, but at the same time the tailing sedan crept up, leaving only one car between them. Their driving skills are good, Hunt noted. He glanced in his mirror and thought he saw two people in the front of the white sedan. This concerned him because a professional strongarm outfit would typically not send one man alone to commit a theft. So it appeared it was now two-against-one.

Hunt saw an opening ahead on the right and switched lanes. He noted the sidewalks were crowded with window shoppers and open air cafes. A normal city scene, with innumerable dramas besides his no doubt playing out at this very moment. But he was focused only on the red light up ahead, and the green sign next to it reading, CENTRAL PARK, with an arrow pointing right. He took advantage of a driver creeping into the crosswalk before coming to a complete stop at the red to change lanes, now second in line to make the right.

The beginnings of a vague plan had formed in his head as he waited to turn, cursing the fact that NYC was one of the few cities where a right turn on red was illegal. He would have turned anyway, watching the white car jockey for position one lane over and now only one car back, but the driver in front of Hunt wasn't turning so neither could he.

The light turned green and Hunt was annoyed to see the driver of the car ahead of him still not moving as he chatted with an attractive female pedestrian who was in the process of crossing late. Horns began to blare behind him. *Believe me, I don't want to lag anymore than the rest of you.* Then he caught sight in his rearview of the white sedan's passenger-side door opening, a black-shoed foot and slacks-clad leg extending from it.

Hunt leaned on his own horn as the driver of in front of him turned around to offer an obscene gesture. He stopped in mid-motion when he saw a man in a suit jogging toward Hunt's car. Thinking he was an irate motorist looking for a confrontation, the driver ahead of Hunt jammed on the accelerator and ripped through his right turn, leaving Hunt in the clear. He, too, pressed on the gas while turning right just as the man on foot reached his door. He saw a hand swipe for the handle and pulled, but Hunt's precaution in locking it now paid off. The accoster was forced to let go of the handle as the Camaro accelerated into the right turn under Hunt's smooth driving.

As soon as he completed the turn, Hunt checked his mirror in time to see the door slam shut on the white sedan. The last he saw of them before he pulled out of sight on the new road, they were beginning to change lanes, no doubt to make the same right turn. Hunt caught up to the cars ahead of him as quickly as he could without being reckless. He had bought some time, but he had no illusions that it would be a lot. His eye caught another green sign up ahead and he locked his gaze to it: Central Park, left. Hunt merged into the left lane and again sped up until he reached the traffic ahead.

Looking left to the new avenue he was a bout to turn onto, Central Park West, Hunt saw that it was congested, adjacent to the famous park. Deciding it was worth it, he pulled into the left lane to wait. He waited through one green light cycle, then another, before being the first car at the light. On the left side of the street he spotted a billboard *for e-Bucks,* Tyler Harding's company, now in arrears due to Harding's untimely death.

Hunt glanced in his mirror as he waited for the last light he needed to make the turn. Just as the light switched green, he saw a white sedan roll into view almost a block behind. He accelerated through the turn, mindful that he would need to hit the brakes soon, but hoping he might make the turn without being spotted.

The new thoroughfare bordered the park on the right side. Hunt was not familiar with the city, and had never been to the park at all, so he had no idea what part of it he had reached. But he had heard it was large, with many different sections. To his right there was a thin stand of trees with a meadow beyond where a few people had picnic blankets spread out. Hunt kept pace with the traffic, not wanting to slow down for the sake of a good glimpse of the park. But as he watched the white sedan speed up in his mirror, he knew he would not be able to shake them by car. They probably knew the city much better than he did. The car had New York plates, after all, and did not appear to be a rental like his. He continued driving in the lane bordering the park while the white sedan gained on him one lane over.

Scanning the road ahead, Hunt saw an opportunity when the line of traffic slowed in advance of a red light with a heavily populated crosswalk.

Hunt came to a stop in back of another car waiting for the light and put the Camaro in park. He scooted over to the passenger seat, picked up the crate and opened the passenger-side door. He exited the vehicle, kicking the door closed behind him and fast-walked onto the sidewalk, where he did his best to insert himself into the moderate pedestrian traffic. Hunt dared not turn around to check the progress of his pursuers. Instead, he surveyed his surroundings. Ahead, the city sidewalk bordered the park for as long as he could see, semi-crowded with pedestrians. To his left was the busy street, and to his right, the sprawl of Central Park itself.

He eyed the park interior while mingling with the walking throngs. He passed a wide open grassy field, but farther on he could see a thin stand of trees. He continued moving with the crowd while monitoring the street nonchalantly for the white sedan. So far no sign of it, meaning it had already passed or was still somewhere behind. Hunt guessed the latter. When they spotted his Camaro parked in the street, they would no doubt stop to check it out and that should buy him some time. He reached the trees and abruptly turned out of a group of Japanese tourists. He walked into the wooded area.

So this is Central Park, Hunt thought as he skirted a clump of shrubs in order to stand behind a grouping of tall trees that screened him from the street. Looking around, he noted he was alone in the stand of trees, although still partially visible from the sidewalk and street. He knew very little about its layout other than it was a large rectangular shape in the middle of Manhattan Island. Deciding to venture further into the park, Hunt moved from the sidewalk through the trees.

Hunt's preconceived notions of the urban park would have led him to picture beer bottles, soda cans and other flotsam littered about, but this part of it, at least, was free of trash. It looked like any other northeast woodland area he'd been in. He even knew that the park featured varied terrain, including marshland which was why it was deemed unsuitable for development in the mid-1800s. At the same time, he was aware it was all a carefully planned and maintained space, one that appealed to many different types of people—businessmen making deals, school nature walks, family picnics, teens partying, drug addicts shooting up—it was all here at one time or another, if not at the same time. And now, as he slinked to the far edge of the treed area, it was host to a chase after a pre-Columbian artifact. *New York*, Hunt thought: *If you can make it here, you can make it anywhere.*

Hunt stood on the edge of the tree line and stared out at the green, sloping expanse in front of him. He had some cover between him and the street now, but before him lie only open space, and with only a few people occupying it, laying down reading a book, or sitting and eating. A peaceful, ordinary scene, to be sure, but one which Hunt's very presence made anything but. He decided to wait out his pursuers here in the wooded area rather than risk being viewed in the open space.

While he waited, he took steps to minimize being recognized. The suit and tie had to go. He stripped the jacket and dropped it on the ground before covering it with a pile of fallen leaves. He rolled his long-sleeved shirt sleeves up to make it look like he wore a short-sleeved shirt, and unbuttoned it down the front. He had just finished tying the necktie around his head in a Rambo-style headband when he heard voices somewhere in the woods behind him.

Hunt stooped and picked up the crate with the artifact, then froze. He heard a twig or branch snap, but still saw nothing. The air was still with zero wind to disturb it. Was someone coming? He didn't want to panic and accost an innocent bystander, but at the same time, if he was forced into a physical confrontation with his pursuers who outnumbered him two to one, he wanted first strike. He also began to doubt his decision to hide in the woods as he hefted the crate containing his prize that was worth over a million dollars. Maybe he was better off in plain view of the city crowds. With this in mind, Hunt started to move out toward the edge of the woods, where he could see more open green space.

But as he started to walk, the noise behind him intensified. Hunt turned around as he walked for a moment too long and snagged his right foot on a tree root, losing his leather loafer. He heard the noise behind him stop, as he also paused his movement. He didn't want to turn back, knowing that whoever it was back there had heard his stumble, and was listening for him now. But he needed the shoe to navigate the terrain, manicured and planned as it was, and to make good time.

Onward. The naval historian moved to his shoe and pulled it back on his foot before taking off running. He avoided thick brambles but tried to keep some tree cover behind him as he made his way toward the open green area. As he broke from a careful walk to what he hoped would pass for a stealthy jog, a large bird of prey he recognized as a red-tailed hawk swooped onto the ground a few yards ahead, grasped a squirrel in its talons and took to the air again. He sympathized with the squirrel even though he accepted that acts of predation were a part of nature. He, too, was being hunted. The footfalls behind him grew heavier as they broke into a run, and he could no longer deny that he was their prey.

The damned crate was slowing him down. Hunt hunkered into a thick stand of ground-level vegetation bordering a cluster of tall trees. Once concealed, with heavy breath he opened the crate and removed the golden Muisca raft, dropping the crate on the ground. He tucked the raft carefully under his shirt, cradling it in his right elbow. He listened for sounds of those chasing him, but heard nothing. No doubt they were listening for him, too. Then he heard the snap of a twig, the shuffling of feet on dry leaves. He ducked out of his place of concealment and started to move again.

The edge of the woods lay a few yards ahead. He could see families lying on the grass beyond. Hunt began to run. He feinted left, even tossing a handful of sticks and rocks in that direction as a simplistic attempt to throw off his attackers' sense of his whereabouts. The ploy worked, at least momentarily. Turning around, he stole a glimpse of the black man from the auction house, the one who had been the runner-up bidder for the Muisca raft, jamming a foot down into the ground, pivoting toward the rockfall and then sprinting in that direction.

Hunt took off toward the grass at a full run. He was counting on the fact that the would-be thieves wouldn't be so brazen in public view of the sun bathers and picnickers that dotted the lawn. One never knew, he was all too aware, but being waylaid alone in the woods wasn't very comforting either. Hunt hit the gently sloping lawn at a sprint, made awkward by having to hold the Muisca raft under his jacket while he ran. Heads turned to gawk at him as he bolted through the tranquil scene, but he didn't slow. In fact, he sped up slightly while shouting, "Be careful everyone, dangerous men after me!" He was pleased to see a woman pull out her cell-phone in response.

Ahead, the grassy area transitioned into another wooded environ to the right, and what looked like a trailhead to the left. Central Park is wilder than I thought, Hunt couldn't help but think as he scanned right, left, then right again before moving on to the trailhead. Any illusions he might have harbored that his pursuers were merely gentlemen of means who perhaps had too many martinis at lunch and became sore losers when they lost the auction were quickly dispelled when the first gunshot rang out. Hunt saw a thin tree branch fall to the ground about fifteen feet in font of him. *High and right*, he thought in a nano-second. He had more than enough experience to know not to give the shooter time to correct his aim.

He took off running down the trailhead, barely catching the sign reading, *To Hallett Nature Preserve*, in his peripheral vision. Off-limits to the public for nearly a century and re-opened relatively recently, this area of the park was known for having particularly lush growth. He ran onto a dirt trail about five feet wide, with a rope railing on either side suggesting visitors stay on the path. The trail was too straight for Hunt's liking, though, and so he jumped it on the right side before his would-be killers could make the trailhead and get a bead on him. He pushed brambles out of his face as he plowed deeper into the unmanicured vegetation. Unseen animals skittered out of if his path around him, but he paid them no mind. A thorn tore into his neck and he stifled a vocal outburst that would have given away his position.

Behind him he could hear people shouting. He hoped it was the fallout of the gunshot in the quiet park, with authorities already on the way and the gunmen running away scared. But the next noise he heard dashed that hope.

"This way!" a man's voice commanded. It came from the part of the path Hunt had just strayed from. The Omega founder beat feet through the underbrush, once again sacrificing some stealth in order to gain distance. But before long the plant growth was dense enough that he was forced to slow down, to hunch over in order to pass beneath hanging branches and clusters of unforgiving underbrush. After making limited headway in this manner, he stopped his movement and concentrated on a new sound. It came from in front of him. Not a human noise, but a constant splashing and gurgling.

Water. Some kind of running water, probably a stream, Hunt thought. Then he heard the crunch of earth and snapping of twigs somewhere behind him, and he knew his pursuers couldn't be all that far behind him. He ran along in an awkward crouch so that he would stay hidden in the brambles, but it was slower going than he would have preferred. He snaked his way through various openings in the bush, meandering through a maze of thickets until he became disoriented and wasn't sure he was going in the same direction even though he could still hear the rushing water. He continued through the maze, but while attempting to maintain travel in a more or less consistent direction. He gripped some whip-like, leafy branches and brushed them aside. He spotted a tunnel-like passage that emerged into open space ahead.

Hunt smiled as he peered through the opening. It had crossed his mind that if the undergrowth became too thick, he'd be forced to retrace his steps back to where those who chased him lurked. The sound of water rushing was much louder now. Hunt moved toward the opening, becoming more confident as he was able to transition from a crouch to a stoop and finally, to a normal walking position. His view of what lay beyond the opening was obscured by tall grasses that extended some distance back into the living tunnel. He parted them as he passed through, and was not surprised to see a small stream, small enough to jump across, bubbling its way across the grassy shelf.

He was surprised, however, to see that only ten feet away it flowed over the edge of a cliff.

Hunt walked along the stream, noting that it flowed out of an even more tangled section of the vegetation he had just picked his way through. Looking right and left, the plant life choked out any sort of easy exit. Curious as to what lay straight ahead, Hunt followed the brook to the edge of the plateau and found himself staring straight down a nearly vertical cliff, punctuated with jagged outcroppings on the way down to a pond.

Has to be about forty, maybe fifty feet, Hunt thought with a frown. As much as he didn't want to, he resigned himself to the fact that he would have to make his way either right or left through the bushes if he was to avoid backtracking. He had just started to move to the right-side barrier of plant life when the sharp crack of a stick—from behind him—caught his ears. Listening intently, he was then able to discern careful footfalls through the bed of brambles he had just traversed.

They were coming for him.

Suddenly the right side potential exit seemed awfully far away, and it was closer than the one via the left, which required him to ford or jump the steam. He heard a man shout, "I see him!" from inside the vegetation tunnel, and Hunt knew he only had time to go one way.

The first man burst out onto the clearing just as Hunt reached the edge of the cliff, where the brook's water tumbled over on its way to the pond down below. Hunt saw him reach for his hip, and he knew he had to take a chance. Being unarmed, that meant to escape rather than engage, and there was only one way to do that from here.

Hunt felt his leg muscles burn with the sudden exertion as he launched into a brief sprint. By the time the sprint morphed into a leap, a second gunman ran out onto the plateau. Hunt barely had time to take in the smattering of park visitors on one of the shores of the pond as he plummeted. He thought the water had looked deep enough from the few seconds' worth of assessment he'd had from the top of the cliff, but in mid-air he felt much less certain. He felt the spray of the waterfall hitting his skin just before he splashed into the pond.

He braced himself for the impact by curling into as tight a ball as he could, cannonball style, and making sure he entered the water head up. He felt the sensation of water pressure on his ears as he plummeted rapidly beneath the water's surface. By the time he felt the tickle of aquatic plants on his back, beneath his uplifted shirt, most of the drop's energy had been diminished. He impacted the muddy pond bottom with a mild thud.

Opening his eyes, he found it was easy to see the light representing the surface above in spite of the cloud of silt his jump had stirred up. Hunt kicked off the bottom, hoping for quick acceleration to get him moving in another direction before the shooters could get a bead on him from above. The mud bottom was loosely packed, however, resulting in a weak push-off. Still, he used his arms for an underwater breaststroke that took him gliding through a cloud of silt. At least it will keep me from being seen right away, he thought as he kicked his way toward the surface at angle.

The first thing he saw when his eyes broke into air was a skyscraper in the distance, reminding him that he was indeed still on the island of Manhattan. He gulped a huge breath into his lungs and then dove below the surface again, making it harder for the gunmen to shoot him if that was their aim. They had fired at him already, so Hunt was taking no chances as he resumed his stealth breaststroke toward the nearest shore, one that happened to be unpopulated. He kicked along through the murky water, needing one more breath to reach land. Hunt scrambled out onto the hardscrabble grass and wasted no time inserting himself beneath some sprawling tree branches that overhung the pond. They would shield him from line of sight to the top of the waterfall.

Hunt glanced at his dive watch, a graduation gift from his grandfather upon completing naval officer school. He noted the time, wanting to keep track of how many minutes passed from the time he exited the pond. He had no doubt that those chasing him would be finding their way down here once they realized they couldn't get a shot off. Or, if he was really lucky, Hunt mused, they didn't see him come up from the pond and now thought he was dead at the bottom after hitting his head or having a heart attack.

Hunt lowered himself to the moist ground and inched closer to water's edge, where a gap in the hanging branches afforded a peekaboo view of the top of the cliff. He saw a man standing up there peering intently down at the pond. The fact that he wore a three-piece suit made it that much more certain it was one of his pursuers from the auction and not a random park visitor. Time to move, Hunt thought.

He crawled back to full concealment and then rose to a standing position. Although he was soaking wet, he was physically fine, able to flex his body parts without feeling pain. But after his hands passed over his shirt to pluck off a few muddy leaves that still clung to him, a pang of fear jolted his system. He ran his right hand over his shirt again, but felt only wet fabric over his body.

The Muisca Raft! His one-point-three million dollar prize was gone! He forced himself to calm down and think. He definitely remembered uncrating the artifact and inserting it beneath his clothes in order to be able to better evade his attackers. But he double-checked beneath his shirt and pants, in case the artifact had shifted, but it wasn't there. He knew what must have happened.

Hunt gazed into the muddy pond beneath the waterfall. He was scrutinizing the path he had taken from the top of the cliff to the pond itself, calculating where exactly he had hit the water, when he heard a male voice close by.

"Do not take another step or I shoot. Hand over the Muisca Raft!"

CHAPTER 3

I don't have it!" The words rang hollow to Hunt even before they left his mouth. It sounded ridiculous. How could he not have the million-dollar item he had just purchased? And yet, Hunt knew with certainty that it was the truth.

"You lie!" the gunman spat, taking a half step closer to his cornered quarry.

"I'm serious," Hunt countered, glancing about at the ground around them. "Do you see the crate anywhere?"

"Liar! We found the crate on the ground in the woods. The Muisca Raft was not inside it. So where is it?"

Hunt stared down the barrel of the pistol—likely a Glock 9mm, he guessed—while he cursed himself for not crushing the crate into unrecognizable bits before leaving it behind. But it would have made too much noise. He considered his answer to the question at hand. Sometimes telling the truth was the best course, and right now he decided to go that route.

"I tucked it under my shirt after I took it out of the crate—so that I could run faster from you gun-toting maniacs—and obviously, it dropped out somewhere between where you found the crate and here." He glanced dubiously into the pond before adding, "Hopefully not in there."

The gunman eyed him carefully, making prolonged eye contact as if to gauge his victim's sincerity. Then he unclipped a walkie-talkie style radio and brought it to his lips. "Says he dropped it on the ground between where we found the crate and down here in the pond after he jumped."

"Bullshit!" came the immediate and angry reply. "Did you pat him down?"

"Better to have two people for that."

It concerned Hunt that the man had some knowledge of tactical procedure. Perhaps an ex-cop, he thought. He hoped not military, but had to admit it was possible.

"Fine, I'll check for it on the ground on my way down to you. Keep him right there until I get there."

Hunt sighed and said, "I'll save you the trouble. I'll take off my shirt and you can see for yourself I don't have it."

"Take off the shirt. Toss it to me," the guy with the gun on him said. He was not the same man who had done the bidding earlier. That must be the one up top of the cliff now, Hunt reasoned.

"Nice and slow!" the gunman said as Hunt began to move his arms. He had not been a SEAL in the Navy, but neither was he a slouch at combat. Even so, he recognized that this was not yet a suitable opportunity to make a stand or flee. Either way would likely earn him a bullet.

"Okay, no worries, just relax. I'm not going to die over an old statue, okay?"

"Then keep it nice and slow, pal. Go ahead…" The gunman eyed him intently as Hunt lowered his arms to remove his sport coat. His mind was reeling in overdrive, trying to figure out a course of action. He began slipping out of his shirt, keeping his left arm in the air while pulling the right from the sleeve.

"Keep going, nice and easy like that. Toss the shirt in front of you when you're done."

Hunt slipped from the garment, but paused before tossing it. "My phone's in the pocket. Can I grab it?"

"No! Toss it."

Ask a stupid question, Hunt thought. At least his wallet was in his pants pocket. Still, NYC after a mugging was no place to be without a phone. And then, just like that, inspiration stuck him. He made like he was about to toss the shirt but then stopped, his head turned toward the waterfall. "Wait a minute. I know where it is. Look!"

Hunt watched out of his peripheral vision as the robber turned his head toward the waterfall.

Hunt used the distraction as an opportunity. He made his move. He flung the shirt at his attacker and also kicked a stone toward him, launching it into the air. The rock struck the assailant square in the chest a second before the shirt enveloped his head. Then Hunt was running and then diving through the air. He tackled the hooded gunman, concerned that the shirt also concealed the attacker's gun hand, but he knew it was there so he pinned that arm back until he heard the tearing of shoulder cartilage. The resulting scream drowned out the sound of the pistol dropping to the ground, but Hunt was watching for it. He dropped onto the firearm and rolled away from the attacker in one smooth motion.

From a prone position on the ground, Hunt levelled the pistol at the would-be thief. "Your turn to freeze, pal!"

The assailant stood there as Hunt's shirt slid from his head and dropped to the dirt. Hunt rose to a standing position while keeping the gun aimed at the man's chest. Hunt took the opportunity to commit his face to memory. He'd never seen him before today, he was sure enough of that. Caucasian, late thirties or early forties, smooth shaven with scraggly brown hair. Dressed well for the auction today in clothes that fit well, but to Hunt he didn't seem like a man who normally wore such clothes as a job requirement. He could be wrong about that, he knew, but something about the way he carried himself seemed out of character with the high-end clothes. Speaking of clothes, Hunt reminded himself, his shirt was still on the ground with his phone in it.

"Take a few steps back, buddy, I'm gonna take my shirt back." He shook the pistol for emphasis. The thwarted assailant complied, walking a few steps backwards, cringing with the motion's effect on his damaged shoulder. Hunt moved forward, taking extra care to keep the gun aimed while bending down, and took his garment back. He retreated a couple more steps, felt for the bulk of his phone, and then let it drop at his feet.

"Why do you want the Muisca Raft so bad?"

"Why do *you* want it so bad?" the attacker, now at gunpoint, spat.

"I'm a collector of historical items who likes to make sure they stay available to the public."

"Whatever you say, rich guy. Most people don't have over a million bucks to blow on a statue, so why should you care?"

"I have the gun, I'll ask the questions: why should *you* care? You—or your associate, anyway, bid almost as much as I did for the same piece. We both know it's a lot more than it was expected to go for—black market or otherwise. And not only did you lose the auction, but then you chased the winner down at gunpoint to try and strongarm the piece? Am I missing something here?"

"Yeah." The thief's voice was a cold deadpan that gave Hunt pause.

"What's that?"

A beat passed during which Hunt began to grow suspicious, but it was too late. "My associate."

At that a new voice sounded from just behind Hunt and to the left. "Drop the gun or die, Mr. Carter." Hunt mentally visualized pulling the trigger at that very moment, almost before the new voice had even finished speaking, while rolling to the ground in an attempt to duck the shot that would no doubt come. But Hunt had no death wish, nor did he wish to cause anyone else harm, even those who would harm him—if there was any alternative.

"Okay. Don't shoot." Hunt dropped his newfound weapon to the dirt and stood there with his hands in the air.

"You find it?" the thief Hunt had had at gunpoint asked his newly arrived partner in crime. That man shook his head.

"Negative." He jerked a thumb at the pond. "Looks like somebody's going swimming." He wagged his pistol from Hunt to the water. Hunt turned his gaze to the pond's depths and took on a skeptical expression.

"What, you expect me to jump in there with no gear—not even a mask—and find that little statue?"

"Put it like this," the auction loser said. "You're getting into the pond. If you find the Muisca Raft, you get to come out again. Get it?"

Hunt gave him a hard stare. He mentally considered whether he should take his pants and shoes off for the swim, which would make him considerably more effective in the water, but decided against it. He didn't want to be separated from his wallet, for one thing. His phone, though, wouldn't survive submersion, so he decided to try for a compromise by leaving it with his shirt, which fortunately already had his phone in the pocket, but keeping his pants on with his wallet in them.

"All right, here I go." Hunt walked slowly to the edge of the pond nearest the waterfall. "I'm taking my shoes off. Don't shoot."

"No funny stuff."

"Except for taking a swim in the middle of New York City at gunpoint."

"Nothing funny about that," the gunman said, eliciting a chuckle from his associate.

"This would be a lot easier with dive gear," Hunt pointed out.

"I'm sure it would," the gunman said, taking a seat on a nearby boulder without taking the gun off of Hunt. "But you ain't got any, so deal with it."

"Yes sir." Hunt kicked his shoes off and placed them by his shirt. He walked to the edge of the pond and placed his toes in the water, sucking in his breath at the cool temperature. Even in August, the pond was chilly. Hunt put the chances of his actually locating the statue, if it was in fact even down here, somewhere around one-in-a-hundred. He knew from carrying it that it had some weight to it. With the pond bottom being soft mud, it meant that most likely the Muisca Raft was sitting under a couple of feet or more of soft sediment. As soon as he got near the bottom, it would cloud the water intolerably.

"Get a move on, Mr. Hunt." The gun barrel aimed at his mid-section reminded Hunt that this was not a choice. It also occurred to him, as he flexed his leg muscles in preparation for the dive, that these people, whoever they were, knew his name, no doubt from the auction registry. It was possible to remain anonymous but Hunt had not opted to go that route, preferring instead for those who knew of his business mission with Omega to tremble in fear as he built his reputation in the treasure hunting and cultural artifacts communities. He knew, of course, that he was far from having that kind of impact on the black market antiquities trade —or even the legal market, for that matter——but he wanted to at least open the conversation about transnational antiquities trafficking to anyone who would listen.

Current company included, Hunt thought dourly as he flexed his calf muscles. He wasn't sure who they were, that is, who they worked for, yet, but he thought he had a fairly good idea. If he was right, it didn't make him feel any better.

Hunt cleared his thoughts while taking a deep breath. Then he executed a clean forward dive into the pond.

CHAPTER 4

The shock of the cold water did little to affect Carter Hunt's progress as he swam across the pond. He had steeled himself for it. He operated on the idea that the Muisca Raft must have been dislodged from his person as he impacted the water after jumping from the cliff. Guided by that simple premise, he headed toward the waterfall to begin his search, iffy as it was.

Hunt could almost feel the gun sight aimed at him as he plied the chilly waters of Central Park toward the waterfall. It didn't take him long to reach the spot where he estimated he'd landed when he had jumped from the top of the cliff. When he could feel the spray of the waterfall on his face, he gazed skyward. The sun was overhead and creating a thousand prisms reflecting through the mist cast off the water on its way down from the cliff, with a dazzling blue and white backdrop of sky and white puffy clouds behind that.

Hunt turned to look at his robbers. Sure enough, both stood close to shore, eyeing him carefully, though he currently had no gun trained on him. He guessed it was because he was in the middle of the pond and therefore could neither threaten them nor escape from here. Still, he was glad not to have a weapon aimed at him.

Somehow that simple reality lessened the pressure he felt and allowed him to think clearly for a moment, while continuing to swim. He eyed the waterfall, this time gauging what might lay behind the falling stream of water. Whether he recovered the object or not, if these people worked for who he suspected they work for, then his odds of survival after either, A) coughing up the Muisca Raft or B), proving to them that he had no idea where it was and was therefore useless to them, were nil. So he calculated the odds of success of various escape routes: the opposite pond shore, where a few people could be seen sitting on the grass not all that far away. Or a fake recovery. He could clutch something in his hand and say, "Look!" before throwing a ball of mud in their faces, then make a break for it. Or he could find out what options might lay *behind* the curtain of water that cascaded into the pond.

He knew that none of these were truly viable options, but out of them, if it came down to it—and it appears that it would—he would check what was behind the waterfall. Hunt dogpaddled his way a little closer, the spray from the water hitting the surface of the pond and smacking him hard in the face now. He glanced about, putting his position in a framework of reference based on his previous whereabouts. This was as good as it was going to get. If the ritualistic metallurgical work was down there, this was his starting point to dive for it.

Hunt began to tread water as a way of resting up for his breath held dive. He spun until he faced the men who held him at gunpoint, and saw that one of them did, in fact, have a pistol pointed at his head now. Probably because I stopped moving, Hunt thought. He raised a hand and made the thumbs down sign, a universal diving hand signal that meant "I'm going to descend."

Hunt saw the gunman nod at him while his associate started walking toward the pond. Underwater, Hunt swam down at an angle, trying to get to the bottom below where he thought he had entered the water earlier. He opened his eyes to make sure he wasn't going to smash into a boulder or submerged tree or other obstacle, making sure to always keep one hand out in front of him in case he did run into something solid. The last thing he wanted was to smash his head on something unforgiving and pass out down here. He knew the two goons standing watch above weren't lifeguards. He continued swimming his way down. He hadn't yet gotten close to running out of breath when his vision discerned the brown plane that represented the bottom of the pond.

Hunt knew that to get too close to it would mean that he would disturb the mud and cloud the water, ruining his chance to see the actual bottom, and hopefully a gold object resting on it. He opted to stay six feet from it while his blurry gaze scoured the bottom. Nothing. He could see nothing right off the bat that would—*wait, what's that?* A shiny object off to the right caught his attention. Remaining underwater, he swam to it, noting the silver color indicating it was likely not the Muisca Raft. He plucked it out of the mud, and even without a mask, he knew what it was. *Beer can. Should have known better.* He let the item drop back to the bottom and made his way to a different part of the pond bottom, where the sound of the waterfall's thundering was even louder.

Beginning to feel the urge to breathe, Hunt eyeballed the bottom in search of a telltale golden glint. He kicked his legs in order to glide over the aquatic floor. By the time he felt a serious need to breathe, he had still not come across anything out of place, and so he surfaced for breath. He faced the waterfall upon breaking into daylight, and immediately turned to the right to check on the thieves. Still there, eyeing him expectantly with not one, but two guns pointed his way.

Rather than engage them in conversation and waste his breath even further, Hunt opted to continue his search, as fruitless as it may be. He took another deep breath and submerged again into the muddy brown void. He swam down to the bottom and this time patrolled a different area of the pond floor while making his way to the waterfall where it impacted the pond. While swimming, he thought about the possibility that the gunmen may simply shoot him and leave him for dead after too many failed attempts. He had seen their faces clearly, after all, and so they may worry about being identified later. But so far, at least, they did not appear overly concerned about law enforcement intervention. Perhaps, Hunt thought, as he kicked over a patch of algae, checking in between the plants for metallic objects, this was because they worked for the powerful organization he suspected was behind all this.

The water beneath the waterfall was a whiteout haze of bubbles and whitewater. Hunt skirted around the edge of it, just barely able to make out details of the pond bottom. He began to feel the need to take in air again. Knowing that surfacing directly beneath the waterfall wouldn't be a good place to gulp air, he decided to continue swimming underwater until he was behind it. He kicked a few more times while the waterfall's impact roared above him, and then he saw the wall of rock ahead. Hunt surfaced and looked around.

In front of him was the base of the cliff from which the waterfall tumbled. He turned around to see the river of water cascading into the pond. He couldn't help but notice that it shielded him from view of his robbers. He turned back around to glance up the cliff again, assessing his options. Could he escape the gunmen by climbing back up the cliff? He eyed the smooth, wet rocks in the waterfall's splash zone, noting they were slippery with moss and algae growth. It would be an exceedingly difficult proposition to climb them, and then even if he succeeded, what was the rest of the climb like….His gaze travelled upward, scouting out a climbing route. But he hadn't gotten far above the wet rocks when his vision caught a gleaming object nestled in the near-vertical rock wall.

Hunt wiped water from his eyes to make sure he was seeing things clearly. There! Not all that high up the cliff—perhaps fifteen feet—lay an unmistakable glittering of gold. He scrutinized it further to make sure it wasn't another can or other trash. *No, it's the Muisca Raft.* It had become lodged in the rocks so that not all of it was visible, at least from this vantage point, but he knew that it was in fact his dropped auction prize.

Hunt knew that too remain silent too long, or hidden too long, could trigger gunshots, so he called over to them. He didn't want to be shot off the wall while climbing lest they think he was trying to escape. This antiquity, as alluring as it was, was not worth his life.

"Hey, I think I found it!"

"Where are you, Carter Hunt? Do not try anything!" came the wary-sounding voice Hunt recognized as the one who had bid and lost in the auction.

Hunt swam until he could stand on the pond bottom and put his hands on the mossy rocks. He glanced up at the golden gleam once again to be sure it still looked like the pre-Columbian artifact and then called over to the gunmen. "Don't shoot. I'm behind the waterfall. I see the Muisca Raft!"

"Can you get it?" came the reply, voice tinged with excitement.

"I think so. Climbing for it now." Hunt raised his right foot out of the water to plant it on a solid foothold, a niche in the mossy boulders. Flexing his calf muscle, he sprung higher until he could grab two handholds. He used those to pull him higher still until he found purchase for his left foot on a shallow micro-ledge. Then he continued to climbing, his right foot slipping once but not enough to overcome his hold on the rocks. When Hunt saw the first dry outcropping of rock he had to contain his urge to jump for it. He took the time to make sure his footing was solid and then pushed up until both his elbows were over the dry ledge. From there it was a simple feat to pull himself up onto the small shelf.

Hunt looked upward. From this vantage point, he could no longer see the Muisca Raft, but he guessed it to be just above the next outcropping about ten feet over his head.

"How are you, Mr. Hunt?" came the voice of the gunman. He had moved closer to the waterfall, judging by where his voice originated.

"I think I see it!" Hunt said, genuinely excited about the prospect of recovering the artifact even though it meant he would soon be handing it over to the thugs on shore. To think that it had survived a millennia or more only to end up lost to the world again was disheartening.

"You *think*?" came the hard-edged reply.

"It's metal and gold-colored, whatever it is."

"Coors beer can?" the other thug suggested. Hunt flashed on the other can he'd already seen at the bottom of the pond. "I don't think so, but I'm almost to it. Don't shoot me, I gotta climb up a little farther."

"You try to climb away from us and we'll pick you off that wall like a fish in a barrel," the first thug said.

"Copy that." Hunt returned his focus exclusively to climbing. While mostly free of moss and algae, the rocks here were still not entirely dry, and he was high enough that a fall on this next section likely meant landing backwards on the boulders below. He planted his bare feet carefully on the rocks and eyed what he thought would make a good handhold if he were to jump high enough to grab it. Then Hunt launched himself vertically, enough to gain hold of the small outcropping. He wedged his right hand painfully between two rocks, then used his feet and other hand to propel himself up until he could drag himself to a kneeling position on the semi-dry rock.

Yes.

The artifact was here, in all its gleaming, golden glory. The Muisca Raft. But then, upon closer inspection, Hunt saw that something was not quite right.

Oh no.

The statuette lay on its side on a small bed of lichens, its primary chieftain figure cracked off of the statue at its base. Hunt reached out and picked up the statue, lifting it from the rocks by its base. As he did, he noticed a dull red cylindrical object lying on the rocks.

"No funny business, Hunt! We can't exactly see you but we can shoot through the waterfall if you make us angry."

"Calm down. I've got it. I'm coming back down."

"Don't lose the damn thing this time!"

"I won't." He had no desire to do that, either. Hunt knew he had little time, so he turned his attention to the red object. A piece of paper, he could now see, tightly rolled, but encased in wax.

A scroll. What? Hunt's curiosity was unbearable, even with the specter of gunfire at any second. He had to know what this was, but at the same time, it looked extremely old, and he knew that aged parchments or papers should only be exposed to controlled climates. Besides, he reasoned as he examined the statue itself, the gunmen grew more impatient with each passing second.

Hunt pocketed the wax-covered scroll and collected the damaged statuette. He looked around the rocks for the piece that had broken off—

the Muisca Chieftain—but didn't see it anywhere.

"It is time for you to come down, Mr. Hunt." One of the gunmen intoned.

"On my way! I've got the Muisca Raft!"

"Hurry up."

Hunt cursed under his breath as he once again tucked the valuable work of art into his waistband. Knowing this type of carry method had failed him before did not inspire confidence, but the reality was that he needed two hands free in order to safely descend the damp cliff. With a last, unsuccessful look around for the broken piece of the artifact, Hunt began his descent.

He planted his left foot into a solid hold while maintaining his grip on the edge of the ledge. There was no getting around the fact that he would have to slide-drop down a section where there were no holds, until he reached a spot to plant his right foot. From there it looked routine, Hunt thought. His fingertips were sore already from the effort thus far, but he blocked out the pain, glanced down one more time to lock in his target, and then let himself fall.

Hunt's right knee smashed into an irregular boulder, causing him to grunt in pain as a trickle of blood sluiced down his shin. But he held his place on the watery cliff.

"Don't drop it again, you clumsy oaf!" one of the gunmen taunted.

"I've got it," Hunt said from behind clenched teeth. He reminded himself that losing his temper in this situation would not help him. *Focus on the downclimb.* Hunt took a deep breath and resumed his descent, carefully planting each foot and hand, testing the holds before committing, the sound of the waterfall tumbling into the pond behind him like a white noise soundtrack that helped block out any distractions.

When he reached the wet, moss covered boulders at the bottom of the cliff, Hunt adjusted the artifact in his waistband. He made sure to telegraph his intentions to the gunmen. "Okay, I'm at the base of the cliff now. I'm going to jump into the pond and swim to you. Don't shoot."

"You still have the Raft?"

"Yes. I'm holding onto it. I will not drop it." Hunt said this to himself as much as to the strongmen. As much as he detested handing it over to anyone else, he had no desire to lose the work of art to the bottom of a New York City pond, either. He pressed the artwork firmly against his side with his right hand while preparing to jump. He carefully turned around 180 degrees until he faced the backside of the cascading waterfall.

"Here goes nothing!" Then he jumped out into the pond, to the left of where the waterfall hit the surface. Hunt made sure to clench the statuette on impact, even switching to a two-handed grip once he hit the water. He opened his eyes underwater, even amid the maelstrom of churning waterfall whiteout bubbles, just to make certain he was kicking toward the light. Upon reaching the surface, he took a breath and began swimming with one arm—the other holding the statuette against his waist—toward the shore, where the two gunmen eagerly awaited their ill-gotten prize.

During his remaining pond swim, Hunt thought about his next course of action, but there was really only one choice. He wasn't going to die over this artifact. He had spent over one million dollars of his own money to try and do the right thing, to place it in a museum for the people of the world to enjoy, appreciate and learn from, but that old expression, *you can't win 'em all* was definitely at play here.

Hunt reached the pond shoreline and gazed up at the two gunmen, both of which had pistols pointing directly at his head. He could see no other people behind them.

"On your knees!" the one who had bid in the auction grumbled. "Now!"

Hunt followed instructions until he was at eye level with the barrel of a Glock pistol not six feet away.

"Get the artifact," one instructed his associate. Hunt noted that he did not use a name to issue the instruction. The second gunman held his pistol, also a Glock 9mm, at the ready as he approached Hunt, who had a conspicuous bulge on the side of his soaking pants.

"Just keep your hands up and I'll grab the Raft. You lower your hands and he's gonna shoot you. Got it?"

Hunt informed the lowlife that he did indeed get it. He kept his hands up while the goon extracted the Muisca Raft from his waistband, and then held it up for inspection.

"Hey, it's busted!" he exclaimed while walking the artifact over to his associate. "The big guy is missing!" the second man said upon viewing the damaged statuette.

"Sorry," Hunt said. "Must have happened when it fell down the cliff."

"Do you have the missing piece?" He eyed Hunt's pants as though he could be concealing it.

Hunt shook his head. "No, I looked for it up there, but didn't see it."

The robbers' next words, directed to his accomplice, made Hunt's spine tingle. "Check it out." The same man who had taken the Muisca Raft from him walked back over to Hunt. "Keep your hands up. I'm just going to pat you down."

"Great." The single word dripped with sarcasm as the antiquities bandit proceeded to pat Hunt's pant legs down, moving up to the pockets. Although he didn't yet know what the scroll was, Hunt knew it had come out of the Muisca Raft and so hoped with every fiber of his being that they wouldn't find it.

He felt the man's hands pass over his back pockets, then the front left, and finally the front right. He briefly patted it down, but as he was feeling for a piece of metal, Hunt was dearly hoping the little wax-covered scroll would be indistinguishable from his pants pocket. The thug finished his pat-down and stepped away from Hunt before looking to his associate and shaking his head. "He's got nothing."

"You guys can climb up there and look for the missing piece if you want. Or maybe it fell into the pond, But I gave you what you wanted. Can I go now or are you going to kill me in the middle of Central Park in broad daylight?"

Hunt tensed as he waited for the answer, but it came surprisingly fast.

"You are free to go," said the one who had done the bidding.

Hunt lowered his arms. "Thanks. Why do you guys want that thing so bad, anyway, may I ask? No reason for it to be bid so high."

"You can ask, but we're not going to tell you. Same reason you want it, probably. Have a nice day." He waved to his co-worker and the two of them started toward the city at a brisk pace. Hunt stood and watched them until they were out of sight to make sure they actually left the area. Satisfied he was now alone, he walked over to the edge of the pond and retrieved his shirt, shoes, and phone. After dressing, he walked away from the pond, lest he was still being watched from a distance. He didn't want them to think he was lingering near the waterfall in order to retrieve the broken statuette piece, or to see him using his phone in an attempt to call the police. He walked up and away from the pond until he reached another grassy field.

On the edge of it was an unoccupied park bench. He went to it and took a seat, again taking a look around to make sure his attackers had truly left. Seeing no signs of them, Hunt put his hand in his pocket for the scroll. A pang of adrenaline rocked his system as his fingers felt only wet fabric. But after adjusting his position, he felt the wax-covered scroll and removed it from his pants.

None the worse for wear following its ordeal, Hunt peeled off the outer wax covering to reveal a grayish paper beneath. Then he carefully unrolled the scroll until its full length, about six inches, was exposed. Immediately Hunt recognized a map—a map of what looked to be the northernmost regions of South America, including part of the Amazon rain forest. But what really caught the treasure seeker's attention was the legend at the bottom of the map.

It read, *El Dorado.*

CHAPTER 5

Providencia, Colombia
Caribbean Sea

Although part of the nation of Colombia, the island of Providencia lay almost 500 miles away, out to sea. Off the beaten yachting track, the isle was home to lush explosions of blooming foliage tumbling down steep hillsides into a placid, azure sea. Tucked away into one of a series of U-shaped coves, making it easy to miss from the air or otherwise, was a white mega-yacht at anchor. Out of sight of the island's towns, the craft had been here for three weeks without attracting any attention.

The humongous yet sleek vessel boasted two swimming pools and a helipad, and thanks to state-of-the-art automation, could be run by a crew smaller than that needed by a ship less than half its size. Tropical sunlight glinted off endless stretches of tinted salon windows. The name of the craft was spelled out in golden lettering on its hull: *Historica*. For the yacht's owner, a Greek man rumored to be in his fifties and sporting thick black stubble on a face with classic Greek lines, the seclusion represented a place to conduct uninterrupted business, though he was not immune to the surrounding beauty.

Presently, Daedalus reclined in a lounge chair on one of the upper sun decks, a tray of smoked salmon and tropical fruits within reach along with a glass of rare champagne.

The bubbly had just been cracked by one of his hospitality crew, and he now prepared to toast the success of one of his latest ventures, yet another antiquity sale.

"Won't you toast with me before your ride, baby?" His request was directed toward a bikini clad woman with a spectacular figure who could not have been much more than thirty years of age. She turned away from the staircase leading to the lower decks and sauntered back over to him.

"You know I will." She took a flute from him and held it out. "What are we cheers-ing this time?"

"I just completed another deal. Made a nice chunk of change. Enough to keep us floating about for a few more weeks, at any rate." He waved the hand not holding the glass around at the uninterrupted natural splendor.

"I'll drink to that!" The blonde clinked glasses with Daedalus, chugged the sparkling wine in two quick gulps and set the flute down on the tray. "Coming with me on the waverunner?" He looked doubtful, so she added, "Just a quickie?" with a wink.

A bubbly tone chimed from a device on the table next to the food tray. "I've got to take this call, babe."

She shot him a mock withering stare. "How do you know? You didn't even check to see who it is."

Daedalus smiled patiently. "Only my trusted associates have the number for my satellite phone."

His friend's smile turned genuine. "Well then I'm glad I'm a trusted *associate*." She turned and patted her backside. Daedalus laughed while not bothering to explain to her that she had one of his cell-pone numbers, none of which had service in this remote location.

He flashed her a winning smile. "You go on, have fun! I'll see you for dinner." After she blew him a kiss and bounded down the stairs, Daedalus picked up his satellite phone. The smile disappeared when he saw the caller's number. He had thought it would be a follow-up call from his last deal, the one he had just toasted to. That had involved a black-market sale of a statue, but one that was considerably more recent in origin compared to most of the objects of his dealings.

Daedalus was a shrewd and adaptable operator, and he was quick to recognize the rising tide of American dissent and capitalize on it. After a rash of vandalism directed toward historical statues, particularly in the Confederate South, Daedalus had instructed his operatives to steal a particular statue from its place of former honor in a smallish southern town. He didn't even remember the name of the general it honored—it wasn't Grant or Lee or whoever the famous ones were—just some Civil War player who had done enough at one point to warrant a statue erected in his name in some Podunk little town.

So he had sent his paid hoodlums there to knock it down under the guise of civil dissent and hyper-political correctness, cancel culture, whatever you wanted to call it. Daedalus called it a business opportunity. He knew that due to the controversial nature of the statue in modern times, that it would be worth money to some. Sure enough, he had put out his feelers and found a Good Ol' Boy network willing to pay a decent sum for the piece. So his thugs quietly invaded the sleepy little town, knocked down the statue with a monster truck and dragged it away.

After the success of the first piece, he'd repeated the process throughout the South a half-dozen more times, including today's finalized deal. History belonged to everyone, he had heard many times by detractors of his wealthy collector-driven business. And he agreed with that. But what his detractors didn't seem to grasp was that in many cases, the current "cancel culture" included, having the works of art in the hands of a private collection actually *increased* their longevity. These Confederate war statues, for example, Daedalus was fond of telling anyone who would listen, would likely have been completely obliterated by the same angry mobs who claimed to care so much for humanity. Instead, Daedalus had rescued them and placed them in the hands of people who truly appreciated them. This held up for other areas of the world, as well, Daedalus was sure. In the middle east, for example, where he had started his illustrious career in black market antiquities. Those nations were perpetually at war, and it was only a matter of time before they blew up their own historical artifacts, anyway. But because Daedalus' company acquired them and sold them to private collectors before that could happen, they still lived on, preserved for the future, whatever that may hold.

Accepting the call, Daedalus held the device to his ear, not being one to trust speaker phones to discuss sensitive matters. "Yes, Phillipo how are things?" Daedalus' brother was his second-in-command of their "import-export" business, as he liked to refer to it. The fact that he was calling him now could only mean that there was some kind of breaking development on the New York City pre-Columbian auction matter. It was a longshot—one of Daedalus' pet projects, but forget about Confederate statues—the auction objective was to acquire a piece that may or may not—but *may*—lead to nothing less than the real life proof of the storied El Dorado legend! So it wasn't his bread-and-butter level dealings, but a hail Mary longshot. Daedalus made sure to always have one of those in play, and for now this was it.

Forget everything else. Daedalus was in this business to rise to the top, not to dabble in petty baubles. The lost city of gold! For him it represented the very pinnacle of his profession, which was why he had authorized bidding of over one million U.S. dollars to acquire it, and failing that, the use of brute, lawless force to steal it from whoever did. He was hoping that this call meant they had won the auction, but at the same time his experience told him that if the news were that good--that simple-- he would have heard earlier since the auction concluded hours ago.

"I am sorry, Daedalus, but we did not win the auction for the Muisca Raft."

Daedalus exhaled heavily as he turned his head to the side and watched his girlfriend zipping off toward the beach on one of the waverunners. He spat back into the phone.

"One-point-two million dollars was not sufficient?"

"No, the final bid was one-point-three million."

Daedalus pulled on his lip while reflecting on this for a moment before speaking. "It's weird that it would fetch such a high price….unless someone else knows what we know. Or what *I* know, anyway. The statue is not merely a statue if my old friend Tyler Harding was correct. So I expect you will move on to our contingency plan?"

He heard his brother clear his throat nervously. "We already did, that, Daedalus."

"You don't sound pleased. Did you fail in that, too?" His tone and words were a reminder of who was the boss.

"Yes and no. The good news is that we did run the contingency plan and we did recover the artifact. Or part of it."

"Explain."

Phillipo recounted the chase through Central Park and how they robbed the statue but that it was damaged in the process.

"This auction winner—he sounds unusually capable for someone spending that kind of money at one of these society affairs. I assume you got his name?"

"Carter Hunt."

Daedalus slowly pulled the phone away from his head and stared at it while contemplating the serious turn his hail Mary pet project had just taken.

"Him again. Wonderful. Why did your men let him live, Phillipo? You know the trouble Hunt and his…his misguided group has caused us."

"I am sorry, Daedalus, but my men were unaware of who he was. They got his name from the auction, but had not heard of him. I was not personally involved in the auction events, as you know. My men were merely instructed to take the Muisca Raft from the winner in the event that they did not win it themselves."

"I am most disappointed. And the damage—how extensive is it?"

Phillipo described the damage to the Muisca Raft, after which his brother sucked his breath in sharply.

"So is there a cavity beneath the chieftain figure, where it was broken off?"

"Yes, a small, narrow one."

"OK, Phillipo, are you with the piece now?"

"Yes."

"I need you to look at it and tell me if there's anything in it."

"There's not, but okay, I'll double-check. Hold on." He was gone for a couple of minutes, during which time Daedalus watched the woman gliding around the turquoise water of the cove on the waverunner. When Phillipo came back on the phone, Daedalus could tell right away from his tone the news was not good.

"Nothing in it, Daedalus. Wouldn't the auction people have X-rayed it anyway, to check for hidden items of value?"

"Perhaps, but this object was not metal. I'm looking for a scroll of paper said to contain a map to El Dorado."

"According to whom?"

"Tyler Harding."

An uncomfortable silence ensued, after which Phillipo said, "Is there a reason you didn't tell me this map was possibly there and that this was the reason for bidding the item up so high?"

"Operational security, my dear brother. It is nothing personal against you. But if you don't know, then the people you hire won't know, either, and that's the way I need it to be. The golden city is a seductive lure and has a long history of making good men go bad in their quest to uncover its riches."

"I see." The curt response made it clear that, if he did see, Phillipo was not pleased.

"Phillipo, I need you to assure me that your hired help will go back to the Park and make sure the map—it would look like a rolled up old scroll, possibly with a wax covering to help it withstand the ages and even blend in with the statue if X-rayed—didn't fall out of the statue when it broke and is still lying there."

"But it broke falling down a steep cliff behind a waterfall!"

"No excuses, Phillipo! If you cannot get it done, I will do it myself or get someone who can, do you understand?"

"Fine, Daedalus. I just wish you would have told me about the map."

"I also need you to put in place the contingency plan in case the map is not in fact there."

"It could have fallen into the pond and been destroyed by now."

"Possibly. Or it could be on the rocks up the cliff, or even floating in the pond protected by a wax covering. Either way, I need you to confirm it. And I also need for you to handle the third possibility, besides that it is still there or destroyed."

"And what possibility is that?"

"That Carter Hunt has it."

A lengthy silence ensued while Phillipo digested this. Hunt had handed over the relic rather willingly and without complaint, for someone who had just spent over a million dollars on it, hadn't he? He had passed it off as self-preservation but now he wasn't so sure.

"Right away, Daedalus. I will have him tracked, and I will personally go to the park and look for the map."

"Excellent. I know you will not disappoint me and Treasure, Incorporated." Daedalus ended the call and gazed out across the cove. He was almost certain from his brother's account of how willingly Hunt had given up the statue that he had found the map. He had to assume that he found it, at any rate. Daedalus would find out if Hunt were now going to travel to South America, and that would tell him almost for certain. Meanwhile, here he was almost 500 miles away from Colombia. He had intended to stay here in this beautiful secluded cove for another month or so, but he felt like now he should be closer to the mainland in case the map turned out to be genuine. It was supposedly drawn by Sir Walter Raleigh himself, after all. This was not the kind of lead Daedalus could afford to ignore.

The Treasure, Inc. founder picked up a computer tablet from the table next to his chaise lounge and brought up a screen that controlled many of the ship's functions. He pressed a button to began hauling in the yacht's anchor and then messaged the Captain that they were leaving the cove. He heard the whine of the waverunner's engine and looked to see his girlfriend arcing into a sharp turn, squealing with excitement. She'll catch up to the yacht, Daedalus mused. Even the *Historica's* largest tender vessel was faster than the huge mega-yacht. At cruising speed, the waverunner could catch up. He had no time to waste on women. She would catch up to him, he thought confidently.

But the real question was, he thought as he sipped from his champagne flute, would he be able to catch up to Carter Hunt?

CHAPTER 6

New York Harbor

Hunt took a seat on the upper deck of the Staten Island ferry, thankful for the cool breeze on his face. Upon leaving Central Park he'd returned his rental car and caught the mass transportation vessel, hoping to throw off his pursuers in case they decided to find him again. As he looked around to make sure no one was watching, he had no doubt that if they worked for who he thought they worked for, they would soon be chasing him again. Hunt took out the scroll of old paper.

In spite of the traumatic episode he had just experienced, it would seem that he had the real prize. A smile formed on his lips as he unfurled the scroll and examined it in detail. He would have much preferred to do this in a controlled laboratory setting, but circumstances did not permit that and so he would simply have to limit the scroll's exposure to the elements as much as possible. Its parchment was old enough to seem genuine for the same period that Sir Walter Raleigh had explored the regions of South America rumored to hide the city of gold. As a historian, Hunt had long heard passed-down accounts of El Dorado in treasure hunting circles that Raleigh had left a map on his death.

Hunt considered the map in his hands more carefully now that he had some time. A shaded area indicated El Dorado's supposed position, but it was a large area. To Hunt it looked like what is today known as the entire country of Colombia, with the specific region being part of the Colombian Amazon. Still some of the most dense and virgin rain forest on the planet, Hunt thought, shaking his head as he began to consider the enormity of what this document suggested. Was it any better than the same old El Dorado myth that a golden city lay concealed somewhere in the vastness of the Amazon rain forest, a swath of unbridled wilderness too large for any person to really conceive of?

After perusing the map some more, Hunt was convinced of both its authenticity and specificity with regard to the location of the golden city. The cross-hatching on the map did seem to describe an area with actual boundaries, sizable though it may be. After observing a few of the faces aboard the crowded ferry and not feeling like he was being tailed, he placed a call on his cell-phone.

Jayden Takada, Hunt's business partner in his Omega enterprise, answered before the first ring ended. The Asian-American ex-Navy man had served alongside Hunt in their early days of service, but while Jayden had gone on to be a SEAL, Hunt, with his degree in World History, had taken the officer route. Later in their Navy days they had worked together on a few covert operations, and after Hunt retired from the service earlier than expected after receiving a large inheritance from his grandfather, OMEGA team was born. After two high profile capers working alongside Jayden, he had decided to offer his friend a full-time position in his fledgling startup.

"Where you at, Carter?"

Aware that it was possible his cellular call could be intercepted, given the vast resources at Treasure, Inc.'s disposal, or whoever had just bid over one million dollars for the Muisca Raft and then hired the two thugs to take it from him at gunpoint, Carter decided he needed to risk getting specific info across, but that it would be a quick call. "I'm on a ferry in New York Harbor headed for Staten Island. Need air travel right now. What do you have?"

"I take it you mean emergency air travel and not the business-class JFK-to-LAX kind?"

"That's right. The kind where you need to call in a favor, most likely. Very discreet."

"Roger that. Everything okay?"

"For now, but I have good news and bad news."

"Give me the good first."

"I won the auction for the Muisca Raft."

Jayden's voice was exuberant. "Sweet! What's the bad news?"

"A couple of hired goons took it from me at gunpoint in Central Park."

"Geez. I've heard you should stay away from that place at night, but..."

"It was a targeted hit. Same guys who lost the auction as runner-up also pulled the heist."

"Wow, I'm sorry."

"There's good news and bad with that, too, the bad being I no longer have the statue and think it's in the hands of Treasure, Inc."

The heavy exhalation of breath on the other end told Hunt all he needed to know about Jayden's reaction. "Looks like we ordered one heckuva soup sandwich. Just give me the good news, then. I'm looking for air travel as we speak." Hunt could hear him typing in the background as he relayed the account of breaking the statuette and finding the map.

"...so if this document really was created by Sir Walter Raleigh..."

"We've got a lead on El Dorado!"

"A lead that Treasure, Inc. wants, too. I think that's why they were willing to bid so high on the Muisca Raft."

"It's not even the same Muisca Raft as in the Bogota Museum, right?" Jayden asked.

"Right, but it's been vetted as authentic for the same period and out of the same materials, mostly gold. And I mean chemically equivalent gold to the one the museum piece is made from, not just any gold. Gold ore that came from the exact same mountain region near the Andes. I was going to have it sent to our own lab contacts for further authentication and analysis, but so much for that."

"It makes sense there would be more than one Muisca Raft, anyway, since that's the depiction of the main ritual, right?"

Hunt nodded as he looked across the rows of ferry passengers, impressed. "Exactly. Just because there are more than one doesn't mean they're not authentic, valuable, *or* that they were in fact connected directly to El Dorado, if it exists. Which reminds me, let me do one thing before I forget. Especially important."

"You need to pay your phone bill or something?"

"No, actually I need to send off an image of the map. Just in case something happens to it, so we'll still be able to reference it."

"What if it gets hacked?"

"For that very reason, I've hired a computer security expert. If you recall last year, I said I would if we found the Ark."

"Right, and we did! So….is she hot?"

Carter shook his head with a smile while glancing about the ferry. The harbor brimmed with boat traffic as the multi-deck ferry plowed through the slate grey waters. "I said I'd hire a technical person, not find you a date."

"Fair enough, so who'd you hire? And where are they?"

"Working from home, like you. I figured if we could save money by not having a central headquarters, may as well do that, for the time being at least."

"Believe me, you don't want to see what passes for Casual Friday around here, Carter."

"I'm sure I don't. And I'm sure Omega's new tech person doesn't, either. Her name is Kelsey Pawar, she's twenty-nine years old and already retired from her position at a well-known Seattle Internet company in order to run her own consulting business. She still does that but will also be handling our needs on a part-time, on-call basis. She assured me that she understands the sensitive and, at times, emergency nature of our business, and that she will drop evrything to bring us tech solutions as the need arises."

"Uh-huh. Is she single?"

"You can ask her yourself when you call her to erase your tracks after you do an image search online for this map."

"After the fact? She's that good? A hacker?"

"She's even better than that. We're lucky to be working with her. She has personal reasons for joining our cause, something about a mosque in India destroyed by profiteers seeking to sell artwork on the black market. She's what she calls a 'white hat' hacker. She knows how to do it, but only does it for good, or to expose computer security flaws so that they can be fixed."

"Sounds like an angel."

Hunt grew conscious of the fact that time was ticking. "So here's what I need *you* to do: as soon as you have my air transport hooked up, call Kelsey and explain that I emailed you the map image, that you conducted an Internet search with it, and now you need all traces of it erased from other people's phones, servers and routers. She will instruct you from there."

"Oh, I'm sure she will!"

"Stay focused, bro. I'm still floating around New York with a piece of paper that some very bad people have already proven they would kill me for."

Jayden cleared his throat and tapped some more computer keys. "I got your six. So listen, there's a private air strip not too far from where your ferry will dock. By the time you get there, I'll have a pilot we can trust to take you south. The good thing about the New York metro area is that there are a lot of friendly contacts in reasonable physical proximity."

"Unfriendly ones, too, but sounds good. Let me get you started on that image search—*secure* image search," Hunt added for emphasis. He already had standard security that Kelsey had set up on his and Jayden's phones and computers as a preliminary caution, but she would also do what she had referred to as a "deep cleaning" afterwards. "Hold on…" He attached the image of the map to an email and sent it before rolling up the scroll and placing it back in his shirt pocket.

"OK, you've got it. Get back to me when you can tell me where to go. You can get back to me on the map later." Hunt ended the call, looked up and saw that the ferry was drawing nearer to Staten Island. A small fleet of vessels plied the water on either side of his boat--tugboats, pleasure craft, barges, other ferries.

He scanned the New York City skyline in the distance. The enormity of it was at once comforting and frightening. It concealed both him and his hunters. It was a true concrete jungle with dangers no less real than the organic jungle he would be invading to search for untold treasure. But to even get there, he would first have to escape from here. He had no illusions that would be a given.

* * *

The ferry's horn blasted three times in succession as it pulled up to the terminal on Staten Island. It concerned Hunt that he still had not heard back from Jayden yet, since once he left the ferry he had nowhere to go. But at least the huge vessel was jam-packed, and the line of passengers to disembark would buy him some time if he hung back and let most of the rest exit before him. He did not want to have to call Jayden and interrupt him if he was still working out the logistics.

At least he was mostly dry by now after his swim in the pond, although he did leave the seat a little wet when he got up. Hunt killed time waiting by going inside to the ferry's concession stand and purchasing a Staten Island baseball cap, which would hide his face and change his look somewhat. By the time he completed his cash purchase and made his way out to the upper deck, most of the passengers had made their way down to the terminal. Not wanting to be dead last off the boat, Hunt mingled in with the rest of the disembarking passengers on the stairwell leading down from the upper deck.

His phone rang as he stepped onto the lower deck. "I'm getting off the boat now. What have you got?"

Jayden spoke fast. "There's a small airport in the village of Red Hook, upstate New York, a couple hours' drive up the Hudson River. Ex-Navy buddy of mine will have a plane ready there to take you to a bigger airport further South. But first, you have to get to Red Hook."

"Couple hours? How am I going to get there?"

"Amtrak train station about a mile from where you are now. I'm sending directions. It goes to within about eight miles of Red Hook. You'll have to cab or Uber it the rest of the way. I can hook that up for you so it's pre-paid with a different name."

"Roger." Hunt reached the exit of the ferry and walked down the ramp to the terminal dock with the other passengers. "I can pay for the train ticket in cash, so that should be good."

"Right. So I texted you the directions to the train station. Hoof it over there, get on the next train, and by then I should have the results of the image search for you."

Hunt thanked him and slipped his phone back in his pocket. Wary, he looked around the terminal for the two well-dressed thugs, or anyone else who might appear suspicious, but it all seemed like normal activity for a busy ferry terminal. The chatter of gulls circling overhead mingled with the sound of the ferry schedule being broadcast over loudspeakers, and the clamor of hundreds of travelers. He wound his way out of the boat throng until he found a traffic-free spot where he could stand without being in anyone's way. He accessed the address from Jayden and started walking in that direction. He moved at a brisk pace, but not fast enough to attract attention.

Ten minutes later he reached the Amtrak station. Hunt bought his ticket in cash, glad to find out he had a piece of luck: the train was in the station and ready to leave in five minutes. Finally, something going my way, he thought. He boarded the train and made his way to his assigned window seat. He settled in for the three hour ride—Jayden had said two hours but then he remembered that was by car. He checked his phone but so far nothing from Jayden.

Then he heard the loudspeaker announcement that the train was leaving the station, the horn blared and his coach lurched into motion. Once the train got up to speed and the vibrations fell into a predictable rhythm, Hunt's thoughts drifted back to the map. He hoped it was authentic, for all this trouble they were going through. He thought about how large the search area was. The map contained no X-marks-the-spot, only the words *El Dorado* over the wide cross-hatched area.

He was pondering the implications of this when his smartphone lit up. Jayden. He held the phone to his hear, avoiding speakerphone even though no one was seated immediately next to or behind him.

"Talk to me, Jayden. I'm on the train. My phone battery's on the low side, so stay to the point."

"Roger that, you're on the train. I'll be brief. So I've been in touch with our pilot. He'll be waiting for you. Name's Graham, don't worry about his last name."

Hunt said that he wouldn't ask about it. He trusted Jayden not to being someone into this who couldn't be trusted. Treasure hunting was notorious for being a "loose lips sinks ships" type of business, and by now they had seen that firsthand on more than one occasion.

"As for the map image search, I'm not coming up with any exact matches. It does return other old maps, and some of those are of South America. A few have to do with pages talking about El Dorado, but none are the same as this one."

"Good. That likely means this map is not some Crackerjack prize that's not worth anything."

"Like if it was a reproduction of some generic map with the words 'El Dorado' overlaid onto it?"

"Exactly. It appears to be old *and* original, wherever it came from."

"I'll have an Uber driver waiting for you at the station to take you to the airport."

"Copy that. Now call Kelsey and tell her you need that deep cleaning."

"Sounds so tawdry when you put it like that."

"I'm sure you won't mind." Hunt disconnected the call, powered his phone down to conserve battery power and watched the Hudson roll by outside his window as the train made its way north. It dawned on him that if he was going to find El Dorado before anyone else based on this old scroll, that he needed to get about 2,500 miles south to Colombia right away. He had no doubt that the pursuit would not stop. Somebody, probably Daedalus, Hunt reflected, wanted that Muisca Raft very badly, and it had to be because they knew about the map. If he was extremely lucky, it was just an off-kilter collector, not associated with Treasure, Inc. who had no idea about the map's existence.

But if he was extremely unlucky, on the other hand….Hunt distracted himself from the unpleasant possibilities by staring out the Hudson River while the train rolled deeper into New York state.

CHAPTER 7

Caribbean Sea

The *R/V Historica* cut a broad swath of whitewater as it churned through the aquamarine waters of the tropical sea, heading southwest. No land was in sight under the bright blue sky dotted with puffy, white clouds. Still on his chaise lounge on the upper deck of the mega-yacht, Daedalus consulted his handheld device, which displayed the ship's position, course, speed and other information. He was alone up here for the time being, which is how he preferred it when conducting business. His girlfriend had caught up with the yacht, predictably irritated but nothing that couldn't be remedied with a fresh-made pina colada from the full service bar in the main salon. Currently she was taking a shower in their stateroom. A little later, Daedalus would visit her there to calm her down even further, but he still had phone calls to make.

There were always new ventures to attend to. It had recently come to his attention that a trove of Apache Indian artifacts had been uncovered in Arizona, and he believed he could "work with" the archaeologists who had discovered them. This usually meant some sort of bribe to look the other way while some of the finds were appropriated by Treasure, Inc. so that they could be sold off to his clients' private collections. Daedalus had his finger over his contact's number in his phone when an incoming call popped up on his screen. *Phillipo*. News on his pet project, *El Dorado!* He accepted the call with a jab of his finger.

"Yes, my brother, what news do you have for me?"

The slight hesitation told Daedalus that it wasn't good. "I'm sorry, Daedalus, but my operators have searched Central Park for the scroll and were unable to find it."

Daedalus allowed his head to loll back on the chair cushion, watching a cloud drift by overhead. *You knew El Dorado would not be easy. Nothing worth doing is ever easy...* "Then we have no choice to assume that Carter Hunt has it. Where is he now?"

"He's not in Central Park. My operatives are combing the city looking for him now, and I am checking for air reservations at nearby airports."

"You checked all the major ones already? JFK?"

"Checked JFK, La Guardia, Newark Liberty, and some smaller ones including Teterboro and Long Island MacArthur. There are a few more to check but so far his name isn't coming up. He could possibly be using a fake identity," Phillipo finished with. But they both knew it wasn't anything more than a plea that said, *I can't find him but it's not my fault.*

"He used his real name to win the auction, and to check into his hotel, and to rent a car," Daedalus reminded his brother.

"I know this."

"Perhaps he isn't travelling by plane. Did you check busses? What is it called?"

"Greyhound?"

"Yes."

"I'll do that."

Daedalus took a deep breath before continuing. "We have to be prepared to accept that he may have somehow acquired private transportation."

"Like Uber, Lyft, ridesharing?"

"Yes, or even just a friend or associate."

"It is possible."

"What I need you to do is monitor international air travel to Colombia. If he is going to search for El Dorado based on the map, I think it's likely that's where he would go, because that's where both Muisca Rafts were found."

"I'm on it."

"I also want you to put together a resource extraction team. I want them to be in Colombia within two days. They should be armed with both conventional weapons and sufficient technology to communicate securely worldwide and to conduct research as we learn more about the map and location of El Dorado."

"How—"

"Which reminds me," Daedalus said, deliberately cutting off his brother's request for clarification. "I need you to have our information technology people put a trace on Hunt's mobile phone. Find the number, and intercept his communications--that is the goal."

"This is a lot to do, Daedalus. I better get going."

"Indeed. And make sure the resource extraction team is comprised of our best contractors. The absolute best. Even if you have to pull them from other jobs. I will be meeting with them in Colombia myself in a few days' time."

Daedalus sat up in his lounge chair, gazing out across the open Caribbean, the seemingly endless sea of turquoise. But he knew that across its expanse lay South America.

And El Dorado.

CHAPTER 8

Red Hook, New York

The airfield was much smaller than Hunt had expected. And far less crowded. The latter was both good and bad; good, since he didn't have to worry about Daedalus' people hiding amongst a crowd, but bad because he himself would stand out that much more. His Uber driver had rolled away a few minutes earlier and Hunt had watched him drive off down the two-lane road that was the only way in or out to the airfield until his lights had disappeared. Hunt looked around at the airstrip, where he saw not a single other person. He counted four planes, all single engine prop types, and all covered with tarps as though they hadn't been used in some time.

A single small building with a yellow utility bulb outside and no windows was the only sign of human presence. Hunt was starting to wonder if either he had gone to the wrong place, or if Jayden had made some kind of mistake, when the whine of an engine caught his attention. So faint at first he thought it might be a faraway throng of insects, the steady, purposeful drone grew more distinct with each passing second. A minute later he could see a speck darken the sky in the direction of the noise. *Incoming aircraft!* Hunt walked to the side of the building so that he could use it for cover if the need arose.

He watched the airborne object draw near, and before long he was able to identify it as a small Cessna, unknown model. He noted that the airplane was still high in the sky, however, for a typical landing trajectory. Maybe it wasn't going to land here after all?

But then at the last second he watched the nose pull up, heard the motor cut out, then watched the plane start to freefall. Somehow the pilot put it into a controlled glide, easing the nose back down as it descended toward the runway at an angle that Hunt thought was scary steep, though he was not a pilot himself. When it became clear that the plane was going to impact the runway reasonably far from the building Hunt stood next to— whether controlled or uncontrolled remained to be seen—Hunt started to walk toward the runway. He glanced around the sky, looking for any other aircraft that might be incoming, but not seeing any. In spite of the fact that he knew runways were extremely dangerous places to occupy, he walked further out onto it to observe the plane's landing, such as it may be.

At that time, his hearing registered a new sound. Not coming from the plane, but a much higher, piercing wail. *Siren?*

He caught his breath as the single engine Cessna wobbled to and fro, wings dipping crazily as it slanted toward the ground. Then Hunt heard the engine crank back to life as it settled into a controlled descent barely 100 feet above the tarmac. The plane wobbled again and then righted itself before dropping to the pavement. The wheels bounced off the runway once before touching down again and starting to roll. Hunt watched as the plane was rapidly brought under control by the pilot, whose form Hunt could now see hunched over the stick.

The airplane hurtled down the runway toward Hunt. When it reached him the pilot braked, causing the tires to screech, but the craft came to a complete stop. Hunt watched the pilot's head and upper body be wrenched forward against his lap belt as if in a medium-impact car crash. All things considered, however, Hunt suspected things had gone quite well for the pilot given what could have happened. Once the plane was rolling slowly in a controlled fashion, Hunt jogged over to it. He saw the cockpit door swing open as he reached it. The pilot stepped out while leaving the engine idling.

Hunt saw that he was a corpulent man, heavyset and clad in blue jeans and a black leather motorcycle vest, with a pair of cowboy boots. His eye was drawn to the man's metal belt buckle, which bore a stylized Navy SEAL emblem. A Stetson hat framing a full scraggly beard completed the ensemble. The pilot extended a hand, but before he shook it, Hunt glanced at his watch to show his irritation that he hadn't been here waiting as expected.

"Graham Walker, nice to meet you, Mr. Hunt. Sorry I'm late."

Hunt shook the bear-like paw of a hand, making a conscious attempt not to wince in its overly firm grip. "I thought Jayden said you were based at this air facility?"

The pilot briefly held his hands apart in a gesture that said, *I know…* "I used to be, and that outdated contact info on the web is how the J-man— that's what we used to call your business partner back in SEAL Team 8-- found me." Hunt couldn't help but smile at that while the pilot continued.

"The J-man paid me before I had the chance to tell him I wasn't actually here no more, bless his big heart. He was always one of the good guys, you know—I mean, even among us good guys on Team 8." Hunt again gave him a nod before he went on. "But it just so happened that where I keep my plane nowadays was still within range—actually a four hour drive—car drive—north of here. "And I was going to tell him, but then I thought, well, I'll be a little late, but I can still do it. I'm still within range. And God knows I could use the money, and the way he made it sound, you guys needed some private aviation services pretty bad, so….here I am!"

Hunt gave him a hard stare as the siren became even louder. To his surprise, the pilot went on. "Actually, since I know you're a good man and I aim to do business with you, let me be straight." Hunt gave him an appreciative nod while the pilot jerked his thumb back at the plane. The siren continued to increase in volume due to its growing proximity to them. "That's a police siren, and those boys in blue are likely coming for me, so if you need a lift, I suggest we get outta here right the heck now."

Finally something the pilot said genuinely surprised him, and Hunt's mouth dropped open as he looked toward the end of the runway and saw the first red and blue hues of the cop car bar lights. He stepped forward until he was nearly nose to nose with the pilot. "What's going on? Tell me the truth. Is this your plane?"

The pilot nodded. "Yes. It's owned by me, registered to me. But it was in hock when Jayden called, 'cuz I missed a couple of payments on it. So I busted it out of the tow yard in order to come pick you up. Usually I'd be able to slip in there, wheel it out all quiet-like until I can just tow it home real slow behind my F-350, but gosh dang if ol' Robbie didn't get him a new junkyard dog. Rottie, meanest damn thing—"

"Hey!" Hunt said cutting him off."

"Sorry. Hey look, I guess you don't want my ride. I'm just gonna face the music here, then." He turned away from Hunt to literally face the approaching police car with its blaring siren. "Nobody wants me to fly, anyhow."

Hunt watched him start to walk away dejectedly. The police car gathered speed down the airstrip now, heading toward the plane. He considered his options, looking around at the desolate airfield. He'd likely be questioned simply for being here with this pilot and his essentially stolen plane, possibly even brought back to the station for interrogation, eventually cleared but then perhaps required to appear in court as a witness... Meanwhile, Treasure, Inc. was looking for him, and no doubt El Dorado at the same time. And Hunt being detained, even for just a short time if that did come to pass, would be a matter of public record and therefore tell them where he is, while at the same time barring his own search. He looked from the rapidly approaching law enforcement vehicle to the plane, and then back to the pilot.

"Hey Graham!" The pilot stopped walking and turned back around to look at Hunt, who said, "Your landing looked a little sketchy. You think you can fly this thing outta here in one piece before those cops get to us?"

The pilot's face transformed into a look that registered first disbelief, then relief, and then happiness, all in about two seconds. Then the big man waved his arm as he started to run toward his Cessna. "C'mon, get in the co-pilot seat!"

Hunt took off sprinting after him, turning his head to the right to see the cop car barreling toward them. His right foot snagged on the edge of a pothole and he stumbled forward, but did not fall. Still, it slowed him some and caused Graham to look back at him. "Keep going, I'm fine!" he called out to him.

"Been awhile since Boot Camp, eh?" was the pilot's response as he climbed up into the cockpit with surprising agility for a man of his size. Hunt flashed on all the exercise he'd already had today in Central Park. He mentally cautioned himself to step up his game as he rounded the plane's nose and made the co-pilot door, which had already been flung open by Graham. "You're telling me!" Best to be friendly about it, Hunt knew, rather than detail all he'd gone through. Besides, there was no time for that, anyway. The siren overcame the plane engine noise now, even as Graham revved it up in preparation for takeoff. He put the plane into gear even before Hunt had his door closed, and the Cessna lurched into forward motion down the runway while the police car drove up to it from behind.

A white spotlight from the cop car lit up the cockpit of the plane, and Hunt could barely hear the megaphone from the officer over the plane noise, but it was clear they were being told to stop. Graham throttled up as the plane taxied down the runway, picking up speed. The police car reached them and was for now easily able to keep up, which Hunt knew would make things even worse, especially for the pilot, if they were actually apprehended here. He could hear it now: *No excuses, you knew we were trying to pull you over.*

"Seat belt on, man!" Graham yelled as he clicked his own into place with the hand not on the stick. Hunt gladly complied and felt his phone vibrate in his pocket as he clicked it into place. He checked the screen, saw that it was Jayden and answered the call. "Hey Carter, you should be almost to D.C. by now, am I right?"

Carter had to laugh at this. "Listen, *J-man*, I'm going to have to call you back. Remember that soup sandwich you mentioned earlier? Well, this one's the chef special. We're taking off now from Red Hook."

He could hear the genuine surprise and concern in Jayden's voice.

"Taking off *now*? But—"

"Look, I'll have to explain it later, but we're still following the plan, I'll call when I can. Battery's low, anyway. Over and out." Hunt ended the call and pocketed his phone. He looked over at Graham and saw that the pilot had a slight smile on his face as he white-knuckled the plane's controls, coaxing more and more speed out of the little Cessna. But behind them, the cop car still kept pace, and Hunt felt his stomach clench as the police car pulled out alongside of the plane and then began speeding forward.

"They're coming up on our starboard side!" Hunt said, sticking to proper aviation jargon, knowing he was talking to an ex-military man. Graham patted his dashboard. "She's giving me all she can for now. Don't worry, she'll give it to us!"

Hunt wasn't exactly sure how to take that, but it would have to suffice so he turned his attention back to the police. The car was now outside his window, and he was mortified to see the officer reaching out of his open window with a service pistol in the hand not on the wheel, aimed right at Hunt. The fact that his plane's window was rolled up meant that he had no chance to hear what the cop was shouting at him, but it didn't matter, the meaning was more than clear.

"He's gonna shoot at us!" Hunt warned.

"Here we go, here go!" Graham was so excited he literally bounced up and down in his pilot's seat like a little kid on an amusement park ride. And to Hunt's immeasurable relief, just like that, the Cessna's wheels left the Earth. Hunt saw the cop car pass below them and inhaled what was to be a sigh of relief. But by the time he was ready to exhale, the plane was dropping again. Its wheels bounced off the tarmac, and then was airborne again, but this time was just as brief.

The Cessna touched down again. This time both wheels landing squarely on the roof of the patrol car. Hunt felt the crunching of glass and metal as the bar lights, antenna and who knows what other equipment was crushed, shattered and dented. Remarkably, the plane stayed airborne this time, slowly picking up altitude as it gained speed. Looking back, Hunt checked to make sure the cop car didn't actually crash. It had pulled over to a stop.

He reached his phone to call 911—if they were hurt he would want to get them help—but them he saw both officers exit the vehicle and point their weapons at them.

He heard shots being fired and ducked down in the seat, pushing Graham down, too. The pilot shrunk his bulk down as much as possible in the seat while still being able to fly. Hunt heard a *ping* as one of the bullets found its target. "I hope that was something non-essential," he said to Graham. The pilot looked over at him and said, "Unfortunately, pretty much everything on an aircraft is essential otherwise it wouldn't be part of it." He paused to consult his gauges as they passed over the end of the runway while continuing to climb into the sky. "But they didn't hit the engine or the fuel tank, or we'd know it by now. So that bodes well for additional airtime."

"Good to know," Hunt said, still looking down out of his window. "So did Jayden, I mean, J-man, give you a destination?"

Graham looked up from his dashboard and eyed Hunt with a nod. "Yeah, he said Ron Regan Airport in D.C. Is that right?"

"Yeah, and from there I should be able to catch a flight down south."

Graham eyed the compass on his dashboard and made a slight course correction, turning the plane a little to the left. "Okay, we're gonna level out pretty soon at five thousand feet, and from there on out…." He picked up a handheld radio and handed it to Hunt. "That's my weather radio, the built-in one doesn't work. From there on out, I was saying, we should be okay as long as the weather holds up."

Hunt exhaled heavily as he took the radio from the pilot and turned it on to monitor the aviation weather channel. He looked out the window, glad to see clear skies and the ground far below. He knew police must be searching for the Cessna by now and wondered how much information they actually had. And then there was the matter of his next move once they got to the airport in D.C. To take his mind off all the variables and let Graham focus on his job, he decided to look at the treasure map again.

After all, once—and *if*, he was inclined to admit at this point—he even got to Colombia, he had to know where to search. He sought reassurance from the map that it was as specific as he thought—hoped?— it was on first inspection. So he carefully pulled out the scroll and unrolled it. Although the sun was no longer at its zenith in the sky, there was still plenty of daylight left, especially at this altitude. As he stared at the precious paper, he reminded himself to have it mailed off to a lab for safekeeping once he got to Colombia. He had a picture of it now, so he no longer needed the physical specimen.

"Whatcha got there?" Graham asked, glancing over from the pilot's seat.

Instinctively, Hunt turned the map so that his pilot couldn't see it. But then he realized the silliness of his poor attempt at subterfuge. Here he was, desperate enough to have a friend arrange to have someone pick him up in a plane that turned out to be stolen, and he is still okay with that enough to fly with him. How could he pretend that he didn't have something pressing?

"Jayden told me that your company recovers artifacts. He said you need to get down to South America for an expedition to recover one. That's all he told me." Graham took both his hands off the wheel for a moment to raise them in a gesture of supplication. "You don't have to say any more than that if you don't want. I'm just making conversation. We have a couple hours to sit before we shift into a landing pattern." He turned his attention back to the controls.

"It's a map," Hunt said cautiously. "Old-looking, but hasn't been verified yet. It might lead to a treasure somewhere in the Amazon rain forest."

Grahams' guttural belly laugh filled the cabin. Hunt shot him a knowing expression. "I know, it sounds crazy."

The pilot smiled while shaking his head. "It doesn't *sound* crazy, my man, it *is* crazy. One hundred percent batshit."

"Thanks for the vote of confidence."

"You obviously don't need my vote or you wouldn't have gotten this far, brother. Hell, I know people who have a *way* surer thing than what you got, and they can't even take two steps toward it. So good for you."

Hunt shook his head rapidly to clear the cobwebs. Here he was, getting a pep talk from a guy who was currently running from the police after stealing his plane out of an impound yard. Maybe the events of the day were taking a toll on Hunt's mind, fogging it? For some reason he felt the need to justify his actions. In a roundabout way, after all, he had endangered this man's life. They had been shot at while taking off. *The curse of El Dorado strikes again.*

"So I don't think you and I ever crossed paths in the service, did we? J-man said you were an officer?"

Hunt was only too glad to take up the more neutral ground of their common military service. "No, I don't believe we did, but yeah I was a first lieutenant with Third Fleet at Point Loma in San Diego, and that's where I first met Jayden…" Hunt told Graham about some of his work in the military, some of the missions he did with Jayden, joking about how he could only tell him about the non-classified parts.

"Like it never happened!" Graham said with a big smile. The Navy talk and reminiscing about the old days and people they had in common and what they were up to these days flowed freely and easily while they flew onward. So much so that it was the pilot, and not Hunt, who had to break off the conversation first.

"All right, buddy, I need to focus on the landing approach here."

Hunt agreed and realized that he still held the open map in his hands. He'd never gotten around to studying it some more. Now, with the landing imminent, that would just have to wait, so he rolled it back up and pocketed it once again.

Graham held a hand out toward Hunt. "Also, I'm going to need the radio now to communicate with the tower. D.C. area, as you can guess, is heavily enforced, and so I'll need to pretend like we're above board."

No sooner did Hunt hand him the radio than it began sounding a shrill emergency tone. Hunt's eyes widened as he pressed the radio into the pilot's waiting hand. "Oh, don't worry, that's just a weather alert," Graham said.

Hunt had a few seconds to hear a robotic monotone voice intone about a series of squalls that was pushing inland around the D.C. Metro area, with all sorts of advisories being issued before Graham changed the channel over to the airport tower frequency.

Suddenly fat drops of water began pelting the Cessna's windscreen.

CHAPTER 9

Ronald Reagan National Airport
Washington, D.C.

"Windshield wipers don't work." Graham bumped his fist on the dash a couple of times, not out of frustration, but in a legitimate attempt to get them to work. They did not, and the rain only intensified as the Cessna approached the lights of the airport runway complex.

"I take it this isn't a plane to qualify for instrument flight," Hunt said, referencing more sophisticated aircraft that could be flown with instruments only, meaning, it wasn't necessary to see outside the craft.

Graham laughed hard, his whole belly heaving with his mirth despite the situation. "And even if it was, it's been a while since my instrument rating expired. I don't know, might need you to reach your arm out there with a towel…"

Hunt eyed him dubiously and Graham guffawed again.

"I'm glad you're in such a good mood over this," Hunt said. "Not gonna lie, I'm a bit worried myself." He wasn't kidding. Visibility outside the cockpit had shrunk to a couple hundred feet in places, while what they could see of the ground was rapidly closing in with fog. Heavy precipitation pelted the plane's metal skin, creating a bone-jarring percussive rattle.

"Remember this heading, just in case," Graham said, tapping a physical compass bubble on the dash. Hunt read the number aloud to make sure he had it right as Graham turned the plane in that direction, where they could still see a couple of runway lights. Looking out beyond their right-side wing tip, where thankfully a running light blinked its "I'm here" warning, Hunt could see a couple of other blinking white lights through the fog, a reminder that they were descending into a highly trafficked airspace and the danger of collision from not following protocols, especially in low visibility conditions like these, was all too real. He felt for the map in his pocket, wondering if he, too, would become another victim of the golden curse.

His dark thoughts were interrupted by Graham's voice engaging in some technical chatter with the tower, which to Hunt sounded like it wasn't going well. He heard the phrase "holding pattern" followed by some choice curses of Graham's off-air, and then complaints about remaining fuel levels. In the end, Graham was given the choice of landing immediately on an outlying runway requiring them to trek through the rain to the terminal buildings, or to wait in a holding pattern for "five-to-ten minutes" until they could be cleared to land on one of the main runways.

"Apparently they don't know who I am," Graham said, with a mischievous grin on his face.

"And it's a good thing," Hunt pointed out.

Graham pointed off to their left. "So we're taking Door Number Two for a mountain of gold, Bob! Minor outlying runway, here we come!"

"I like your enthusiasm," Hunt said, gripping a handhold, "but let's get to the ground in one piece, shall we?"

"You got it!" Graham put both hands on the control stick and went to work landing the plane at the same time that Hunt's phone rang in his pocket. He fished it out, saw that it was Jayden calling, and took the call, not on speaker.

Before Jayden could say anything, Hunt said, "We're going in for a landing now at Reagan. Weather sucks. Do I have a connecting flight?"

"Sort of."

Hunt clenched the handhold even tighter. "Doesn't sound good.

Explain?"

"Weather's got all the commercial flights grounded for at least the next couple hours. Private planes are allowed to take off for the next thirty minutes, and they have one available that can get you as far south as Miami, but it's got no pilot. It's available for charter, but they said their pilot is not available right now, but that if we could find our own, we could charter it. I can wire them the funds, but I'm waiting to hear back on some pilots."

"I'll call you back after we land."

"Hold on, we're going in." Graham pulled back on the stick to level the small plane out as he dropped in toward the runway. The rain intensified along with the wind. To Hunt it felt like they were riding in a paper cup blown in a cyclone, but somehow Graham managed to control the Cessna all the way down to the tarmac. The wheels touched down, bounced once, skidded once, and then bit down on the asphalt as Graham applied the brakes.

"That was even smoother than when you landed in Red Hook," Hunt marveled.

Graham grinned back at him, yelling to overcome the still shrill whine of the engine and rain bombardment. "Back there I was trying to come in undetected because J-man said you were being followed. A long slow approach is easy to see from a long ways away, so I came in high, deliberately threw her into a stall, and dropped right down, like a poor man's helicopter landing."

Hunt eyed the pilot as he continued to decelerate the aircraft. He had a new level of respect for him at this point. Then he looked outside at the driving rain splashing off the tarmac, at the terminal buildings that looked as though they were literally a mile away, barely visible through the wet haze. He didn't see that he had any other choice than to slog through the cold rain to the terminal, or even to wait in the Cessna if whiteout conditions developed, which seemed possible. In other words, Hunt thought, *I'm stuck here.*

Graham engaged in some more chatter with the control tower and finally shut down the engine, leaving the running lights on so that they were still visible to other aircraft and ground vehicles. He turned to Hunt. "Look, I'm just going to hang out here until this weather clears. Probably only be a couple of hours. Safer than trying to walk to the terminal. You're welcome to wait with me if you want. I'm sure your commercial flight is on hold, am I right?"

Hunt nodded. "Right. Charter planes can leave for the next few minutes, but the only one with suitable range, a Citation CJ2, doesn't have a pilot available. So it looks like—"

"Wait, what? No pilot?"

"Right. On vacation. We didn't have a reservation, this is all very last minute, so—"

Graham reached over and tapped Hunt on the shoulder. "I can fly those."

Hunt returned his stare, looking for any signs of flinching, insincerity, anything that would suggest he was not telling the whole truth. "Are you licensed to fly that class of aircraft? Jets?"

Graham shrugged. "Look, I didn't say I was *licensed* to fly one, I only said that I *can* fly one. I and I can. But it takes a certain number of hours per year to maintain the license and I haven't been putting those in since I started flying small craft. But hey, I can take you to Miami in it. Your call."

The sound of rainfall hammering the small plane's roof and fuselage drummed against their ears until Hunt asked, "You're not making this up?"

"No way. I'm sure I could re-certify today if I took the test and had the requisite hours logged. But it's pricey to maintain, you know, so I let it drop. Flew tons of 'em in the Navy and for the first five years after."

Hunt took out his phone and dialed Jayden. "Let me see if it's even still an option. Jayden answered right away. "J-man, I'm sitting on the tarmac here at Reagan International with your old buddy Graham Walker, who says that he can fly the Citation CJ2 jet from here to Miami. Two questions for you: One, do you believe him..." He paused to look over at Graham, who simply watched the call with interest. "...and two: is that plane still available if we provide our own pilot? You're on speaker."

Jayden's voice, though competing with the drumming raindrops, was audible enough in the cockpit. "If Graham says he can fly it, Carter, he can fly it. He's an absolute a legend in the SEALs. Rumor has it he saved a sharpshooter's life with a hang glider and a bottle of Jack Daniels, but I'll leave that story for another day."

"You'll have to, my phone battery's in the red. But get us that Citation, okay? It's one helluva slog to the terminal from here and I don't want to do it just to find out it's not available."

"Consider it done. And tell Graham I'll wire him his fee now, too."

"Thanks J-man," Graham interjected. "But just one thing…"

Hunt looked over at him while Jayden asked what that was. "I keep telling everybody, it wasn't Jack Daniels, it was Southern Comfort."

* * *

Sitting in the considerably roomier cockpit of the Citation jet, still on the tarmac of Reagan International, Hunt eyed Graham very carefully as the pilot went through his pre-flight checklist, flipping switches, turning dials, and pressing buttons while watching LCD displays. It was considerably more technical than the Cessna, and Hunt would have been lying had he said he wasn't concerned about his safety, Jayden's glowing recommendation notwithstanding.

"Don't worry, I know what at least half of this stuff does," Graham said, toggling a bank of switches on a ceiling panel. But ten minutes later the twin Williams-Rolls FJ44-2C jet engines purred to life and Graham informed Air traffic Control they were ready for takeoff. The thing that gave Hunt the most peace of mind was that he was able to charge his cellphone from a retractable USB cable in the plane's dashboard. He'd call Jayden when they landed in Miami to find out next steps.

"You sure your Cessna's going to be okay here?" Hunt asked.

"They'll tow it somewhere, I'll get a bill. But yeah, it'll all work out. If I take the time to park it all proper-like now, we'll miss our takeoff opportunity. I left the hazard lights on. Another five minutes and they're gonna lock the runway down."

Hunt knew he was right, but at the same time was thankful for his dedication to the contracted job. "Let's go, then. My company will pay the fees for your Cessna in addition to your pilot's fees." Graham shot him an earnest look and then the jet started rolling out onto the runway. This time, the acceleration was so smooth that Hunt almost couldn't feel the asphalt beneath them. But the sensation of speed was definitely there, and in no time at all they were wheels up over the capital city, sheets of rain spraying off the windshield faster than the wipers could wipe them off.

Once they levelled off at a cruising altitude, Hunt once again pulled out the map and unwound the scroll.

"That must be some interesting reading," the pilot said. "But don't mind me, I've got plenty to keep me occupied here until we get to Miami."

"I'm trying to make sure we know where to go once we get to South America," Hunt said, turning the map sideways, then back again. Once again, the allure of the old document drew him in, and for a time he forgot about the driving rain, the fact that he was being chased, that he was in an airplane in bad weather piloted by someone he barely knew...

El Dorado. The letters welcomed his mind back to the search, the quest, the obsession. The old map mostly depicted the country of what is now Colombia, which was, of course a colossal area he knew to be about a half a million square miles, far too many for even several lifetimes of careful, grid-based searching. But the shaded, or cross-hatched part of the map, across which the Spanish words *El Dorado* were written, ostensibly contained his objective. Somewhere in that shaded area, according to the author of this mysterious piece of cartography, lay the lost city. Or, Carter reflected, the home of the Golden Man himself, which he knew was what El Dorado literally translated to. But even if that's what El Dorado did in fact refer to—a man, rather than a city—that man would have been surrounded by untold wealth.

And Carter aimed to find it. To do that, he knew he might need modern cartographical aids like Geographic Information Systems, satellite photography, possibly LiDAR, ground penetrating RADAR and others. He knew all too well that traversing even a single mile of what has been dubbed the Green Hell could take more than a day. Countless people had died in pursuit of various treasures in the South American wilderness, including El Dorado. Because of that, it paid to do a little research first to narrow the search zone.

His thoughts were interrupted by Graham, who by now had been simply babysitting the sleek jet on autopilot as it sluiced through the drenched skies heading south. "Can I ask you a question?"

"Sure."

"This treasure-it's been there a long time, right?"

"That's right."

"So why all the hurry to get to it right now? I mean, what's the huge rush? It'll still be there next week, next month, next year, right, if you don't get it now?"

Hunt looked up from the map and turned to his pilot. "Maybe, maybe not. There is a small but obsessive community of international antiquities traders who follow breaking news on archaeological projects, so that when a new discovery is made that might shed new light on a historic treasure—like this one—" he paused to hold up the scroll. "—it tends to trigger a sudden wave of interest and activity."

"So you're saying other people are also trying to get the same treasure right now?"

"That's what I'm saying."

Graham appeared to think about this for a minute. Then he said, "But do they have a private jet and pilot?"

"They sure do."

At this the pilot's eyes widened and he turned back to monitoring the plane's controls as they flew onward through the weather.

* * *

Miami International Airport

After a blissfully uneventful landing, Hunt and Graham sat in the Citation on the tarmac outside one of the main terminals. Hunt held his phone in one hand and said, "I need to give Jayden a call and see what's up with hooking up my next leg. Do you have a phone that you can use to verify you received your funds for services rendered?"

Graham said that he did not have a phone. "I forgot to grab it I was in such a rush to pick you up."

"I'll check with Jayden that he transferred the money, then." Hunt was about to press the call button when Graham said, "Mr. Hunt?"

Hunt turned his way, finger poised over the phone. "Yeah?"

"I would like to be a part of your expedition, as long as you'll have me. I can fly this very plane—" he patted the dashboard to make it clear—"to Colombia. And once we're down there, well, you know how fast things can change. Amazon's a big place. I can fly all sorts of aircraft, big and small, planes and helicopters, to move you around where and when you need to go. Ground vehicles and boats, too, and I'm also pretty handy as a mechanic, if it comes to that."

Hunt eyeballed the man carefully. He had gotten him this far, it was true, but to join the actual expedition entailed other factors. "You'd need a passport to get us into the country."

Hunt lifted his backside off the leather pilot's seat and retrieved a blue booklet from his back jeans pocket. He held out a U.S. passport to Hunt, who took it and opened it up. He noted that it was still valid although had no stamps less than five years old. He also noted that the first name was the same one he had given him, and that his last name was "Walker." He handed it back to Graham.

"So you didn't have time to grab your cell-phone before you ran out of the house, but you took your passport?"

Graham's expression became sheepish. "Look, my cell account got behind on payment and they shut off my service, okay? That's why I didn't bring it. Now that you paid, me, I'll be able to have it turned back on."

"Let me talk about it with Jayden for a minute. But you understand that this expedition has very real dangers. You probably don't have any recent shots—we'd have to get vaccinations for you in Bogota so that you don't get sick down there."

"*No problemo, amigo!*"

"Do you speak Spanish?"

"Not much more than what I just said. I can order tacos and ask where the bathroom is, that kind of thing."

Hunt laughed good-naturedly. "I don't know that we'll need you to actually trek through the jungle with us, but we'd pay you to be on standby in the city or village with an aircraft to fly us out when we call. We'd get you a satellite phone to stay in contact. Sometimes in the field we work with local guides and may not always need you, but I've learned the hard way it does pay to have our own pilot on standby."

"I can do that."

Hunt stared him down for a few seconds during which neither man's gaze wavered. Then he held up the phone and opened the cockpit door. "Stay here, let me have some words with J-man."

Graham nodded and Hunt stepped down out of the jet. Closing the door behind him, he called Jayden, who immediately began to explain the air travel options, all of which involved some kind of wait time.

"Jayden, hold up. Listen to this. Graham says he can fly this same jet all the way to Colombia, after refueling, of course. And he said he'd like to join the expedition as our pilot. He'd be on standby at the air facilities ready to extract us as needed. He has a non-expired U.S. passport. Do you see any problems with that?"

Jayden's enthusiasm was unbridled. "Wow, hell no! That's great. I mean, no I don't see problems, he's one of the good guys, Carter. I know that. I would trust my life to him. Actually, I already have. I would not be here today if it weren't for him, you can take that to the bank. It's classified, but trust me, he saved my ass when everyone else, including my own government, wrote me off. If he wants to do it, let's help him by having him help us. I know he's had a rough time financially since getting out of the service."

"I'll take that as a 'No,' you don't see any problems with hiring him for this expedition. So here's what I need you to do now: Pay the jet company to extend our rental. Pay Graham half of his fees to fly to Bogota and back up front. And get yourself down to Colombia by tomorrow."

They ended the call and Hunt took a deep breath, inhaling the warm, moist air of the Miami night while looking around at the palm trees framing the terminal buildings, and the Spanish language billboards and signage. He knew the sub-tropical city was only the barest hint of what was to come in the next few days. He thought of all the money he was spending, the trouble and risk he was putting himself through, and reminded himself that he could stop now and go home. Just pay Graham to fly him back to New York, get a hotel and fly commercial back to Los Angeles whenever he was ready.

But then he felt that little scroll in his pocket. If he wanted El Dorado, the time was now. He had a lead on it, treasure was his business and El Dorado was the mother lode. The thought of letting it fall into Daedalus' hands—in effect to be used for his personal profit and enrichment—sickened him.

He opened the plane door and climbed into the cockpit. "Graham, buddy, you're hired!"

The burly pilot's visage erupted into a portrait of happiness and relief. "Hell yes!"

"Let's go find El Dorado."

"Say what?"

"El. Dorado. The Golden One. The lost city of gold." Emboldened, Hunt took the scroll from his pocket and held it up for Graham to see. "That's what the map leads to."

The pilot looked at him as though he was dealing with someone who didn't fully comprehend reality. "Hey, as long as you're paying me, I...I'll fly you wherever you want to go."

Hunt's enthusiasm would not be deterred. He climbed into the cockpit and pulled the door shut. "Just thought you might like to know what we're looking for. If we find it, the whole world is going to know, anyway."

CHAPTER 10

Bogota, Colombia
Elevation 1,660 Feet

Hunt smiled as he and Graham passed beneath the sign reading *El Dorado Café*. They took seats at an outdoor table, taking advantage of the warm, sunny weather after being cooped up in airplanes for the better part of the last two days. A modern city with a population of about eight million, Bogota boasted a downtown with sleek skyscrapers set against a mountainous green backdrop. After checking into a nearby hotel, Hunt and Graham had come here for a bite to eat and to plan their expedition while awaiting Jayden's arrival.

"Air feel thinner to you?" Hunt asked Graham as he perused the Spanish language menu.

"Nah, we're already acclimated from flying in the unpressurized Cessna," Graham joked. They ordered a couple of Pilsen beers and some fish tacos from a passing server before turning to the task at hand. Hunt knew that logistics was the thing that tended to make or break expeditions. Traipsing off into the jungle without a plan—even with equipment—was never going to end well. The key, as with most business objectives, was to apply their available resources in the most efficient way before setting out.

"So we'll be heading south to the mountain caves where the Muisca Rafts were found." Hunt glanced at the wall where gold painted tribal figures similar to those depicted on the rafts adorned the establishment. "Both rafts—the one in the Bogota Museum and the one I won at auction and had stolen from me—have the same chemical signature, meaning they were likely found in the same cave system, which is rumored to be extensive."

"And your map shows that to be the actual location of El Dorado?"

The server returned at that moment with their drinks and Hunt waited to answer until she had left. "It has a shaded area that looks like it includes the caves among other places, but I think that's a decent place to start."

He raised his Pilsen and clinked bottles with Graham. "To The Golden One!" He took a sip before setting the bottle down and continuing the conversation.

* * *

The next morning found Hunt at a post office mailing the carefully boxed scroll to Kelsey Pawar in the states. He had quality images of it on his phone and backed up on a flash drive, so there was no need to risk it to the elements, loss, or theft by carrying around. Another advantage of mailing it to her was that she would get it to a lab to have it chemically analyzed, which might offer further clues as to its origins. Once he had paid and handed it off to the clerk, he met up with Graham to shop for trekking supplies—backpacks, clothing, camping gear, dehydrated food, radios, pretty much everything one needed to spend several days to weeks in the tropical wilderness.

By lunchtime he and Graham had made several trips to their hotel room, filling it with additional outdoor equipment including climbing gear, multi-tools, machetes, flashlights, and even a small inflatable boat.

"All this will fit in the chopper, right?" Hunt asked Ghraham, who raised an eyebrow at the substantial mound of gear.

"Think so. It's a Eurocopter EC-130. Real nice bird. Worst comes to worst, we might have to leave out a few six-packs and some of the ice. The *Aguardiente* is a lot more bang for the buck in terms of space-to-weight ratio," he said, referring to Colombia's hard liquor of choice.

They had decided on using a helicopter as a drop-off and pickup vehicle so as to avoid using local guides. Expedition fast-tracking, Hunt called it. The more he had to ask around about needing a guide, the easier his movements would be for Treasure, Inc., and Daedalus to trace. In some areas of the world, such as the middle east, Hunt had existing relationships with guides who could be trusted to remain discreet. But Colombia was not one of those places. He had seen the warnings, too, posted in the outdoor shops, the national parks, the websites: exploring the wilderness was dangerous without a guide, don't do it, you could wander into FARC guerillas or drug runner territory. Hunt knew these were legitimate concerns.

The rest of the day was spent with Hunt making team arrangements and getting Graham his vaccinations. He watched the local weather stations with a keen eye, but no reports of storms were imminent. Being June, it was not rainy season, but that did not mean there weren't storms or that it never rained. He also learned that the rivers were not yet low to the point of being unnavigable, which happened frequently during the height of dry season. So he was pleased with the seasonal window that fate, if not himself, had picked for his expedition.

By dinnertime, Graham had returned with sore arms and papers declaring him safely vaccinated against dengue fever, malaria, yellow fever and typhoid, and Hunt felt reasonably confident that tomorrow they would be able to set out. He also felt well acclimated to the altitude after a day of moving about the city.

Hunt and Graham ate at the hotel restaurant for dinner, taking an inside table in a space that was semi-crowded with other international diners. By the time the two men had ordered drinks, a well-built Asian-American man in his mid-thirties with a head of thick, wavy black hair stopped at the entrance to speak with the young hostess, chatting with her somewhat longer than was really necessary, before walking straight back to Hunt's table.

He came to the table with a hand raised for a high five, but Hunt stood and hugged him instead, and Graham followed suit.

"What, no brewski waiting for me?" Jayden took a seat. As if on cue, a server showed up and took their order for a new round of Pilsens.

"You hungry?" Hunt asked, offering Jayden a menu.

"I ate on the plane, but seeing as we're heading out into the bush tomorrow, I should take the opportunity for a real meal, am I right?"

Both of his dining companions agreed and the server returned to their table with the beers and a menu. Again, Hunt and Graham toasted to El Dorado, this time with Jayden. Talk turned to reminiscing with Graham over their shared Navy days, and before long more drinks were ordered. Hunt was glad they had such a tight-knit team, for that would be important once they got *out there*, as he thought of it. He'd rather trust his life to friends than hired guns if at all possible.

Jayden had just finished telling Graham about the last time he and Hunt had gone searching for a legendary relic together, and a wild night they had spent in Iraq with a camp of desert nomads, when a woman sashayed up to their table. Standing at just over five feet tall, what she lacked in height she more than made up for in beauty. She wore her long chestnut hair in a ponytail beneath a ball cap with a *Divers Do It Deeper* scuba flag emblem. Her athletic figure was evidence of a strict workout routine.

Hunt's face was buried in his phone reading an email, and so he failed to notice her, but Graham was immediately captivated by the female beauty in their presence. Jayden's face, however, lit up with the recognition of an old friend.

"Maddy?" his voice expressed all the doubt in the world even though he knew exactly who she was.

"Hello boys, I see I'm a little late to the party!"

Hunt looked up from his phone toward the voice and froze in disbelief for a moment before his face broke out into a huge smile. He rose and embraced her warmly. "Well if it isn't world-renowned archaeologist Dr. Madison Chambers! You didn't tell me.....Jayden?"

His friend shrugged and returned a sheepish look. "Wanted it to be a surprise, bro. And besides, she wasn't sure she was going to make it."

"It's true," Maddy said, taking a seat at the table next to Hunt. "I thought I might have to run a dig in Mongolia, but the paperwork fell through at the last minute. So when I couldn't get in touch with you I called Jayden, and he told me…" She lowered her voice and leaned in over the table with raised eyebrows. "He told me you won an auction at Sotheby's that holds a clue to final resting place of El Dorado?"

Hunt eyed her with a gaze that was full of possibility and wonder, but answered simply, "Yes."

Maddy leaned in close to him. "You remember after the Atlantis thing when you asked me if I wanted to join your company and I said I couldn't right then?"

"Yes."

"Well now I have time and I want to join you on this expedition." She held a hand up to stave off the protests she knew were forthcoming. "I'm not asking for a cut of the treasure, if any is found. Only academic recognition. You don't even have to pay me. I'll pay my own way. I just want to be a part of it, be able to publish papers about it. I've been doing Egyptology for so long it's like I've forgotten about the rest of the world, but I've always been fascinated by the legend of El Dorado. I can help you. You know I can. Please let me come along."

"Oh man!" This from Graham. "You can't say no to that!"

Maddy blushed while Hunt turned to his new pilot. "You going to carry her twelve days out of the jungle mountains if she gets sick?"

Graham shrugged. "Hell, you know I would. Fly her out, maybe. Good point, though…" He turned to Maddy. "You got your shots?" He proudly showed her his marked arm.

She smiled on seeing it. "Oh yes. In my line of work as a professional archaeologist doing digs in exotic locales, it's an occupational requirement. I'm good to go. I also brought along my own field gear and equipment, so I won't be a strain on yours."

Their server returned to the table and Hunt ordered Maddy a glass of red wine, which he knew from past involvement with her that she enjoyed. But to his surprise she turned it down and instead requested a Pilsen. "I can be one of the boys."

After yet another round toasted to El Dorado, Hunt grew serious as he turned back to the archaeologist. They had been in a romantic relationship with one another years ago, but their respective careers got in the way, with both of them required to travel the globe on a moment's notice. He still cared deeply for her and didn't want her to get hurt.

"Maddy, this is a dangerous expedition."

She smirked at him. "Oh really? You think I'm not aware of the smorgasbord of dangers Colombia has to offer? I know that you know how to take precautions, Carter." At this came some snickering from Jayden and Graham, but she ignored it and continued. "I held my own in Atlantis, did I not?"

Hunt nodded, acquiescing. "But reasonable precautions will not be enough. Treasure, Inc. is aware of the map and I have reason to believe they will also be down here, if they're not already, looking for the lost city. As you know, they do not play well with others."

Maddy shrugged, took a pull from her beer, and said, "That just tells me you need my help more than ever. We can start with your interpretation of said map. As you know, if you're not reading the thing correctly, you're sending yourself and your team on a wild goose chase. And let's face it, El Dorado is a wild goose chase as it is."

"Even with her it'd only be the four of us," Jayden pointed out. "Three of us, really, since our pilot here will be on standby a lot of the time." Graham grunted an acknowledgement as he chugged down some more Pilsen. "I'll bring some crossword puzzles to do while I'm waiting around."

Hunt's response was to light up his cell-phone with the map image and hand it to Maddy. "I took this of the scroll I found in a genuine Muisca Raft depicting the classic chieftain ceremony."

Maddy smiled ever so briefly—recognizing that she was joining this expedition, which was so different than the more academic, well-planned and government funded ones that were her bread and butter. So much more *fun*. And dangerous. But that was Carter Hunt, she knew.

She took the phone and studied the image while the rest of them sipped from their beverages. Hunt eyeballed the crowd in the restaurant to make sure they weren't being unduly observed, but nothing seemed out of the ordinary. Just a mix of local and tourist diners conversing at tables over plates of hot food, with a few at the bar slightly rowdier, watching a soccer game. Maddy pinched and zoomed the image to manipulate it, magnifying a section here and going for a wider view there. At length she said, "On first glance it indicates this mountainous region south of Bogota. That's where the caves are in which the famous Muisca Golden Raft was found."

Hunt beamed at her. "And that's where we're heading tomorrow."

"To the caves!" Graham said exuberantly while Jayden explored some chips and salsa.

Maddy looked away from the phone, to Hunt. "Can I see the physical map?"

Hunt shook his head. "I mailed it back to the states today, both for safekeeping and to have it analyzed in a lab."

"To date it and determine chemical composition or the plant type used in making the parchment?" Maddy asked.

"Exactly," Hunt said.

"Let me know when the results come in, I'll take a look. Meanwhile, I've had a long day travelling so if we're heading out early morning, I should get to my room. I booked one myself in this same hotel," she add quickly.

"What do we got, one room for the three of us?" Graham asked. "Or are you…" He shifted his gaze in a not so subtle way from Hunt to Maddy.

Hunt shook his head, embarrassed. "It's us three guys in one room. Two beds, one cot. I'll take the cot. Maddy is right: we should all wrap it up and get some sleep. Tomorrow the search begins."

CHAPTER 11

Port of Cartagena
Colombia

The mega-yacht *Historica* was so large that its captain was told, to Daedalus'
ire, that it would have to remain at anchor in the harbor until one of the
cruise ships left its berth. Possibly later today, he was told, if not, then
sometime before tomorrow evening. Not that this would really stop
Daedalus from doing what he wanted. He had numerous tender boats from
which to choose to take him or his staff to shore, and even a helicopter at
his disposal from the helipad on the aft deck. Still, it irritated him not to get
his way, that even after offers of "additional port fees" he was still denied.
That's not the Colombian way, he thought. In his home country of Greece
he could get whatever he wanted, and surely Greece was far more civilized a
nation than was Colombia? Regardless, here, apparently his money wasn't
worth as much. Stepping ashore onto the dock from the yacht would not be
an option for some time.

It will serve them right when I plunder the treasures of their cultural heritage right out
from under them. For that was exactly what he intended to do; it was the sole
purpose for his calling on this port. He needed a little more intel, but that
could be gathered from right here in the middle of the harbor due to an

onboard communications array that would make many municipalities green with envy.

From one of the salons, seated in a Lazy Boy recliner in front of a wall of glass that afforded a panoramic view of Cartegena's twinkling lights, Daedalus placed a call on his sat-phone to his brother. Phillipo answered on the first ring, sounding a little weary. *Good, means he's been working. I pay him more than enough.*

"The field team: is it coming together?"

"Yes, personnel are en route to Bogota now and should be in place there before this time tomorrow. But I have better news than that."

"Good. And what might that be?" Daedalus' tone was one of guarded optimism. He knew from experience that sometimes what his brother considered "excellent" was to him merely "good," what was "good" patently average. But this time he was in for a surprise.

"A known professional associate of Carter Hunt's was flagged purchasing airfare from the U.S. to Bogota. She landed today."

Daedalus held the phone away from his head and stared at it, like it had just done something he hadn't realized it was capable of. "What kind of associate?"

"An archaeologist, Dr. Madison Chambers."

Daedalus nodded to himself. "So this Dr. Chambers, associate of Hunt's, is here in Colombia right now?"

"That's right. We don't know where she's staying yet because she didn't book a package deal with the airfare. If she's in a hotel, she booked it separately after she got there. But we'll find out. And more importantly, we know Hunt's team is starting from Bogota."

"Excellent work, Phillipo. The *Historica* is now in Cartagena, so those resources are available, you know what they are."

"Thank you, brother."

"Have you thought about target search areas—where they might look first, from Bogota?"

A short pause ensued, after which Phillipo said, "If they are guided by the map, then it could be anywhere in Colombia, really."

"But they chose Bogota."

Daedalus could almost picture his brother shrugging on the other end of the call.

"One of two primary international airport destinations used as an entrance to the country, along with Medellin. It doesn't mean for certain that Bogota is their actual jumping-off point for the expedition, but my team will find out."

"Let us pretend for a second that they have no X-marks-the-spot map. As you know these old documents can be quite cryptic even if they are genuine and truthful as of their origination. Their meaning is often obscured by the passage of time."

Phillipo grunted to acknowledge what his brother said, and then Daedalus continued. "Let us also suppose that Bogota is the actual starting point for the expedition, with no other travel to smaller cities or towns required. What are the most notable areas connected with El Dorado in an expeditionary radius around Bogota?" Daedalus stared out at the light evening boat traffic milling about the harbor while his brother answered.

"Well as you know, of course there are the mountain caves to the south where the Muisca Rafts were found, including the latest—"

"Yes, yes, and what else?" Daedalus' impatience could not be restrained. Those caves were well picked over. No doubt there were still some artifacts to be discovered there, but he didn't see how anything of true significance could have gone unfound all this time.

"And there is Lake Guatavita to the north…"

"Yes. Those are the only two around Bogota I can think of, as well."

"Yes, but they are very well known with regard to El Dorado, Daedalus. Both sites have been searched many times over. If they have a map, they could be going anywhere."

"Which would mean you need to follow them. But if that is not possible, I would think those two well known sites are as good as any to begin looking for them. We have the manpower. Divide your team up into two sub-teams--one to the lake and one to the caves. No—correction: divide your team into *three* sub-teams: one to the caves, one to the lake, and one on standby in Bogota in the event that we learn Omega Team has gone to an altogether different destination."

"Our team is twelve men, Daedalus. To divide them into threes would mean only four men per team."

"Four heavily armed, well equipped, well-trained and experienced operators, you mean?"

"Of course, that is the reason we only have about a dozen of them. Verified ex-Special Forces are not cheap, as you know."

"That is fine with me. Three agile, directed teams strikes me as better in this situation than one large team, which would also attract more attention. We do not want the Colombian government or the guerrillas involved."

"As you wish, Daedalus. I will make it so."

"You better. It has been some time since our company has had a real coup, a find of true historical significance undeniable to humankind. *That* is what we strive for, brother. Do not forget that. The daily trading of regional baubles is all well and good, but serves only to finance a discovery on par with El Dorado, which would elevate us beyond compare. I am tired of this pesky Omega Team getting in our way, and who, to add insult to injury, seem to share our—or at least *my*—same vision."

Daedalus thought he detected his brother exhaling sharply, perhaps biting his tongue. He had detected a growing insolence in him over the last couple years, and sought to quell it. He had no need for a disloyal Number Two, even if it was his own flesh and blood.

"It is indeed *our* vision, Daedalus."

"Good. Then go now and make our vision happen."

Daedalus ended the call and stared out at the Cartagena night. Tomorrow, the players would all be here. The game was about to begin.

CHAPTER 12

Pasca, Colombia

A small town about forty-five miles south of Bogota, Pasca was an agricultural community in the mountainous jungle region near to where the famous pre-Columbian Muisca Raft was discovered in 1969. The nearest airport was thirty miles away, ironically named El Dorado International, but since they had a helicopter Graham landed them in a field on the outskirts of town. As they descended, the four of them—Hunt, Jayden, Graham and Maddy—were afforded a magnificent view of the town's surroundings.

Nestled in a small, picturesque valley ringed by lush green mountains, Pasca was loaded with churches both old and new, and with open air farmer's markets. The main roads were narrow but paved while side roads were dirt. A mix of vehicles old and new, from cars to trucks to scooters to bicycles plied the roadways.

Hunt's method for exploring on this outing was to use the chopper to drop in, explore, and then call to be extracted. More like a military operation than a traditional expedition, but he had the resources and knew exactly where he was going, not to mention was competing against another team, so the approach made sense to him. The downsides of the tactic were that with only four of them and no pack animals, they could only carry enough gear and supplies to last a few days before they would need either to be extracted or else to have more supplies air dropped to them. But he thought it should be enough. He hoped it would be, at any rate.

Graham switched off the engine and they all piled out of the aircraft onto the grassy field. On a slight grade, it sloped off dramatically at the far end of it, where the few cattle had been driven by the landing of the noisy machine. They knew exactly where they were going and had already made an aerial pass over the mountain's cliffside caves, which offered absolutely no suitable landing zones for an aircraft of any kind. The plan was to stage the first phase of the expedition here on the edge of Pasca, rig a drop rope, eat a hearty breakfast, and then depart again for the caves, this time to leave the three explorers there while Graham returned to Pasca to wait for the call to pick them up.

The road into Pasca, a two-lane blacktop occupied at any given moment by an unpredictable menagerie of cattle, goats, roosters, dogs, and human pedestrians, lay a few hundred feet away. No structures bordered this particular field, nor was it in active agricultural use, and except for the occasional passing vehicle at this early hour, they were unobserved. They spread a blanket out on the field and ate a hot breakfast they had taken to go from a café in Bogota only an hour ago. The steady hum of insects was nearly as loud as their conversation, and the heat intensified quickly with the rising sun. Nevertheless, they enjoyed the meal immensely—still warm eggs, fresh corn tortillas, beans, salsa, freshly picked vegetables, a thermos of hot Colombian dark roast coffee, and another of fresh-squeezed, pulpy orange juice.

Even though they had been over it before, Omega Team reviewed the plan once more while they ate, satisfied that all of them understood it and all of them agreed it would work, especially Hunt. Although he would not be accompanying them into the caves, Graham's role was no less dangerous, although it was an exposure to danger of a different kind. He would remain in this very field as long as he could, but told them he would move around a bit so as not to attract attention, for a helicopter parked in an inauspicious farming town like Pasca would inevitably draw suspicion.

He did not want to become the target of drug lords or dealers, which is exactly what he would appear like to many. The aircraft itself was extremely valuable, even if only for "chop shop" parts. And so Graham, armed only with a Glock pistol, as were Hunt and Jayden, would have to be highly watchful, nimble, and wary while he waited for the extraction call.

So important was the ability for Graham to communicate with the team that he himself had not one but two satellite phones, one clipped to his belt, and the other kept in a storage compartment in the chopper in case something happened to the first. The field team, meanwhile, carried one sat-phone per person to communicate with the outside world, and walkie-talkies to talk with each other and possibly the chopper itself should it happen to be within range.

When they had finished eating, they left the food scraps in the field, packed up their paper plate trash and stowed it in the chopper. After one last check to ensure that their streamlined field gear, consisting of three small but fully and strategically loaded frame backpacks, was ready to go and readily deployable from the helicopter, the four of them boarded the aircraft.

Graham warmed up the engine and went through a pre-flight systems check while Hunt, Jayden and Maddy belted in, with Hunt occupying the co-pilot seat. They would have preferred a military style chopper with a large cargo bay to facilitate jumps and recoveries, but they had what they had and they were grateful for that. With a last look around, Graham gave them all a thumbs up sign. Seeing no objections, the pilot lifted his mechanical bird straight up into the sky. After hovering there for a minute to make sure all was mechanically and electrically right with the craft, and to get his bearings, Graham turned the craft toward the caves. He accelerated off of the plateau that was the field over the steep drop-off of the greenery-shrouded mountain, like some kind of amusement park ride that elicited thrilled shrieks from his passengers.

The helicopter ride to the cave site took less than ten minutes. Hovering overhead the steep mountain, Graham lowered the chopper slowly and carefully down the mountain face. Nearly a vertical cliff for the portion of it that housed the caves, it represented a serious hike and then climb for anyone attempting to access it. Fortunately, the winds were light this morning, and the pilot had little trouble holding the machine in place about forty feet above the two dark openings in the side of the great green mountain.

Hunt, Jayden and Maddy prepared to drop down to the caves by putting on goggles to protect eyes against airborne tree debris caused by rotor wash or by passing through the thick canopy of trees. They also wore helmets with green camo graphics. Jayden handled the job of opening the rear door and releasing the rope ladder, which had been secured in place at the door before lifting off. He also was to ensure that the ladder payout was smooth and tangle free. He had nightmare stories to tell at the pubs of drop-lines getting caught in an updraft and becoming entangled in the rotors.

"Ready, read, ready?" Graham shouted.

The exit order was Jayden first, then Maddy, and then Hunt, who had to climb back to the rear to where the rope ladder was from the front. Jayden donned his backpack and then crouched with his back to the helicopter's open door. Gripping the hand-holds on the door frame, he lowered his legs out the door until they found the rope ladder's uppermost rungs. From there he made short, easy work of the descent, even though the ladder twisted and gyrated beneath the hovering chopper. Graham kept the aircraft nearly rock steady.

When they saw Jayden pass beneath the tree canopy with a thumbs up, Hunt helped Maddy position herself on the ladder. Once he was sure she was confidently situated, he told her to start and she began her downward climb. While she was still halfway down, Hunt's walkie-talkie, clipped to the shoulder strap on his backpack, squawked with Jayden's voice.

"The Eagle has landed. How are you guys?"

Hunt smiled and depressed his radio's transmit button. "Maddy's almost to the canopy. As soon as she passes under it, I'll start down."

"Roger that," came Jayden's enthusiastic reply. Hunt watched the archaeologist descend the ladder until she became enveloped by greenery. Then he turned to Graham, pointed to himself and gave the thumbs down sign. The pilot returned the OK sign and then Hunt, with a last look around the cabin to be sure no one was leaving anything behind, eased his body outside the chopper onto the ladder.

He looked up as he descended, watching the bottom of the chopper get smaller as he worked the rope ladder. In no time he felt the wet leaves of the canopy brushing over his body, and he switched from looking up to looking down. Between swatches of leaves and branches he could see the faces of Jayden and Maddy staring up at him.

"Almost there!" Jayden called up to him. The rope ladder reached to about six feet above the ground, and he made the drop as the others had done, bending his knees on impact under the weight of his pack. As soon as he had recovered from his jump, he pressed the Talk button on the walkie-talkie clipped to his backpack shoulder strap.

"OK Papa Bird, three baby birds in the nest. You can fly away now, over!"

"Copy that, baby bird. Papa Bird out."

The helicopter began a slow ascent, to make sure the rope ladder didn't become entangled in the trees. They had known that he would have to fly back to the field with the ladder dangling, since on the return flight he would be alone in the bird, but Graham said he had done it before and would be no problem. Hunt only hoped that no one up by the road would see the chopper flying with the ladder out, because that would certainly raise questions, but it was a chance they had to take, and at least it was still early in the morning.

A few seconds later Hunt's radio crackled with Graham's voice saying he had cleared the canopy with the ladder and he was good to go. "Good luck, *tres amigos!*" The trio stood there, faces tipped skyward, until the chopper had flown from view.

They cinched their packs tight, checked the ground for any gear that might have been shaken loose and dropped during their descent. Finding none, Hunt pointed toward the yawning black mouth already visible through the foliage. This was a very wild place, he knew, with zero signs of human presence. No trailheads, fences, not even a scrap of litter was to be seen anywhere.

They walked toward the cave, three abreast, Maddy in the middle. At its entrance, they stood and looked around. They knew from their aerial survey that another cave opening—they didn't want to call it another cave altogether since they might connect somewhere underground—lay about a hundred feet away to their right, with yet another approximately fifty feet below this one on the cliff. They weren't sure exactly which one the finders of the 1969 Muisca Raft had used, but Hunt knew this was the same cave system.

After checking that the LED lamps on their helmets worked, as well as making sure a working handheld flashlight was at the ready for each team member, they walked up to the cave entrance and stared inside, allowing their eyes to adjust to the dimness.

The lip of the cave entrance was perhaps five feet above Hunt's head. A small flock of green parrots flew out of the cave, startled by the humans' presence, and took noisy, squawking flight out into the airspace away from the mountainside. They waited a few more minutes to see if anything else wanted to leave, while gazing into the entrance. Hunt shined his flashlight beam into it and saw a mound of rock in the middle of a cavern, and what looked like narrower passages leading out of sight to the right and left behind that, with the right-side passage being higher elevated than the left.

"I think it's time," Hunt declared. "You ready?"

Both Maddy and Jayden answered in the affirmative, and then the three of them walked into the mountain cave.

CHAPTER 13

Six beams of light, three from helmets and three from handheld flashlights, explored the confines of the cave's outer chamber. Hunt was familiar with rumors that much of the cave system here was unexplored, and that even what has been seen by human eyes still holds many mysteries for those who are able to look closely enough. He was also aware that many an expedition had focused on this region since the discovery of the Muisca Raft in 1969, and that with each passing year, the archaeological and cultural finds became less and less significant; low hanging fruit, the law of diminishing returns, Hunt reasoned to himself.

Looking upward, Hunt judged this antechamber to the cave system to have a ceiling that was about twenty-five feet high at its peak in the middle of the space, which was as of yet not so much underground as carved into the side of the mountain. Looking back out through the entrance, drops of water fell from overhanging foliage against a backdrop of blue sky and the blazing ball of fire still rising in the morning sky. The floor of the cave was solid rock, and dry.

"Could make an awesome living room right here, you know?" Jayden said, framing his hands around the cave entrance.

"Natural ambience, privacy, million dollar view..." Maddy added, running with the joke.

"Local God included," Hunt said, as he moved off toward the rear of the chamber, playing his flashlight beam on its walls, which so far were unbroken and featureless. The crunch and scuffing of boots on the cave floor echoed in the space as the three of them slowly and methodically made their way to the rear of the antechamber. Noting nothing of real interest in the main chamber, they turned their attention to the pair of passageways that led deeper into the heart of the mountain.

On the right side of the antechamber, a small cleft in the rock yawned its presence at the top of a rocky rise. On the left side, a larger opening beckoned downward. Jayden played his light beam on its walls and saw that it quickly sloped out of sight at a steep angle. Maddy walked back and forth, alternately shining her light on the entrance to both passages.

"Door Number One or Door Number Two?" Jayden spoke the obvious question aloud.

"Right side goes up, left side goes down," Maddy stated, her gaze following her light beam up into the righthand passage.

Hunt turned to his spelunking companions. "Why don't Maddy and I go right, and Jayden, you go left—a little ways in—just to recon it and see if there are any obvious dead-ends." He tapped the walkie-talkie clipped to his backpack strap. "Then we'll radio each other to report what we found."

The strategy agreed upon, he and Maddy walked up the incline until they reached the entrance to the righthand tunnel. Jayden, meanwhile, moved to the large left-hand passage and entered it unceremoniously. He shone his light about the new area and saw that there was a wide, head-high tunnel leading down at a forty-five degree angle. Clicking his walkie-talkie's transmit button, he said, "Going down."

"Copy that," came Hunt's reply from the entrance to the right-side passage." He and Maddy scaled an incline until they stood at the entrance of the small cleft in the rock wall. Through it Hunt shone his light and studied the upward-sloping tunnel. Narrow and low, to traverse it required them to stoop and proceed single file. Hunt led the way with Maddy close behind. He could see that the passageway curved left up ahead while becoming even steeper. "Real steep leading up in this one," Hunt said into his radio, as much to test the communication link was working as to impart not-so-critical information.

"Copy," Jayden returned. "Pretty easy walking over here, still heading down." He ambled down the wide tunnel, pausing here and there to inspect a glint on the cave wall, which turned out to be flecks of quartz crystals reflecting his light beam. He continued his way down until he reached a "fork in the road," as he described it to Hunt over the radio. The tunnel he had been following ended at a large knob of rock, but two more tunnels led away and down on both sides of it. He peered down both of them in turn with his light, and noted that both looked about the same. They each led further down into the mountain at about the same angle as the main tunnel, and both curved gently out of sight about twenty feet down, toward each other.

"Dead end here," Hunt reported from the right-side passage. He and Maddy had reached a vertical blind end of what amounted to nothing more than a wormhole of rock. "Stay put, we'll meet you where you are."

Down at the fork in the road, that was fine with Jayden, who promptly shrugged off his pack, took from it a canteen and then used his pack as a seat while he chugged water. Down here it was noticeably hotter than it was outside, which was hot to begin with, and the humidity was the same. While he drank and waited he stared at the cave walls, whose glittering content seemed to be increasing with depth. He reached out a hand and picked with his fingers at a piece of crystal. After a bit he was able to wiggle it loose so that he held a tooth-sized chunk of pinkish rock between his fingers. He was no geologist, but he knew it wasn't a precious stone of any kind. Semi-precious at best. Still, he pocketed the chunk to have it identified later. When that was done he heard the crunch of footsteps descending the passage.

"Down here," he called up to Maddy and Hunt.

"Fork in the road, eh?" Hunt said upon reaching Jayden, who stood and shouldered his pack once again while Hunt and Maddy took a breather and drank some water of their own. "What do you think," Hunt asked, "same approach—you take one, Maddy and I take one, explore a little ways and then touch base?"

Jayden nodded. He knew that Hunt never wanted to leave Maddy alone in the cave, which was fine with him. Jayden pointed to a reel of line dangling from his pack. "Remember, if too many forks come up and we have to worry about getting lost, to start laying out line."

Hunt nodded. "For now, let's say that neither you nor we will proceed past another branch-off. This is just to see how far each passage goes."

With that understanding, Jayden set off alone down the right fork while Hunt and Maddy took the left. The passage Hunt and Maddy followed was only slightly more constricted than the main one that led to the fork, and after their experience with the wormhole, it seemed positively roomy, so much so that they were even able to walk upright side by side.

Jayden encountered something more puzzling not long after starting down the righthand fork: a hairpin turn that continued downward at a slightly less steep angle. He noted the quartz crystals that glittered in his light while he made his way around the sharp turn. He had to stoop just slightly after it straightened out again, though it was still as wide as before. He walked what seemed like a long ways in the same direction, without much variation in the tunnel topography itself. He paused to flick off his headlamp and flashlight after a time and marveled at the utter pitch darkness, the total absence of light that made itself known. He thought about how, were he to somehow end up in here without a light source, how completely helpless, how dead, he would be. Of course, all of them carried redundant light sources and extra batteries, as well as fire-starting tools, but even the thought of it was enough to install a grave and well-founded fear.

Jayden turned his headlamp back on but left the flashlight off to conserve battery power, though he still carried it in his hand in case he needed it fast. He resumed his trek down the long passageway, still needing to lower his head most of the time to avoid the ceiling. He spotted his first emerald in the ceiling of the passage, a dull green crystal that jutted from the ordinary rock like a beacon of light. It made him wonder if anyone had ever been here. For if so, wouldn't they have taken the precious gemstone? It was large, nearly the size of a golf ball, and that was only the part of it he could see protruding from the tunnel ceiling. Jayden paused to remove a small rock hammer from his pack. He'd brought it along since they were searching for El Dorado, the land of gold, and so some of the simple tools of a field geologist would come in handy to find out whether they were in the presence of gold.

He chipped around the emerald, digging into the ceiling around it. As he struck the rock, the percussive blows of the hammer echoed around the narrow chamber, and he reminded himself that he didn't want to trigger a cave-in, and should only hammer what was absolutely necessary. But this gem was huge, and he wanted it not for personal gain, but for possible trade in an emergency situation, for sample comparison to other emeralds—those associated with the El Dorado legend. While gold was the paramount substance associated with the legend, emeralds were also part of the story, and part of Colombia's rich mining history. Some of the finest emeralds in the world came from this country, Jayden knew, and he could see why when the stone came free into his cupped hand. It was larger than a golf ball because an additional crystal had extended deeper into the ceiling, holding it in place., Jayden could see that he broke it off and that a vein of it continued deep into the ceiling, but what he had chipped away was a chunk with a cylindrical rod attached to it. He lifted his hand up and down to feel its heft. He was still marveling at how large it was, and began to wonder if it was really an emerald and not some other exotic green rock—malachite, perhaps?—that wasn't worth as much, when his radio crackled with Hunt's voice.

The transmission was breaking up and he only caught bits and pieces of it, something about a room, but Jayden tapped his walkie-talkie's transmit button and spoke. "Come again, Carter, you're cutting out, over." He wanted to tell him about the emerald, but needed to hear the reason for his call first.

"....out into a ....room, over."

It occurred to Jayden that the walkie-talkies were at the limits of their range, which likely wasn't that far, having to transmit through tons of rock. "You're still breaking up. We need to be careful not to get out of range..."

He paused to see if Hunt could hear him and switched off his headlamp to conserve battery power since he was just standing their while transmitting. In the darkness, he was about to transmit again when he realized he could see something in the direction he had been going. Not a specific object, there was not enough light for that, but he could *see* the tunnel wall up ahead which meant that light had to be coming from somewhere in that direction.

He picked up his radio again. "Hey Carter, I can't quite hear you but I've got something to check out up ahead. I see light, over." A reply came back that was nothing more than static. Jayden flipped his headlamp back on and started walking toward the light he had seen. The tunnel itself was still the same as it had been, including walls that fairly glittered with quartz and the occasional emerald, which he no longer stopped to extract.

He tried the radio once again along the way, but this time received nothing but silence in return. As he neared what he could now see was a bend in the tunnel, he turned off his artificial light and was greeted with obvious daylight coming from the left. He followed the curve of the tunnel, noting that leaf litter and twigs now carpeted the tunnel floor. He didn't see how he could have looped all the way back to the same antechamber entrance, so it was with confusion that he rounded the corner.

He was greeted with a stunning view of open sky framed by a cavern entrance draped with hanging vines. It was clearly not the same chamber they had started from, this one being smaller overall and leading back to only the single tunnel from which he now emerged. He directed his flashlight beam to the ceiling and walls of the cavern but found no other tunnels or chambers. He walked out to the edge of the cavern and took in the majestic, absolutely stunning view. He looked down on a thickly forested valley far below, covering many square miles and being surrounded by steep green mountains thrusting around it on all sides.

Craning his neck to look up, he saw another opening in the cliff about fifty feet above and realized that was where they had entered the mountain. He had come through the antechamber there and wound his way down here. Looking to his left, he saw another yawning chasm abut 100 feet away.

Directing his gaze straight down he found a near vertical face, enshrouded with foliage and short trees. Then his radio blurted out Hunt's voice, and he realized he could hear actual words again.

"Jayden, do you copy? Over." Jayden palmed his radio and held down the transmit button.

"Hear you loud and clear now, Carter, over."

"Where are you?"

Jayden was about to answer when he was distracted by a moving object in the sky, flying from left to right in the middle of his panoramic view of the rain forest valley. A surge of adrenaline shocked his system as he realized it was a helicopter. But it was white in color, not the bright red of the one Graham was flying. He told himself not to panic, that it could just be a tourist sightseeing helicopter or some sort of government aerial survey. But this was a remote part of Colombia and deep down he knew those things were not what this was.

Without taking his eyes off the moving aircraft, Jayden intoned into his walkie-talkie: "Carter, I think we might have some trouble."

CHAPTER 14

Hunt and Maddy exchanged concerned glances. They stood in the center of a small chamber, lesser in area than the antechamber they all started out in, but the roomiest part of the cave they had come across since then. Hunt spoke into his radio.

"What sort of trouble? And where are you?"

Maddy walked slowly around the new space while Hunt stood in place and radioed with Jayden.

"I came out in a cavern that opens on the edge of the mountain—about fifty feet straight down from the one where we started."

"Are you lost, as far as retracing your steps?"

"Negative."

"Injured?"

"Also negative."

"Then what's the problem?"

"I'm looking out across the valley and there's a helicopter flying low and slow over the middle, at about my same altitude. It's not Graham's bird."

Maddy stopped in her tracks and turned to look at Hunt, who said into the radio, "Get in touch with Graham, give him a head's up that there's another helo working the area and see if he knows anything about it. Maybe he heard some airband chatter, over."

"That's a wilco," Jayden replied, using the military jargon that meant *will comply*. "How are you two lovebirds doing?"

At this Hunt saw Maddy blush, and he couldn't suppress a grin despite the serious situation. "The *archaeologist* and I," Hunt said, stressing Maddy's team role, "have found a small chamber. We're checking it out now to see if it might lead anywhere."

"Copy that. I'll get off the horn with you now so I can call Graham."

The radio exchange completed, Hunt and Maddy made awkward eye contact. "So what's it looking like in here," Hunt asked, eager to change the subject. "Dead end?"

"Not quite sure yet." Maddy moved to one section of the cave wall.

"How do you mean?" Hunt put down his walkie and replaced it in his hand with his flashlight, which he began to aim around the walls and ceiling.

Maddy crouched in front of one corner of the cave. "Look at this." She pointed a finger at something Hunt couldn't discern yet. He walked over to join her and started to shine his flashlight on whatever it was she was interested in, but she covered the beam with her hand. "No don't, it might startle them."

He paused for a second. "Startle *who*?"

She grabbed his hand holding the light and gently guided it until the beam was aimed away from the hive, but still illuminating it in its periphery. "I think this is a beehive."

Hunt knelt down and turned an ear toward the object. "I do hear a faint buzzing." And then they saw a dark little blob rise from the object and move off through their air between them. "Bees!" Maddy exclaimed.

"I didn't think bees lived in caves," Hunt said, staring at the hive.

"I don't think it's their preferred habitat, though I'm not an entomologist. But....and this is going to sound a little *out there*, if you will…"

"That's okay, just hit me with it." Hunt kept a close eye on the hive.

"They may have been placed here on purpose, long ago, by people."

"On purpose? For what purpose?"

"Mind you this is pure speculation on my part, but ancient peoples like the Muisca tribe are documented as having utilized beeswax to make the molds that they then poured molten metals into, such as gold and silver." Another bee emerged from the hive and took to the air.

"So the Muisca were beekeepers, cultivating them to have a ready supply of wax for the metalworking molds?" Hunt asked, eyeballing the buzzing hive.

"Precisely. Furthermore, they would even keep more than one species of bees because each produces its own distinct variety of wax, and they used the different waxes for various, specialized purposes."

"I never knew that," Hunt said sincerely, looking into her eyes.

"So it could be that they used this cave system, or one like it, as sort of a natural apiary. It is not impossible that these critters here—" she nodded to the hive. "—are direct descendants of bees that were used to make the very same molds that created the Muisca raft itself."

Hunt's radio suddenly blared static at a loud volume. He was crouched close to the hive, and the noise seemed to irritate them, since lots of bees began pouring out of the hive—dozens, and by the time Hunt and Maddy got to their feet—hundreds.

"You're not allergic, are you?" he asked Maddy while backing steadily away from the rapidly evacuating beehive.

"No. You?"

"Not that I know of."

"Good." It occurred to Hunt that should they be swarmed by bees in this confined space, they may not be able to do much about it. They would be stung many times over. He turned down the volume knob on his walkie-talkie. "Let's try not to disturb them. Give them some space."

They backed away from the hive into the middle of the chamber.

"Don't they have to pollinate flowers?" Hunt said in a low voice after they had reached a safer distance.

"They do, so they must be able to get outside from here. Maybe the hive is capping a narrow fissure in the rock that connects to the outside."

Hunt looked around the chamber, sweeping his beam over the walls, floor, and ceiling, careful to avoid shining it on the beehive. "I don't see any other passages except for the one we came in by."

Maddy stared at the hive. "We'd have to relocate it to find out for sure. But it certainly is a possibility. We didn't see any other bees until we got to this chamber, right?"

Hunt indicated his response with a nod. "I didn't, but let me ask Jayden. I'll try reaching him again." He tilted the radio that was clipped to his pack strap toward his mouth and said, "J-man, did you happen to see any bees— that is, bumblebee type insects-- on the way in?"

To their surprise, the ex-SEAL's voice came back almost immediately, and clear enough to be heard against a background of only weak, intermittent static. "Funny you should ask. I didn't see any until I got out here. But now that you mention it there are a few bees—queen bees? Bumblebees? Don't ask me what kind—flying around the opening to this big hole in the wall that I'm standing in. Not a whole lot, but a few."

Hunt and Maddy stared at each other with open mouths. "Looks like your theory is confirmed, Dr. Chambers," Hunt said. Then he said into the radio, "Copy that, Jayden. Standby, we've got to take a look at this hive here for a minute and I'll be back in touch, over and out."

Maddy nodded while looking at the hive. "Yep, somehow they're getting outside from there. But since they don't seem to be going this way..." she swept an arm at the tunnel they had come in from, "the hive itself must be concealing another exit."

"Let's check it out." Hunt drew the machete that hung from a scabbard clipped to his belt. Maddy shot him a concerned look, which he addressed by saying, "You step back to the tunnel entrance in case they go crazy. The hive doesn't look that big, but we can't see how far down it extends into the rock."

"Right," Maddy said, already walking over to the tunnel entrance. "And I hate to disturb the bees, I really do, but we need to see what kind of fissure or perhaps even passageway that hive is concealing."

In response, Hunt raised his machete and walked to the beehive, pausing when he was a couple of feet away. One or two bees flitted about the vicinity and a throbbing hum emanated from inside the hive. He took one step closer and turned around to check on Maddy. "Ready?"

She nodded. "Be careful."

"After I strike it, I'm going to run back to where you are. Be prepared to run into the tunnel if necessary."

She nodded her agreement and then Hunt raised his machete over the hive. He made a couple of slow practice swings, aiming to bring the tip and middle portion of the blade sideways across the hive as close as possible to where it protruded from the cave floor. "Here goes…" He warned, drawing the long blade back to deliver what he hoped would be the severing blow.

He sliced the blade into the bottom portion of the hive with a guttural cry from the exertion that echoed against the chamber's stone surfaces. The blade cut through most of the hive but embedded there, not quite all the way through. Bracing himself against his right foot, he slammed his left into the middle section of the hive while pulling back on the blade at the same time. Achieving what he had intended, the hive toppled onto the cave floor while the machete came free into the air, still held by Hunt. He back-peddled away from the fallen hive.

A swarm of bees flitted out of their broken home, clouding the air over the center of the chamber. Hunt reached Maddy and the two of them crouched in a ready position while shining their lights on the center of the chamber. The buzzing intensified as more and more bees poured out of the opening.

"Seems like there's a lot more than could fit in the little part of the hive," Hunt guessed.

Maddy agreed, and as they watched, more and more of the stinger-bearing insects filled the cave air. After a few minutes, the rate of new bees flying into the cave slowed, and the ones that were in the cave began attaching themselves to the ceiling, where they crawled around in confusion. Only one or two of the insects made their way as far as Hunt and Maddy. After a few more minutes, Hunt felt it safe enough to return to the hive site.

Hunt swatted away the few remaining bees that remained in the space above the hive and peered into the cavity revealed by its destruction. A jagged portion of hive still clung to the inside of what looked like a narrow fissure, as Maddy had predicted. To get a clear look, Hunt thrust his machete down into it and cleared most of the remaining beehive away, the pieces falling beyond the reach of his headlamp into a flue-like crevice in the cave rock.

"Maddy, it's like you said. Narrow chute that leads down out of sight. The hive extended down into it. Suddenly a Hunt felt a sharp pain on the side of his neck and realized he'd been stung. A buzzing noise intensified in the air around him, and then he heard Maddy's voice calling out to him.

"Carter get back, they're dropping down into the chute!"

Hunt sheathed his machete and swatted away bees with his hands while backpedaling again toward Maddy, who still hung back at the entrance to the tunnel. He tripped once over an irregular patch of rock on the cave floor, but quickly regained his feet, turned and ran the rest of the way to her.

"Are you all right?" she asked breathlessly.

Hunt put a hand on the side of his neck. "I got stung. Hurts like a mother, but I'll be fine. I'll *bee* fine, get it?" He added the humor to demonstrate that he wasn't worried.

She chuckled in spite of the situation, then pointed to where the hive had been. A thick column of bees now poured into it from the ceiling, like a dark funnel of smoke going up a chimney, but in reverse.

"So forgive me if I don't walk over there to see for myself," Maddy said, "but is the chute large enough for us to fit through?"

Hunt replied in the negative. "It is for the bees, that's about it."

* * *

Jayden checked his walkie-talkie battery level after using it to contact Graham. He had told him about the chopper he'd seen, but Graham hadn't seen or heard anything about it himself yet, so he told him thanks for the heads up and that he would take precautions. Pleased to see that the device still had decent power remaining, he was about to check in with Hunt to tell him he was going to start the trek back into the tunnels, that he would meet them perhaps at the fork in the road, when he heard a persistent buzzing noise that seemed to be growing louder.

The former SEAL turned in the direction of the auditory disturbance and was surprised to see a dark column twisting out of a small hole in the cavern ceiling. It took him a few seconds to process the fact that they were insects, then a few more seconds to understand that they were bees. He recalled the radio chat with Hunt asking about bees and backed away from the incoming swarm, the outlet for which was near the rear of the cavern, by the tunnel entrance.

Jayden backed up until he stood on the edge of the opening in the cliff, very careful to plant his back foot against a small rock there so that he had both a landmark of the edge and solid footing. To his astonishment, the bees continued to flow from the opening in the ceiling, a thick rope of winged drones that spread out as soon as they descended into the cave and swarmed around the entire cavern. It soon became apparent that he would not be able to get back to the tunnel without being attacked by the main swarm. This left him little alternative than to consider his options from the edge of the cliff.

He knew that above him was the antechamber they had entered the system in, and that to the left was another open cavern. Peering down he also noted a rocky ledge after a drop of about fifty feet. He did his best to recall the side of the mountain as viewed from the chopper right before they dropped onto the face. Yes, he was certain, there was another cavern below. This was important to know because he didn't want to strand himself on the side of the cliff, but at the same time, the bees were relentless.

He felt the first sting right through his pant leg on his left thigh, and knew it was time to go before he was enveloped by the swarm. Turning to face the drop, he forced himself to concentrate. The height was too far to hope for the best and slide down. Normally he would rig a climbing harness and belay rope, but there was no time for that, not to mention he was alone with no one to belay him. So he unclipped a climbing rope he fortunately had looped on the outside of his pack for easy access. Then, as the edge of the swarm reached him, he hurriedly looped the middle of his 100' climbing rope around a jutting boulder of rock so that about one half of the rope fell off either side of the rock, down the cliff.

Holding one side of the rope in each hand, Jayden walked backwards down the cliff. He knew that should the rope slip up and over the rocky knob that he would fall backwards fifty feet. He was a skilled though not expert climber as a result of his military experience, and so did not possess the fear that an amateur would have. He did not allow the possible negative outcomes to interfere with what his body needed to do right at this moment.

Looking up as he descended, he saw the bulk of the swarm flit away, back into the open cavern. He still felt a couple of bees crawling on his exposed skin—his hands, his neck, but he paid them no mind as he worked his way down. Fifty feet, though a frightening distance to fall from, was not that far to go and in only a few more seconds, he his feet dangled into open air as he reached the opening of another cavern in the cliff face. Passing down, he caught a glimpse into this new cavern until he planted both feet on the rocky platform he had seen from above.

Satisfied he was on stable rock, he pulled the rope down from one side until it came free from the boulder above and dropped into a loose pile at his feet. Still wary of the bees, he shrugged off his pack, knowing there would likely be a few stragglers hiding beneath it. He swatted at his clothes until no more bees flew away.

Then, after a last glance around which showed only the pure desolation and rugged natural beauty of his location, Jayden gathered his rope and pack and stepped into this new cavern.

CHAPTER 15

Pasca Colombia

Graham Walker was on high alert. He sat in his bird in the same field he'd eaten breakfast in with the team. He'd returned there after dropping them at the caves, and was preparing to move to another location to avoid sitting in any one place too long, when he received the radio call from Jayden. Hearing about a potential "enemy chopper" in the area, he informed Jayden that he'd keep his eyes and ears open—both organic and electronic. Not ten minutes after the communication, he heard what was to him the unmistakable sound of a chopper in flight. Grabbing a pair of binoculars, he scoped the aircraft and watched it as it flew across the valley.

At first he had told himself it's probably an aerial tour, eco-tour, something like that, for tourists. But, while those could be found in more inhabited parts of Colombia, Pasca was not one of them. Besides, he could see no logo of any kind airbrushed on the side of the craft as was per usual with a commercial operation. Nor was the aircraft identifiable as being part of any sort of government unit, national or local. It simply had a solid white paint job. He couldn't read the tail number from this distance, even with binoculars, but he had seen enough to put him on edge.

He had pulled a woodland camouflage net he'd taken along for this very purpose and covered his helicopter with it, so that from any distance it just looked like a small rise in the grassy field, and viewed from above it would make it nearly indistinguishable from the ground. But now, sitting inside the craft, light muted by the camo net, he was worried. Monitoring dual bands on his radio, the airband used in aviation, and the walkie-talkie channels used by Omega's field team, anxiety began to creep in.

The airband had been uncharacteristically silent. In most parts of the world, he could always hear some chatter from other aircraft, from air traffic control towers, but today so far he'd received nothing but radio silence. It meant that either this newcomer bird was using a non-airband channel, which was illegal everywhere in the world and usually not as effective for communicating in the air, or avoiding communications altogether, not checking in with whatever business headquarters or military base or whatever facility it had ties to. There were only two possibilities that he could think of to explain that kind of behavior, and both were bad news.

It could be the infamous and long-running rebel group FARC (Revolutionary Armed Forces of Colombia), he thought with a pang of fear. He was more than happy to be associated with Hunt's team, but at the same time, as bad as his financial situation was back at home, he had no desire to be shot up with a bunch of automatic weapons in the hands of drug guerillas or freedom fighters or whatever kind of rebellious groups there were around here these days.

And then it could be this group that Hunt and them were so worried about, what was it called? He racked his brain for a moment and then came up with it: *Treasure, Inc.* He knew Hunt said they had shot at him today, but for Graham's money, he'd rather go up against them any day than face a drug lord's hired killers or the FARC or something like that. *No gracias, amigo.*

He debated if he should move again or stay here. Being in the air raised his profile considerably due to being visible and loud, while also burning fuel. He had an extra portable tank with him, but it wouldn't last for long, just an emergency reserve, really, the like red portion of a car's gas gauge below the "E." He needed to keep a certain amount in reserve to be able to extract Omega Team and then make it back to Bogota, which was above the halfway mark. If he couldn't do that, he'd have to find fuel around Pasca, which would raise a lot of questions. Fortunately, this particular helicopter could use regular car gas, which gave him a lot more options. Even so, he was hoping not to have to refuel at all.

It turned out not to be a helicopter that made up his mind, but a Jeep stopping on the side of the road at the edge of the field. He noticed that the traffic on the road had increased since he landed in the field for the second time. Most of the traffic whizzed by the field either on their way to or from the village. For those seeking scenic vistas for photo opportunities, there were better stopping points along the long and winding road than here. So it was with surprise that Graham watched the green Jeep Wrangler heading away from town slow down and then come to a stop on the side of the road in front of the field.

Graham grabbed his binoculars and trained them on the occupants of the vehicle. There were three of them and they all wore camo gear. The looked like hunters to him, and the Jeep bore no insignia or logos of any kind, but seeing the long guns put him on edge. His radio channels remained silent. If they were after him, he needed to move now. He waited to see if it was merely a pitstop to fix something with the car, or maybe to urinate onto the edge of the field. But when one of the men started pointing into the field, with the others nodding, and then they started walking into it, he sprang into motion. He exited the aircraft and hurriedly removed the camo tarp, knowing as soon as he did they would see him.

He flipped the switch to start the engine, praying that he would have enough time to warm it up. This was a fast-starting chopper, but he would be pushing it all the same. While it warmed up, he wadded up the camo net and dragged it into the chopper. Then he got back into the pilot's seat. The party of gunmen had taken notice of him now, and stopped moving into the field. He tensed, for if they stopped it could mean they were about to draw their rifles on him.

A large flock of birds took to the air at that moment, rising out of the field a few yards from the helicopter, startled by the engine noise.

Graham breathed a sigh of relief as he saw two of the men aim their rifles at the departing flock and fire. One of the birds fell from the sky and plopped into the field. He saw two of the men high five each other and start walking in that direction.

Just hunters. Now that he had the chopper started, he decided it was best to change locations anyway. He had been sighted by these hunters, after all, and the noise of the engine starting could no doubt be heard for miles, and so he proceeded with taking off out of the field. He rose and from a controlled hover, and thought about where to go while spinning around in a slow circle.

The road had light but steady traffic on it now, lorries and cars and even horseback riders traversing up and back to and from town. Pasca itself was visible from this vantage point, the brown stone of its churches dotting a larger tapestry of green vegetation. His radio channels remained silent. Graham considered the great cliff itself where he had dropped his team. It dropped off into that completely wild, undeveloped valley the other chopper had flown over. He pointed his aircraft in that direction and decided to go that way. He'd do a flyby once past the caves, then up and over the mountain, loop back and fly to the outskirts of Pasca and find a different place to set down.

He took a low approach, not rising into the sky above the forested valley after he passed over the edge of the field, but instead continuing in a straight line as the land broke away beneath him. He eased the craft's nose lower so that he flew low over the treetops, the top of the canopy like a verdant green floor beneath the helicopter's skids.

Soon he looked over to his left and saw the mountain wall rushing by. He slowed the craft to orient himself, looking for the cavern where he had dropped the team. He had to look up to see it, but there it was. The entire cliff face was pockmarked with them, he could see. He resumed forward travel, passing close to the cliff, maintaining a steady but minimal distance above the rain forest canopy.

After passing by the cavern system he turned his attention to the rain forested valley floor. It stretched on as far as he could see form this low vantage point. He looked but couldn't see even the slightest break in the veritable wall of vegetation. He had served a jungle tour or two in the service, and while not unacquainted with tropical forests, this was without a doubt the wildest place he had ever found himself in, nothing short of a riot of plant life concealing God-knows-what.

One thing was for sure, Graham thought as he peered down at it in awe. There was no possible landing zone down here, anywhere, anywhere at all. The entire valley was enclosed on three sides by the steep, green mountains, so he opted to hug the mountainsides all the way around, and then rise above the open field again before looking for a new landing spot in which to hide. The whole round trip should take less then ten minutes, he calculated. He pulled a Colombian cigarette from his shirt pocket it and lit up, exhaling the smoke out the window. *This job ain't so bad.*

He neared the end of the first mountainside and followed the curvature to the right. Glancing over to the wall on his left, he saw none of the dark spaces puncturing the green mountainside marking the caverns, as with the side where he'd dropped Omega Team. Looking to the right he stared across the long dimension of the valley, the field at the opposite end not visible from this low altitude.

He flew until he reached the third cliff wall, then turned right. When he reached the end of this one he would ascend and pass over the field. He turned his attention back to the wall, and again noticed no openings in its green façade. He was about a quarter of the distance across the long valley wall when he saw a splotch of unnatural color far off to his right. He looked away and then back again to clear his head and make sure he wasn't seeing things.

Then his heart sank, for rising out of the jungle was the white helicopter Jayden had warned him about. It occurred to Graham that, since he had noticed absolutely zero openings in the canopy, that the valley floor must be slightly higher in some places, and the helicopter pilot had exploited that, knowing they would not be visible from Graham's altitude along the opposite wall.

Well now what, cowboy? Graham had been in helicopter combat before, and he did not like the aggressive posture the bird had taken as it rose quickly into a stationary hover, its nose pointing to follow Graham's own bird's course. Sure enough, a few seconds later the unknown helicopter bolted forward, flying low and fast just over the canopy toward Graham. He knew that if he varied both his speed and altitude that it would make it harder for them to plot a course towards him, so he pulled back on his collective and rose up the face before promptly diving down again half the distance to his previous altitude. He veered out toward the middle of the valley more, too, since he didn't like the cliff wall so close on his left while conducting evasive maneuvers. It had been a while since he had to fly like this, and he knew he was more than rusty.

For its part, the aerial challenger held up well, hanging back more without trying to anticipate each and every move on Graham's part. It veered out more into the middle of the jungle floor, then paced its adversary laterally, disregarding its ups and downs. Graham was too preoccupied with his flying to notice the rear door of the enemy chopper slide open, and a human figure holding a long gun take up position in the open doorway. He took his craft as low as he could, until leaves and palm fronds brushed against the underside of his craft.

Graham was skillfully navigating the canopy and valley wall when his windshield suddenly fractured into a spiderweb of cracks. He could still see straight out ahead of him, but the righthand portion of the windscreen was nothing more than a whiteout of broken laminated safety glass.

I've been hit! Normally he might have suspected a bird strike, a falling chunk of rock from the mountain that fell from high up and ricocheted off the cliff at his same height, but he knew that wasn't it. He'd been shot. And that realization brought this situation to a whole other level. Graham shifted tack and tactics, a surge of anger-driven adrenaline guiding his actions. He put the aircraft into a sharp right turn and then accelerated as fast as the chopper's engine was capable of toward the combatant aircraft.

As soon as he was on course, he reached for his Glock pistol and gripped it in his right hand while holding the thrust lever with his left. He knew what he had to do. He pulled up briefly to dodge an errant treetop that protruded from the rest of the canopy, then homed in on his target. The enemy chopper had turned toward the middle of the valley and distant caverns wall, starting to flee. No doubt they had seen the damage done to Graham's craft.

He needed them on his left side so that he could shoot out his window which also afforded a clear view compared to his ruined windscreen. The craft was larger and faster than his own, but the larger size also afforded a bigger target They had not been expecting his offensive maneuver, since Graham was able to catch up to them by the time they headed in the opposite direction. From slightly below and behind, like a shark, Graham thought, he aimed the barrel of his Glock at the chopper's body where he knew the gas tank would be, and squeezed off three rounds.

One of them ricocheted off the skids, while two missed their mark completely. He kept after them, straining his craft's engine to the breaking point, but his adversaries' more powerful engine began to work in their favor, carrying them to the fringes of his pistol's effective range. Out of rage, Graham fired off another shot, but it, too, missed.

And then, just as he had mentally given up but not yet given his machine the controls to turn around, he felt an impactful thud which instantly caused his helicopter's engine to lose power. The rifleman had found his mark from the platform of his fleeing chopper. Black smoke began to issue from Graham's engine, and he knew that he had mere seconds to do something that proved not to be the wrong thing. Helicopters were not like planes, whose wings enabled them to glide for some distance in the event of an engine failure. No, the moment a 'copter's engine ceased functioning, that aircraft plummeted back to Earth straight down from wherever it was, and straight into whatever lay below.

In this case, that meant somewhere in the middle of a massive, uninterrupted, dense jungle occupying the valley floor, ringed with steep mountain walls on three sides. Graham eyed a cluster of treetops poking out of the main canopy and turned toward them. He was losing engine power fast, his gauge dials and lights going crazy, system alarms braying. He wanted more trees to break the one-and-a-half-ton chopper's fall once gravity took over. As soon as he was over the tall clump, he switched off the engine. He was going to crash—he didn't even think it could qualify as a crash-landing, simply a crash--but at least he could choose where he crashed.

He also needed to stop the rotors before they came into contact with the canopy at 450 RPMs, which he knew would be catastrophic. He flipped the switch combination to shut down the engine, praying that the circuitry to even shut itself down was not damaged. He mumbled a little prayer of thanks when he felt the vibrations cease along with the industrial whine, and for a split second, when that helicopter was higher than it would ever be again, all was quiet but for the distant whine of his enemy, flying toward the cavern walls.

And then pilot Graham Walker braced himself for the impending jungle crash. He holstered his pistol, knowing that if he lived he would need it, not to mention he didn't need it getting tossed around on impact and accidentally going off. His seatbelt was already fastened, and he didn't usually wear a helmet but he remembered the rental facility guy telling him about all the safety equipment on board, including a helmet. So he reached back and grabbed it and put it on. He had just buckled the strap when he saw the first flash of green and felt the first bumps of what would be a multi-level crash, through a layered tree canopy and then with whatever the ground terrain was. He hoped for water, but didn't give that much chance.

On the next substantial impact, probably a tree branch, he heard the crunch of breaking glass, and then the craft bounced violently to the left. It was jolted in different directions and at different angles each time it came into contact with another substantial tree limb or trunk on the way down to the forest floor. Graham felt like a ragdoll in the pilot's seat as he crashed down through the forest canopy.

It took him a while to realize he had stopped moving. Large branches, coconuts, and even loose parts of the aircraft itself continued to rain down on top of the downed helicopter for some time after it came to rest. Graham was still seated and belted in, but now in a nearly upside-down position. He felt weary, groggy, like he could fall asleep easily, but somewhere in the back of his mind he knew this was not a good idea and shook it off. Forcing himself awake, he slowly turned his head. Feeling a sharp pain when he turned right, he tried left and found he had more range of motion in that direction.

But seeing the blood on the dashboard, then on his arms,, really woke him up. Feeling his face revealed a wet stickiness that led straight to his painfully sore nose, and he knew he'd broken it when it hit either the thrust lever or the dashboard itself. *Sonfabitchsonofabitch*....he grumbled to himself. It wasn't only the physical pain, the loss of the rental helicopter his new company would have to somehow pay for, or that he could easily have been killed, but his ego suffered a hit right along with his body and the helicopter. For all his decades of flying, this was the first time he'd ever crashed a helicopter. He wasn't proud of it. Yes, he'd been shot out of the sky and so it wasn't really his fault, but he still felt like he'd let himself down, let Omega Team down. And now here he was hanging upside down in the middle of the Colombian high altitude rain forest by himself, with unknown mercenaries who obviously wanted him dead. What if they spotted his wreckage site and came after him on the ground, hunted him down like an animal?

That thought got him up and moving. He unsnapped his seatbelt and gingerly worked out of it, exploring the pain-free range of motion of each limb as he tried any new type of motion. Looking out the window he could only see a cacophony of green leaves and branches. He rolled to his right, feeling soreness in his back but nothing that seemed broken or that prevented him from ending up on his hands and knees in the passenger seat. He felt the entire craft rock back and forth, causing the trees supporting it to creak, and he cautioned himself not to shift his weight too quickly lest he send the precariously balanced helicopter crashing an unknown distance to the ground. From there he was able to kick open the passenger-side door, which was tilted toward the ground.

On processing what he saw out the window, Graham got the shock of his life. The jungle floor was not ten feet below him. He experienced a chill as he saw the mound of boulders clumped together on the ground beneath the downed 'copter. Had it not hung up in these trees a few feet above the ground, Graham would have been smashed into those rocks. Given the extent of his injuries even with the trees softening his landing, he preferred not to think about what would have happened had he landed on the boulders.

Graham thought fast. He needed to get out of here before either the 'copter fell the rest of the way to the ground or the people who shot him down came by for a visit. He had a small school-style backpack that he used for personal items like cell-phone, lunch, etc. But now he stuffed it with all useful supplies and gear he could scavenge from his crashed airship, including the binoculars, a small flashlight, the food he had, a canteen of water, and the walkie-talkie Hunt had given him. He was especially grateful for the latter since the plane's electrical system was powered off and so he could not use its radio. He was tempted to see if the 'copter still had battery power, because then he might be able to use the radio, which had a more powerful transmitter and more bands than the handheld walkie, but he wasn't willing to risk it. There could be a fuel leak and turning on the electrical system could send a spark…

He also stuffed the cargo net into his pack, figuring it might be useful for constructing a shelter or concealing his location. He considered the compass on the dashboard. He did not have another one, and he did not have one of those fancy smartphones that could run a compass app. He remembered from when he was flying a few minutes ago the compass bearing that would lead him to the cavern wall that made up the opposite side of the valley. Although he could look at it now and start off in the right direction, he was aware that it wouldn't take long before he veered off course, without a compass to consult along the way. He pried the compass bubble out of its mount with a screwdriver and dropped it into the outer compartment of his little backpack.

Once he was loaded and had taken everything of practical survival value from the helicopter, including his backup sat-phone, and placed it in either his backpack or pockets, Graham stepped out of the aircraft's passenger-side door. Then he let himself hang down until his feet were only three feet or so above the boulders, and let himself drop.

Knowing he was coming down on an uneven surface, he worried about twisting an ankle, of being stuck here unable to even walk, which would no doubt spell his doom from any number of ways. But his two feet landed firmly and without pain on one of the big rocks. He kept his balance and then, conscious of the fact that he stood beneath a haphazardly dangling helicopter, he stepped off the boulder pile and took a few steps out on to the jungle's dirt floor. Moist and carpeted with plant matter, it had a springy feel to walk on. He looked back on his hanging aircraft and shook his head. *Bye-bye birdie.* He felt lucky to have survived.

He listened for signs of the other chopper, for sounds of a hunting party on the ground coming to make sure the job had been finished, but there was only the presence of heavy, unadulterated rain forest. Birds, insects, the rustling of leaves. He knew there was an awful lot of jungle standing between him and the rest of his team, or between him and the road to Pasca. Either way, he knew he had better get started.

Graham Walker shouldered his backpack, checked his holster to make sure his gun was at the ready, and took a last look back at his crashed 'copter. Then he set off on foot into the jungle.

CHAPTER 16

"All the bees left down the chute." Hunt said this as he shone his flashlight on the cave ceiling, before sweeping it around the walls and back to the center of the cave where the wrecked hive lay on the ground. A couple of errant worker bees flitted about, landing on their fallen house before taking off again, but the thick swarm was nowhere to be seen or heard.

"I certainly hope you're right." Maddy began to walk around the cave, slowly inspecting its periphery, the parts that were cast in darkness or deep shadows without viewing them with a direct light source. "I know there are no other passageways that lead anywhere from here, but I'd just like to inspect more carefully before we leave back the way we came if that's okay."

Hunt agreed and also moved slowly about the chamber, examining its features. He reached an outcropping of rock that formed a kind of natural alcove and stepped inside it. Sweeping his beam along the wall there, he caught his breath as he saw color on the otherwise dark rock.

"Maddy, look at this!" She walked over and shone her light on the wall of interest.

"Wow! Oh my! Look at that detail!"

The two of them crouched down before an intricate painting directly on the cave wall. Mostly reddish in color, and occupying a rectangular patch of cave wall about two by three feet, the painting depicted various figures both animal and human. Four-legged animals, birds, even fish were presented. A series of squiggly lines and stippled patterns was interlaid between the different figures, creating a rich tapestry of obvious artistic merit.

Hunt retrieved his cell-phone from his pack, lit the device up and took a series of pictures of the cave painting, both in its entirety and close-ups of particular features. Maddy continued to thoroughly inspect it while he did this, standing to inspect the upper border of the ancient work of art. "Incredible! Crudely rendered yet richly detailed at the same time."

"Can you say for certain it was done by the Muisca tribe?" Carter asked.

Maddy slowly nodded. "It certainly looks that way. To be one hundred percent certain, I'd need images of it to compare to verified, similar works. And a pigment analysis of whatever they used for paint—probably a berry extract--wouldn't hurt. But if I had to put money on it, I'd say Muisca. And that's just by looking at it." She waved her arm around at the cave. "Add to that the fact that we are sitting in known Muisca territory, and it becomes even more likely it's Muisca." She continued walking along the upper border of the piece, and then paused, looking some distance above the artwork at an irregularity in the rock.

"Carter, check this out, would you? You're taller than me." Hunt walked over and aimed his flashlight at the area on the cave wall above the painting she indicated. An indentation in the rock wall seemed to contain an anomaly of some type. He squinted at it. On first glance it looked like a fallen chunk of rock from the cave wall itself. But after standing on his toes and aiming his light more precisely, he could see that it was not a piece of rock, but some sort of manmade object.

"Possible artifact! I think I can reach it. Here, hold my light." He handed her his flashlight and flipped on his helmet's headlamp so that he could be hands-free. He stood on his toes and stretched his right hand as far above his head as it would go, which was to the base of the mystery object.

"I could give you a boost…" Maddy started, but Hunt's hand wrapped around the object. He pulled it toward the edge, circling his fingers around it. "I got it."

He pulled his hand down and they stared at a clay figure of a tribal human sitting in his palm. Mostly brownish, but highlighted with red and yellow features, the sculpture was about five inches tall. Portrayed in a sitting position, the figure appeared to be male, and sported large circular earrings and a colored sash around its waist.

"Incredible! May I?" She took the figure from Hunt's hand and turned it over, examining it from all angles. "Oh, Carter, this is fantastic!"

"It's not gold, though."

"No, but it's definitely pre-Columbian, most assuredly Muisca. We're definitely in the right place." She looked about the cave as if to divine what other treasures it held.

Maddy and Carter proceeded to extensively photograph the figurine, and then he put it back on the rocky shelf where it had likely been for centuries.

"I see no reason to mention this find to anyone, " Carter said, making sincere eye contact with Maddy. "There are many like this one that have already been found. Let this one be, where it belongs."

She looked deep into his eyes and nodded.

"Onward to the big prize," Maddy said at length. "El D."

"Yep. Speaking of which, we should touch base with Jayden soon." He and Maddy walked about the rest of the cave, searching high and low for any more artifacts, but found no more.

"I pronounce this chamber searched and its finds categorized," the archaeologist said.

"Interesting," Hunt noted. "A clay figurine and a beehive that may indicate they were making molds for molten metal."

"Let's see what else this cave system holds."

Hunt tried his walkie-talkie but received no signal back from Jayden, not even static. "We're probably separated by too much solid rock," he guessed. "Let's make our way back to the 'fork in the road' and go from there."

Maddy agreed and they moved to the entrance to the tunnel. After a last look around the chamber, sweeping their lights over all parts of it, they turned and walked back into the tunnel system. Although they knew where they were going and had a plan, Hunt felt a nagging concern tugging at his consciousness. Something he had told himself would not happen had come to pass.

The team was separated in the cave system.

CHAPTER 17

Jayden flipped on his helmet light. He took the first look at his surroundings in the new cavern he had dropped into. He especially looked for bees, but didn't see any. That was the strangest thing, he thought. Once he felt safe that he was not about to be swarmed, he paid more attention to the cavern itself. This one was longer and narrower than the previous two, more like an extension of an internal tunnel. After a perfunctory examination of this outer cavern, he found there to be nothing of interest. He tried his radio one more time, repeatedly calling on Hunt's channel and hearing absolutely nothing in return. He tried a scan of all channels, in case for some reason he or Maddy had switched frequencies, but heard nothing on any of them. He even specifically called for Graham, who he knew could monitor the walkie-talkie channels, but nothing came back from him, either.

Somewhat concerned now at having been separated from the rest of his team, he considered his options. He moved to the rear of the outer chamber, where only a single tunnel led deeper into the mountainside. Although this passage looked much like the others in terms of its layout, including how he had to stoop to walk through it, something about it immediately set it apart.

The walls glittered, not with crystals but with small flecks of gold. He halted to eye some of it up close. He had heard of pyrite and how it superficially appeared like gold but was actually called "Fools' Gold," and couldn't say for certain what these particles were. But they looked like gold, and they were in the land of El Dorado, so he took it as an encouraging sign and kept moving. The passage took him a long way straight back before it started to curve right and down. He could feel the strain on his calves as he plodded down the solid rock slope. The air was very still and stale in here, like there was not a lot of exchange with the outside atmosphere. Sweat trickling down his face, he was glad for the moisture-wicking technical fabrics he wore that maintained breathability in hot, humid environments.

Jayden was beginning to wonder how long a single, unbranching tunnel could run, when he saw a break in the corridor up ahead. At first he thought he had gone all this way for another dead-end, because the tunnel was blocked by a wall of rock. But technically, he saw, it wasn't a dead-end since a hole in the cave floor opened into a space down below. Jayden trained his flashlight on the jagged opening, and as he did, he felt a flood of emotions.

An impressive space waited down below. He wanted to see it. But at the same time, he cared about his personal safety, and descending alone into an unknown space in a cave system he was already very deep into was not the most prudent thing. He also did not want to let his team down. He was lucky to be working with a good friend, with such capable people whose business mission was a truly worthy cause. Were he not doing this, Jayden knew he would probably be doing underwater welding and things like that, installing communications cables. Not that there was anything wrong with that, but treasure hunting, in spite of its unpredictability, was altogether so much more exhilarating, like living a real-life dream that never ended. Because the prudent thing to do right now, separated from his team and out of radio contact, was to turn around and go back to the cavern that opened on the cliff, and wait there until he made radio contact. The outdoorsman in him knew this. Shining his light down into the new space, he gave it fifty-fifty odds that he would not be able to get back up again if he went down that way.

The explorer in him won out. He saw a pool of water down there. He saw glittering objects. He was going down there. Jayden looked around for a way to rig a climbing rope but didn't see any obvious solutions; nothing to wrap a rope around as he had done earlier to drop down the cliff. He sat on his knees pointing a flashlight down into the pit. If he were going to get down, he would have to make the drop without the benefit of a rope.

He thought he could hang down from the edge and drop maybe ten feet to a flat cave floor. From there, he'd have to wing it. He took a last look around to make sure he wasn't leaving anything behind, and then got into position to drop. He gripped the edge of the tunnel floor. He let his limbs go taut. He felt his fingers begin to lose their grip on the rough rock, and then he let go and flexed his knees.

He softened the impact by going into a forward roll to transfer the energy of impact over a longer period of time before coming to a stop. He came to rest in a crouching position staring at a shimmering pool of water, shimmering only due to the artificial light from his headlamp, otherwise pitch black would reign. He stood and eyed his new surroundings, but what he could hear is what got his attention: running water.

The circular pool had one outlet breaking its circumference, and that was a small stream that flowed straight back to the wall of the chamber, where it disappeared into a cleft of rock. Jayden stabbed it with his flashlight beam and thought he might be able to fit through it, should there prove to be no other way out, though he hoped it wouldn't come to that.

He walked to the edge of the pool and stared into its water. The bottom appeared to be flat rock no different than the rest of the cave system. Its depth was about chest height for Jayden were he to stand in it. He turned away rom the pool for a minute to assess the rest of this new environment. He glanced up at the ledge from where he had dropped into this new world. He saw no easy way to get back up, no rock formations to jump off of, and it was far too high for him to jump up and grab the edge.

He walked around the roughly oval shaped chamber, his head not more than a few inches below the low ceiling. Spotting a pile of something in front of the cave wall, he moved to investigate. So much of the cave looked the same that any other material, no matter the color, no matter the size, stood out like the sorest of thumbs. Jayden exclaimed out loud to himself upon coming to the pile.

It was not a pile at all, he could now see, but rather a display of clay figurines. Warriors in repose, mothers with child, even animals. One of the figures commanded his attention. A clay figure about a foot high and decorated with an elaborate headdress held his hands together. Between them was an actual nugget of gold, about the size of a coffee creamer, though irregularly shaped as if it had come that way out of the Earth.

Now we're on the right track, Jayden thought, taking out his cell-phone. He snapped off a series pf photos of the artifacts, especially of the gold-bearing one, but left them *in-situ*. Finding this small cache of treasures buoyed his spirits, for it meant they had stumbled onto a location not previously discovered. He backed away from the trove and wiped his brow, taking a deep breath. He could see why, though. It was oppressively hot down here, a little harder to breathe. He knew that he had entered the realm of serious caving while now essentially a solo spelunker. *Not good.* He had discovered enough to make the team happy, and at this point he just wanted to regroup with his team so they could share what they had found so far and go from there as a group.

But first he had to find a way out of here. He drank some water from his canteen and then turned his attention to the natural room in which he found himself. As he noted earlier, the central pool poured into a small stream that flowed through a cleft of rock. He began walking around the space, aiming his light to its far corners, searching for passages that were outlets leading out of here. By the time he had circled the pool and come back to his pack where he'd left it on the floor, he had discovered no additional passageways or caverns. Frowning, he stared up at the level from which he had dropped down. That was the only way out.

Or, he told himself, aiming his flashlight to the cleft of rock through which the stream flowed....*Through there*....

Jayden knew that water in caves was extremely dangerous indeed. Any rainfall occurring outside could suddenly and without warning increase the source of the cave water, causing flooding inside the system. That meant that for anyone in a stream or pool in a cave, if it did not have a lot of accessible overhead space, they risked drowning in the event of a sudden downpour as the water level rose to the top of the cave.

He walked over to the gap in the rock wall where the small stream entered it. He aimed his light to the ceiling of the fissure, then back down to the water itself. The stream here was shallow, only a foot or so deep. The crack was just wide enough for him to fit through sideways, though not while wearing his pack. Shining his light inside the fissure, he saw that the stream carried on for some yards straight away until it sloped down out of sight. Jayden withdrew from the claustrophobic space and breathed deeply in deep contemplation. It was either forge ahead into this watery space, which was in no shape or form a safe thing to do, or he had to somehow go back up the way he had come.

He gazed back up at the lip of the tunnel from which he had dropped down here, hoping that viewing it from a different angle would allow him to see some solution which had previously eluded him. No such luck. The ground below the tunnel lip was featurelessly flat. Jayden walked over to it and stood there, arms stretched high. He flexed his legs a couple of times and then tried his best standing high jump, noting that his fingertips were still at least two solid feet short of the tunnel lip. Then he eyed his pack on the ground and had an idea. Maybe if he stood on it and then jumped, he could grab the level above and pull himself up? He could tie a rope to his pack first with the other end fastened to his belt, so that when he got up he could haul his pack up behind him....

He put the plan into motion, dragging his pack over and even situating the items inside it to maximize a jumping-off point to stand on. Then he tested it out, standing atop his backpack. It gave him nearly two additional feet of height, but even with his redistribution of items to make for a smooth surface, it still felt giving and unstable. He tried jumping and found that he was not able to jump as effectively as he could from the solid rock floor. His fingertips still fell well short of the tunnel shelf every time, and soon he became winded and needed to take a break from the exertion.

It was just not going to work, he thought, now sitting on his pack. He palmed his walkie-talkie and transmitted on their team channel as well as scanning all channels, but heard absolutely nothing. Noting that the battery power was not at full capacity, he swapped out the batteries for a fresh set in case that would make a difference, but it did not. Fresh out of ideas, Jayden resigned himself to the reality that unless he wanted to simply wait here and hope that someone found him, he was going to have to see what lay ahead in the stream tunnel.

He mentally retraced his route thus far in the cave system, and didn't see how Hunt would be able to come across him. He had dropped down the cliff from one cavern to another below it, so there was no reason to think they were internally connected in a way that Hunt and Maddy could follow. Jayden yelled out loud in frustration, listening with his head in his hands to his vocal outburst bouncing of the cave's endless rock.

Then he rummaged through his pack and looked for something he didn't need that he could leave behind a sign that he had been here. He decided he could live without a T-shirt (*"Hog's Breath Saloon, Key West"*), and wadded it up into a ball. He wrote a quick note on a piece of notebook paper ("I was here, went down into pool room, through stream tunnel," and he noted the time and date. He folded the note and put it inside the shirt. Then he threw the T-shirt up onto the tunnel floor, where it would likely lay for eternity, but at least if Hunt and Maddy did come this way, they would see it.

After another moment to reflect on the fact that he had no other choice, Jayden dragged his pack over to where the stream flowed through the rock wall. He didn't bother putting his pack on since he wouldn't be able to fit through the cleft wearing it. Instead, he took a tarp out of it and tied it with a rope around the outside of the pack, to give it a waterproof cover. Then he shoved it in front of him sideways through the cleft in the rock until it splashed into the shallow stream on the other side.

Jayden slipped sideways through the same opening, and standing in knee-deep water, picked up his backpack and put it back on. Then, after situating his gear and turning on a flashlight, he began plodding through the stream toward the downward slope he could see ahead.

CHAPTER 18

Port of Cartagena
Colombia

Daedalus paced the upper deck of the *Historica* while its chopper, affectionately referred to as the *Helicoptera,* approached for a landing on the helipad. His sat-phone lit up in his hand and he answered it, but only long enough to say, "He's coming in now. I'll get the briefing from him and call you back," before pocketing the phone and turning to face the incoming aircraft.

He stood and watched the landing. Viewing the chopper through binoculars, he checked to see that the pilot was the only person aboard, which he was. The field team should all have been dropped off in the mountains. He was about to lower the binoculars when he caught sight of a marred area of white paint low on the chopper's left side. *What happened there?* As he told his brother, he would find out firsthand soon enough. He picked up his regular cellular phone and dialed the pilot's number. He watched as the man ambling across the helipad paused to fish out his device, looked at the display to see who was calling, and then looked up in his direction and waved.

"Georgio, I would like to meet with you right now on the upper deck."

"On my way." A few minutes later and the pilot was climbing up the stairs to the deck Daedalus occupied. The Treasure, Inc. founder welcomed his pilot, a short, stocky man with curly, jet black hair, by waving his arm at a tray of food and beverages. "Please, help yourself."

"Thank you, Daedalus." Georgio, whose former career was flying helicopters for Greece's Hellenic Air Force, availed himself of a bottle of sparkling water and some tuna sashimi.

"So you were able to drop our field team in the target area?" Daedalus said, not giving Georgio a chance to eat.

The Treasure, Inc. pilot nodded, hurriedly swallowing his raw fish. "Correct." He licked his lips and smiled. "Have you heard from Phillipo yet? I already briefed him via encrypted satellite phone."

"No, but I wanted a firsthand account before I talk to him."

Georgio plucked another piece of sushi from the tray and poised it near his mouth. "Mmmm, okay. First of all, there is some minor damage to the helicopter that will cost something to repair."

"I noticed," Daedalus said, his voice stern.

Georgio nodded and smiled, apparently unconcerned. "It does not require grounding. We can still safely use it as long as we need to."

Daedalus nodded and Georgio continued. "So, I dropped the field team in two sub-teams of two, as we talked about. Two in the middle of the cliffs outside an open cavern, and two on the jungle floor near the base of the cliff with the caverns. All of their gear went with them, including the scoped rifle they used to—" Suddenly he paused, a mischievous smile overtaking his features. Ah, but you don't know about this yet."

Daedalus tented his hands and eyed his pilot with curiosity. "Know about what?"

"After the first cave team was dropped…" He went on to recount how they were able to literally shoot down Omega Team's helicopter.

Daedalus leaned forward, keenly interested. "So it is still there, wrecked in the jungle?"

Georgio laughed, nearly spitting out his sushi. "Of course it's still there! It will always be there, it's in the middle of nowhere."

Daedalus gave him a hard stare before asking, "And its pilot? Is he dead?"

Georgio chugged some water before answering. "Probably."

At this, anger flared in Daedalus' eyes. "Probably?"

Georgio paused eating and drinking to stare at his boss. "Well yeah, Daedalus. *Probably*. The ship didn't explode or set on fire, that we could see. We shot the motor, hydraulic fluids and gas leaked out, and it crashed down into the jungle."

"So you don't know if he died in the crash."

Georgio threw up his hands. "Of course not. But even if he didn't, he's completely screwed. His aircraft is wrecked, and he's alone, probably with minimal gear, in the middle of a high elevation rain forest with whatever injuries he sustained in the crash, separated by miles from his team, who are presumably in the caves." He chuckled at the hopelessness of the predicament. "If he's not dead, it won't be long before he wishes he was."

CHAPTER 19

Graham Walker had begun to wonder if he should go back to his crashed helicopter and await rescue. The bright red aircraft would be easier to see than him, after all; he'd always heard that in survival situations it was best to stay with the craft, whether it be an aircraft, car, boat, whatever, to increase odds of rescue. Even when taking into consideration that whoever had shot him down might find him first, he was seriously weighing whether trekking through the jungle alone to find his team was a risk worth taking.

Already the insects feasted on his flesh. He had no repellent with him. He thought there might be some in the chopper's first aid kit he had taken, but it was small and its contents more meager than he would have thought. There were some bandages, Band-Aids and antiseptic, things like hat, but nothing really useful like inspect repellent or drugs.

Even though he had the compass he pried from the helicopter and therefore knew he was walking in the right direction--toward the cliff with the caverns—he still felt like he was making hardly any progress. He had no way to know how far he had gone, without a GPS device, and this jungle all looked so much the same. Down here on the forest floor he did not have the benefit of instant awareness of his position as he did flying above the canopy. Hardy cycads, a primitive palm-like tree and towering ferns competed for space on the forest floor, while the soaring canopy trees blotted out the sunlight from high above.

He stopped frequently to use his walkie-talkie. He followed the protocol Hunt had established, which is not to refer to anyone by name, nor to say the word "Omega." At this point he thought that to be silly, since the only people within range of the walkie-talkies besides Omega were the people trying to take Omega down. But he followed protocol anyway, omitting names altogether and just broadcasting, "It's me, anybody read?" Over and over.

He was in the middle of saying it yet again when he was smacked in the face by a moth so large he thought it was a bird. Disgusted, he put down the radio and started walking again, stepping over a mound of rock here and some exposed tree roots there to make painfully slow forward progress. With added stops to check that he was still on track with the compass heading, the going proved to be tortuously slow.

Sweat streamed down his face, his hair and clothes wet with either sweat or water from passing through wet leaves, and Graham began to fantasize about where he'd be right now had he not taken off with Carter Hunt in Red Hook. Even a jail cell with its three hots and a cot was preferable to this, he told himself as he forced his way through more itchy plants without the benefit of a machete. The plant life was so thick he felt like he was in a damned cave. Here there were no trails or paths whatsoever, just a profusion of chlorophyll.

He found there was none of the exotic allure that people conjured when they watched a rain forest video or simply imagined walking through a real rain forest. None of the one-with-nature communing that looked so peaceful, with butterflies flitting about a shady glade, warm furry creatures approaching cautiously from their leafy hiding places. He would have been hard pressed to articulate it, but this was so much more demanding than that, and worse still, so much more *confusing*. He'd spent time in jungle climes in the service, but it was different with the support of a squad. At least there a guy had gear, supplies and some kind of communication network that worked most of the time. Even had he been shot down in wartime, which never happened to him personally, someone on his side would know where he was and what happened.

Now he felt like he was almost completely winging it. Sure, he told himself: he did have an objective now, to reunite with the team. Oh, and then help them find El Dorado, he thought bitterly, causing himself to literally laugh out loud as he ducked beneath a clump of head-high ferns. I'm going crazy out there, he thought. He sung, or hummed if he didn't know the words, all the songs he could think of, mostly classic rock, songs about getting out of this place and breaking on through or to keep on keeping on....

The approach worked so well that after a while he realized it had been some time since he checked his compass. *Great.* He'd been pushing through pretty hard and thought he deserved a short break while he checked his heading, so he took a seat on a downed tree whose trunk was at the perfect height to serve as a mossy bench. Graham consulted his compass, lining it up with the direction in which he had been travelling. He felt ill when he saw that he was now significantly off course, having strayed a number of degrees from his initial heading.

Telling himself not to cry about it like a little baby, Graham reoriented himself based on the correct heading, chugged some of his now precious canteen water, and set out again. Knowing he had tacked on extra distance to an already exceedingly difficult slog didn't help his spirits any, and after a while it was all he could do not to succumb to feelings of desperation. He kept his head mostly down and watched for hazards about to be underfoot, not caring to see the never-ending wall of impenetrable greenery that threatened to envelope him.

He stopped to rest again at the trunk of a tall tree with water dripping off of it from above. Took another compass heading, telling himself he would not let that happen again. Although back on track now, he had already gone far out of his way, the damage done. But since he didn't know exactly which part of the mountainside he needed to come out on, he figured it wasn't all that critical. He would get to the base of the mountain and go from there. He heard birds flitting from branch to branch. At least that's what he thought they were. He couldn't be sure because he could see birds, but still hear other sounds.

He set out walking again, but for some reason couldn't shake the sensation he was being followed. He told himself that he was only tired, his senses beginning to play tricks on him. Or that he was spooked by being shot down, and attributed the feeling to being hunted by the same bad actors. But he continued to hear the occasional snap of a twig or rustling in the foliage, whereas earlier all was quiet. Or was he simply noticing it more now? Time blended together with the forest itself as he plodded on, one foot in front of the other when he could, hands pulling branches out of the way when he couldn't pass. On and on he trekked through the forbidding environment, face and hands badly scratched, feet sore, head weary.

Obsessively checking his compass, he trudged on, mentally kicking himself for not having packed a "ditch bag" in the event of going down in the jungle. He told himself that if he was to continue in this line of work, he'd have to up his game. For now, he'd just have to tough it out. He watched his shoes as they stepped, wary that one misstep could turn an ankle and then he'd really be done. So he watched his feet, and as his right foot was about to come down on a dried palm frond, he anticipated the crackling sound it would make and was therefore surprised when he heard a crunching noise *before* his foot landed. Some distance away, but not all that far, maybe ten or twenty feet.

He froze and looked around, head on a swivel, as he would have said in his military days. He could see nothing, though, not even a bird moving. Shaking his head to clear his senses, he looked around yet again, and still he detected nothing more than the forest itself. He told himself he wasn't used to the bush anymore and continued forging his way through the greenery, now wearing his aviator-style sunglasses for eye protection even though it was dimly lit on the forest floor.

He grew hungry and thought about the leftover breakfast food he had in his pack, but forced himself to keep marching on, not wanting to stop to eat. He also knew he needed to conserve his food since he had no idea where more would come from at this point. He glanced up for a change and jerked his head back as he came almost eye to eye with a green tree snake coiled in a dangling branch.

Jesus, are these things poisonous? He stared at the creature unmoving, but the snake didn't move either. Graham decided he would be the one to shy away first, and slowly bent his knees so that his head was lowered down from the serpent. Then, with the same sloth-like motion, he moved himself sideways until he felt he was far enough away to stand up and run. He barreled through the underbrush until he encountered a thick wall of scrubby plants he would have to stop to deal with. But he had avoided the snake.

Graham was in the process of figuring out the best way to navigate past the wall of thorny plants in his way when a sound shattered the stillness of the rain forest. He jumped with the suddenness of it, with how out of place it was. Then his radio bleated again and this time he recognized a voice. Hunt's.

"...see smoke from chopper. Do you copy me, over?"

CHAPTER 20

Hunt and Maddy stood at the edge of the same cavern Jayden had dropped down from earlier. They noted that a few bees skittered about, but not the thick swarm they had loosed in the cave. They stared down at the jungle spread out before them. A wispy trail of dark smoke in the middle of it issued from Graham's downed helicopter, which naturally gave them both tremendous concern. Hunt looked at it again through his binoculars, but could see only the broken treetops where something large had obviously disturbed them. Hunt immediately put out radio calls, and after waiting a couple of minutes, finally got a response.

"Yes, yes, Carter—sorry, no names—"

"Graham, it's okay. Never mind the protocol for now. Take it easy and tell me what happened. But first, are you injured?"

"Broke my damn nose, that's for sure, hurts like a mother, and I've got various little bruises and fractures, but overall I came out of it rather good. Damn bug bites are the worst thing now."

"Glad to hear it, copy. We'll get you medical attention as soon as we can. And we've got bug spray waiting for you when we link up." Hunt looked out across the rain forest, knowing his pilot was stuck down there somewhere. A thought occurred to him. "I don't suppose you have any flares on you, from the chopper?"

"That's a negative. I didn't see them and didn't have time to look before I bailed out. I was lucky I have my little daypack and the first aid kit I did get."

Maddy shot Hunt a concerned glance, but Hunt shrugged. "Probably just as well you don't use one. It would also tell Treasure, Inc. exactly where you are, and that you are alive. They might think you didn't survive, which would be an advantage."

"True. I'll take whatever edge I can get at this point. So about my position. I did manage to take the compass from the 'copter and have been taking bearings. But I sill have no idea where I am relative to you. I can't see anything above the canopy."

"What compass heading are you using?"

Hunt pulled a simple compass of his own from his backpack and held it level with the horizon. Then he oriented it using the same heading number Graham had been using, but 180 degrees in reverse, since he was looking in the opposite direction.

"OK buddy, I see your intended course from the accident site." Hunt thought that as thinly veiled as the euphemism was, it was better than saying "crashed helicopter" in case anyone was listening in. "Turns out you would have ended up pretty far away from us, more toward the other end of the valley. So let me give you a new heading, okay?" Hunt took a bearing to the fallen chopper, calculated the reverse direction that Graham would need to use coming from his location, and told him the new heading over the radio.

"Copy that heading. "After confirming he had the right number by saying it back to Hunt, Graham asked where exactly they should meet up.

Hunt knew that the privacy codes on their walkie-talkie channel, which were really nothing more than specific squelch settings, might not be enough if Treasure, Inc. had brought a radio specialist along. But right now he just had to hope that they didn't. He told Graham, "We'll be somewhere nearby the base of the cliff, in an area that offers concealment. Don't panic if you don't see us right away, we'll be there waiting for you. First we need to get down there, so no huge rush on your part."

Hunt was surprised to hear laughter emanate from his radio speaker. "There's no rushing down here, buddy. You'll see."

They signed off and Hunt turned to Maddy. "How are your climbing skills?" He looked down from the cavern to the forest floor far below.

"I've done it before, is about all I can say. Under supervision. It's not part of my actual job description." She gave him a smile that said, *I hope you know what you're doing.*

Hunt nodded. "I'll set everything up and walk you through it. Right now, help me by laying out whatever climbing gear you do have—ropes, carabiners, chalk, pitons, hammer, anything like that."

"You got it." She went to her pack while Hunt did the same, readying the climbing gear to make their descent. When Hunt's equipment was laid out, he walked back inside the cavern to the tunnel entrance at the back. From there, he transmitted from his radio, looking for Jayden. He wanted to tell him they were descending to the rain forest floor.

"J-man, long time no hear buddy, pick up?" He repeated various versions of the "where the heck are you" message and then waited, but no reply came.

Maddy looked up at him as he walked back out to the edge. "No word from Jayden?"

Hunt shook his head. "He must be deep inside the tunnel system. But don't worry. He knows what he's doing. Right now we've got to help Graham."

Hunt helped Maddy to rig a climbing harness and showed her what to do, and what not to do. "I've always wanted a man to show me the ropes," she said, cracking a suggestive smile.

He laughed, shaking his head. "Just make sure you don't actually fall for me, okay?"

Her eyes widened in mock surprise. "Not funny!"

"Let's do this." Although he couldn't have known, Hunt selected the same outcropping of rock to anchor their climbing rope that Jayden had used earlier. He and Maddy would descend at the same time, side by side, each using their own rope, both of which were looped around the same anchor rock. Hunt knew that it was far from ideal, but it was all they had. Looking down, he could see a ledge of some sort, so he would reevaluate the rigging when they got down there.

He and Maddy backed up to the edge of the cliff, as Jayden had done, and then walked down backwards. They took it slow, with Hunt letting Maddy set the pace, which wasn't all that slow, he was pleased to discover. They rappelled down the cliff without incident until they passed in front of the open space that was the cavern Jayden had fled to when escaping the bees.

"Wow, another cavern!"

They continued lowering to the ledge, but then Carter halted them. "Check it out!" He pointed down to the ground, where a recent set of boot prints was imprinted in the dirt, a few small plants recently crushed.

"Jayden landed here!" he said, lowering them the rest of the way to the cavern ledge. He helped Maddy get out of her climbing gear and then the two of them entered the chamber. The cool air felt good after the exposed climb down. Maddy shed her pack and sat while Hunt dropped his and kept walking to the rear of the cavern.

"Looks like this one only has one exit, straight back." He examined the cavern floor to see if he could find more footprints, but it was mostly solid rock this far inside and he didn't see any.

"You're not going into the tunnels, are you?" Maddy sounded concerned. Hunt knew she definitely did not want to be left alone, especially with the separation from the rest of the group.

"I'm going to stand in the entrance to the tunnel and try to make radio contact with Jayden. We know he was on the ledge out there, so..." Then he shone his beam into the tunnel, saw that it was navigable, and tried simply shouting his name in that direction. He listened for a reply until the echoes died, but he got no answer in return. Then he tried via radio, but there, too, he was disappointed.

He walked back to Maddy with the news. "Not getting anything." She eyed him with an unwavering gaze without saying anything. To Hunt, that was even worse than if she had come out and said, "Everything's going to crap."

Because it was. He couldn't deny that. Jayden was missing, and his pilot shot out of the sky, trekking alone through a dangerous, even hostile environment. And a much darker thought took hold over his mind. What if the same team who shot down Graham also came across Jayden and shot him down as well? Inside one of those tunnels or caves, no one would ever hear it or even know about it for a long, long time.

He told himself that until he knew what happened, that worrying about it was time wasted that could be spent reuniting with his team. He told Maddy. "Come on, we've got to go find Graham."

Out on the ledge they rigged the climbing gear again. Hunt had a more difficult time finding a suitable rock on which to rig the ropes, but he found two medium sized trees and was able to use both of their trunks to his satisfaction. Once again they put their backs to the cliff and walked off the edge, descending the mountain face.

Hunt glanced down at the jungle as if he would see some sign of Graham, but he was greeted with only the unbroken expanse of trees that he knew would be waiting for them when they got down from this cliff.

CHAPTER 21

For a while Jayden was able to walk on the side of the subterranean stream, sort of a rocky shoulder that, while requiring him to stoop, made for easier going than wading through knee-deep water--water that was on the cold side, too, at this elevation. But as he neared the slope, the shoulder narrowed to the point that it was easier to trudge along in the steam itself. He had to be diligent with his flashlight, though, since it would be easy to miss the bottom dropping out from under him if it suddenly became much deeper, such as a depression in the bottom forming a natural pool. So he walked carefully while staring mostly at the stream bottom. Soon the entire tunnel began to slope downward.

At first the slope was somewhere between gentle and steep—at enough of an incline that he had to concentrate not to slip, but at the same time still easily walkable with his backpack on. As he walked with both his headlamp on and a flashlight beam in his hand, he noticed a profusion of glittering masses underwater and in the tunnel walls. Quartz, emeralds, and gold ore. He picked up a loose nugget of what he was nearly positive to be gold (not pyrite) and pocketed it for later analysis.

As he moved downstream the incline became gradually steeper, and the water rushed a little faster. It was this latter force that necessitated him to move slowly, even more methodically, lest he slip and fall into the stream.

He did not want to have to walk around in here soaking wet. Because he moved more slowly, he was able to notice increasing detail on the bottom of the stream. It became more and more golden, with larger gold chunks peppering the bottom. They were not loose, but embedded into the cave bedrock. Above him, the tunnel ceiling sparkled with similar ore.

Jayden continued working his way downstream, noting that the dimensions of the tunnel itself remained little changed. He stopped here and there to examine a particularly large chunk of gold or emerald. He was staring at one such area of interest when he heard splashing coming from somewhere behind him. He stopped all movement to better be able to hear. Was it only the rushing stream? No, he was sure that, as he continued to listen, the splashing was caused by human footfalls. Someone else was walking downstream! Thinking they must have found his note left above the pool, he called out: "Carter! Maddy! I'm down here!"

No answer came, but the splashing went on, getting closer. Jayden rose to a standing position and called for his friends again. Still no reply. If anything, the footfalls increased in pace and loudness. Soon the first beams of light from the new arrivals landed on the cave ceiling in front of Jayden. It seemed like the type of beam light looked different, like they were not the same kind of light that Hunt and Maddy had been using—maybe halogen instead of LED?

He wasn't exactly sure what, but something didn't feel right about this and so he switched off his flashlight and then his headlamp, leaving him in near darkness but for the bobbing, wayward light beams of the newcomers walking his way. The stream occupied the entire width of the tunnel here, so with no higher ground to go to, Jayden remained standing in the stream, stock still. Silently he undid the catch on his pistol holster, and noiselessly again he withdrew the weapon without taking his eyes off the bouncing lights coming closer with each passing second.

Then he heard a voice. Male. Only a couple of words, softly spoken, but enough to know it definitely wasn't Maddy, and the accent gave away that it wasn't Hunt. On edge now, Jayden began to walk slowly downstream again, not allowing his movements to create any splashing louder than the naturally rushing stream. He put his flashlight underneath his shirt to filter the light, then switched it on. He picked his way downstream while listening to the louder, wet steps of his pursuers behind him. Their lights occasionally played across the tunnel walls not far behind Jayden. When he saw their lights he picked up his pace as much as he dared, but whoever they were, they were not concerned with stealth and so easily kept pace with him as they moved downstream.

The streambed was very steep now, and Jayden wondered how much longer he could go before he slipped and fell on his backside, since the weight of his pack drew him backwards on the incline. But the question was answered for him by the cave itself. A few yards ahead, his light picked out a change in topography. It looked like the stream ended, and Jayden feared that it ran into a narrow rock crevice too small for him to fit through, or possibly even completely submerged. But as he walked cautiously to where the stream disappeared, he saw that the situation was altogether different.

The sound of rushing water also became louder, which was a grave concern since it meant he could no longer hear whoever was chasing him. He turned sideways so that he could look both downstream and upstream by moving only his eyes. When he saw flashlight beams playing on the cave ceiling about twenty feet behind him, he switched his gaze back to the stream.

It didn't end here, he could see, but dropped off at a very steep angle, not much better than vertical. Creeping close to the edge, he was wary of slipping and being washed down the waterfall. For that's basically what it is, he thought. A subterranean waterfall. He looked back upstream and saw the flashlights only ten feet behind him now, and heard two different strange voices. They were almost to him. He wished he knew who they were, but they must be pursuing him, which meant they didn't intend to ask if he wanted to go to lunch sometime.

Turning back to the waterfall, Jayden got down on his belly in the stream, tensing with the cold water and flashing ever so briefly on his SEAL training days on the beach in San Diego. He took his flashlight out from under his shirt and stuck it down over the waterfall. He whispered a choice curse word as he saw how long the drop was. Not necessarily survivable, he thought. If he were not being chased by people who aimed to kill him, he would not have considered going down it.

But as the voices became nearer, and he glow of their flashlights bathed the tunnel behind him, he knew he didn't have much choice. He could either take his chances with whoever these people were—whether that involved a two-on-one gun battle, or an exchange of words that led to him being taken prisoner—he couldn't know. With a last glance down the waterfall, he picked out a few details far below and then made his move.

CHAPTER 22

Graham Walker's spirits were buoyed after talking with Hunt on the radio. He bashed and marauded his way through the prickly forest, caring not for the litany of minor scratches and bug bites he endured, nor for the spiderwebs that assaulted his face. He checked his compass religiously to make certain he stayed on his new course that would reunite him with his team, hardly slowing his pace to do so.

About an hour after the radio exchange, the downed pilot heard a new sound. He stopped moving to assess it more carefully, cocking his head to one side like a hunting dog. A bubbling, gurgling sound that he recognized as running water. He checked his compass heading and saw that it was almost in line with his prescribed course, so he decided it was worth taking a look. His canteen was nearly empty already, and so taking in some fresh water and topping off his canteen would be worth a small deviation from his course.

Graham pushed his way through foliage so dense he could not see more than a foot in front of his face while the sound of rushing water became clearer. He scraped away numerous creepie-crawlies he could not identify in the slightest and had no desire to. Minutes later he swatted away a broad palm leaf and stared with surprise into open space, something he'd seen very little of since crashing into this unbridled wilderness.

A small brook babbled from left to right in front of him. Narrow enough that he could ford it with one giant step, the waterway nevertheless appeared to be a promising source of drinking water. He looked left and right, but found that the stream quickly curved out of sight in both directions, enshrouded in greenery. Graham knelt at the stream and cupped both hands into its clear, flowing water and splashed his face. The coolness felt wonderful and reviving, and he repeated the act several times, also lapping water like a thirsty animal at the watering hole.

When he looked up, he was staring into the eyes of two humans.

They stood on the other side of the bank, about ten feet to his right. Naked but for loincloths and elaborate body paint, both held spears, not at the ready, but gripped in one hand with the butt end resting on the ground. The taller, skinnier of the two also had a bow and arrow slung over his shoulder. Neither of the tribal men appeared either threatening or frightened themselves, but merely curious. They simply stared at him as if witnessing something unusual, which no doubt Graham's presence here must be to them.

Very slowly, Graham raised his wet face from the stream while maintaining eye contact with the strangers. He couldn't help but notice that both of the men were adorned with what appeared to be gold jewelry— necklaces, earrings, and bracelets.

"*Hola amigos.*" Graham clumsily tried Spanish, even though he knew that they most likely only spoke and understood their own tribal dialect. Corroborating this fact, the pair of tribal men remained mute, expressionless, and unmoving.

Suddenly Graham heard a clicking noise off to his left, but before he could turn to see what it was, the taller tribal man's head rocked violently back with a splash of blood and he crumpled to the ground.

Instantly the other tribal man disappeared, backing into the foliage as though he had assimilated himself into it. Another shot was fired and Graham saw the soil erupt in a powdery plume from the ground where the other tribal person had stood one second earlier.

And then Graham himself turned to look at the murderer who had just shot dead the tribesman. He had time to see only a man in camo fatigues, fully kitted out with a high caliber hunting rifle. When the barrel swung Graham's way, he, too backed into the jungle, seeking its cover and protection. He did a kind of backwards crabwalk into the leaves, until he could flop over onto his belly, push himself up and start running. He didn't know or care which direction; anywhere so long as it was away from the killer hunting him. For it was he that the assassin wanted, Graham knew. The tribal man was only collateral damage, an innocent bystander whose death the triggerman would no doubt justify by calling him a threat. Scary tribal warriors with spears and arrows, and all that. Graham knew the type, and that made them all the more worrisome.

He ran pell-mell through the rain forest, slashing his face open on saw palms and thorny leaves. He was some distance away, though it had been anything but a stealthy evasion, before it even occurred to him that he carried a pistol. He remember his skepticism when Hunt had presented him with it in the hotel room in Bogota. Now it seemed like his only lifeline, however thin.

Not only was he sorely outgunned by the rifleman, but he highly doubted that gunman was working alone, so he would be outnumbered, too. Knowing that at any moment a high caliber round could come ripping into his body or head, Graham sought a place he could shelter and hide just long enough to take defensive aim with his pistol.

He found it in the root pit of a fallen tree. The tree, one of the tall ones that made up the canopy, had recently been struck by lightning and toppled, its root ball pried from the Earth, leaving an open pit. Graham ensconced himself in that pit, even dragging leafy branches around the edges of it to conceal him further. *Who am I kidding?* Graham thought, taking a chance and cracking off more branches of the fallen tree to drag into place over the pit, concealing the opening entirely. He crawled down in it and waited, knees drawn up to his chest and pistol aimed up with a shaky hand. Were they highly observant, his hunters would notice the tree's root ball in the air and deduce that there was a hole in the ground large enough to hide a man. They might even see the freshly ripped branches on the fallen tree and make that connection. But even given those possibilities of deduction, Graham still thought this gambit to have slightly better odds of survival then blindly running through the rain forest waiting to be gunned down like an animal.

He heard footsteps approaching and knew he did not have long to find out if he was right. He tensed inside the covered pit, literally like a cornered animal as his hunter neared. The shooter was running fast. He heard him grunt a monosyllabic word, at least he thought it was a word, and then he could see part of the man filtered through the bed of leaves covering the pit. He wasn't stopping.

The next thing Graham knew, a pair of boots were dropping into the pit, the branches that had been covering it pressing down on Graham's body. He could tell by the look of absolute shock that Graham's hiding place had acted like a pit trap, catching his hunter by surprise.

And Graham knew he had to take advantage of that element—take advantage of it right now or die. His pistol was an advantage in quarters so close the hunter's rifle could not be raised. Graham had time to take in camo face paint, dark eyes wide with fear and bewilderment before he felt a fist in his gut knocking the wind out of him. But his pistol remained in his right hand and he pulled the trigger with it aimed at his opponent's chest.

The report was loud in the close confines even though the soft earth absorbed much of its impact. Graham saw the fire dim in his assailant's eyes, but put a second bullet into his chest just in case. Then he aimed his gun up and out of the pit, bracing himself for a second attack by the deceased operator's partner. He heard footsteps crunching on the ground nearby.

Graham grabbed the rifle from his opponent and pulled it away from him. He knew it was much more powerful than his own weapon and he could aim it up and out of the pit, so he adopted it for this new fight. He found he was so nervous he literally shook with fear. He was trapped in a small pit with a dead man he had killed after nearly being killed himself, and now he was about to face down another would-be killer.

He moved the barrel of the rifle in a circle around the pit, trying to cover any angle from which the dead man's squad mate might approach. Then, even though he did not yet see the foe, he heard gunfire and saw dirt explode up around the edge of the pit. Graham shrunk down as far as he could go and pulled the dead man's body over him as a human shield while keeping the rifle aimed up. He heard footsteps moving away from the pit and thought maybe he had scared the attacker off.

Not willing to take the chance of leaving the pit where he could be picked off like a prairie dog leaving its hole, Graham continued to frantically move his rifle around the pit circle. He was expecting another close quarters attack, and that's why he was taken so off guard. The second gunman had climbed onto the fallen tree trunk, where he now lay and took aim at Graham from above, like a sniper. Graham instinctively moved to raise the rifle in his hands but the tip of the barrel jammed into the dirt side of the pit before it got anywhere close to a firing position.

Yelling in frustration and desperation, Graham dropped the rifle and yanked his pistol out of his holster, but it was too late. The sniper had a bead on him, and a thin smile crossed his face as he held his breath and began smoothly squeezing the trigger.

Graham was still in the process of raising his pistol, knowing he was going to be too late, when a long piece of wood suddenly stuck into the side of the sniper's head. He still pulled the trigger on his rifle, but the impact had moved him way out of position, so that the bullet went harmlessly up into the canopy. Then the rifle itself dropped to the ground and the shooter's body began to slide from the fallen tree trunk. Graham heard the soft thud as the lifeless corpse came into contact with the rain forest floor.

And then, taking the shooter's place on the tree trunk, the tribal man he had seen before, the shorter partner of the one who had been shot, appeared standing on the tree trunk. His spear was held at the ready and he carried the sniper's rifle in his other hand, but when he saw Graham in the pit and made eye contact with him, he merely leapt off of the tree and fled in the opposite direction into the jungle.

CHAPTER 23

Under a sky that had grown progressively grayer since they began their descent, Hunt and Maddy hung from their ropes on the mountain cliff. They had gone about two-thirds of the way down the mountain, having to stop and re-rig the ropes a couple of times on the way.

"Looks like smooth sailing from here on out," Hunt predicted. "How you feel?"

"Good, but my feet will welcome level ground again." Maddy paused to check her footing. They were about to start down again when they heard a gunshot ring out. In the quiet of the rain forest, it shattered the stillness and reverberated off the mountains for what seemed like a long time.

Hunt immediately transferred his ropes to his left hand and grabbed his holstered pistol with his right. "Where'd that come from?"

"Not sure." Maddy pointed toward the middle section of the jungle valley, not that far from where they would be once they reached the ground. "Maybe over there."

Hunt looked to where she was pointing but didn't see any obvious activity. Then he checked to make sure a bullet hadn't hit higher up on the cliff, which could trigger a rockfall, but he didn't see any indication of that, either.

"Graham's down there somewhere on the forest floor," Hunt said, springing straight out from the cliff and letting his feet land again to test his footing. "We should get down there. Ready for some fast-roping?"

"You bet. I kind of feel like a target pinned to the wall like this."

"At least there's more plant cover for the rest of the way down." Maddy saw that it was true. Higher up there were portions of the cliff that were bare rock, which made two human bodies stand out that much more than they would against a mottled green and brown background.

The two explorers resumed their downward climb, sliding down the anchored rope with their backs to the jungle, which was nerve-wracking to them both but also the fastest way off the cliff without falling. Now and again Hunt would crane his neck around while descending to check their progress. Much closer now, he could make out individual trees as opposed to the blanket of green the forest looked like from higher up.

And then the second shot rang out.

To Hunt it sounded like another discharge from the same firearm in the same location. Maddy cried out in fear and Hunt gripped her shoulder. "It's okay. I don't think they're aiming at us or either we'd be hit or we'd have heard a round bounce off the cliff somewhere around us."

"You really know how to cheer a girl up, Carter. So what do we do?"

"Keep going!" He and Maddy once again resumed their rappel down the cliff. On the way down, Hunt tried the radio once more. "Anyone copy, over?" He repeated the message.

He wouldn't mind hearing from either Graham or Jayden at this point. It scared him how wrong everything seemed to be going, and now with ground shots fired. He didn't want to alarm Maddy, but he silently pondered what kind of skirmish they might be dropping into. His single pistol suddenly seemed woefully inadequate.

They descended onto a break in the cliff, not a cavern but a concave overhang that required them to freefall straight down the rope in mid-air until their feet came into contact with the cliff again. From there it was easy going until they reached the base of the cliff, which was really just the uppermost portion of a hill that sloped down to the rain forest floor. They collected their climbing gear and hurriedly attached it to their packs while scoping out the forest with what little vantage point they had left. Hunt also took a compass heading to orient himself to the path Graham was supposed to be taking, though with shots fired, he accepted the possibility that he may no longer be on course.

Then they jogged down the hill to the valley basin, knowing they were not silent in the process but willingly sacrificing stealth for speed to no longer be a sniper target. As soon as they stood among the tree trunks, Hunt drew his pistol. He stood close to Maddy and said in a low voice, "Down here we need to be stealthy. No talking above whisper, and try to avoid stepping on anything that would make noise." Maddy silently nodded her understanding and Hunt again checked his compass, then pointed off to their left.

It began to rain as they started to move. At first it was merely steady and light, but as they walked into the heavy plant cover of the jungle floor, a genuine downpour broke wide open.

CHAPTER 24

Port of Cartagena
Colombia

Daedalus stepped out of the shower in the bathroom of the *Historica's* exquisitely appointed master suite and slipped on a robe. He'd been thinking that the time might be right to get more personally involved in the El Dorado affair. He did not want his reputation to become that of an exclusively "hands-off" CEO. He was a modern treasure hunter who sought his prizes mostly from behind a computer and phone, it was true, but he did not want those who did his dirty work for him to think he was not capable of getting his hands soiled himself. He walked past his girlfriend who still lay nude on the bed, now playing one of those mindless games on her smartphone.

"Sweetie, I may be off the ship for the next couple of days on business. I trust you will be okay?"

She looked up at him and smiled while reaching for a frozen cherry from a bowl of them on the bed. "I'll be fine, D. See you when you get back!" She winked at him and resumed her game while the home theater TV mounted on the wall played some reality TV show that he knew was nothing more than a contemporary soap opera. His mother had watched the scripted ones when he was a boy; he hadn't liked them then and he didn't like them any better now.

Knowing that the sun would be starting to set soon, he left the salon for his preferred place of conducting business on the upper deck. He radioed his chief stewardess that he would be there in a few minutes and so would like a light supper and drinks prepared for him. Then he navigated the ship's stairwells, hallways, decks, even an elevator, stopping to chat briefly with a crew member here and there, before walking out onto the uppermost deck. He was pleased to see an array of hors d'oeuvres and a club sandwich waiting, along with a silver tray of beverages on ice.

He reclined in a chaise lounge and had a bite to eat while he began to check his messages in the usual order: sat-phone first, then business cellular, then personal cellular, then e-mails. He had a voice-mail left by his brother on the sat-phone, which meant he was trying to talk to him in person. Without listening to the message, Daedalus called Phillipo back. His call was answered on the first ring.

"Daedalus! You heard my message? So—"

"I didn't hear it. Just tell me."

"We shot down Omega's helicopter over the jungle. It—"

"I know, I already took a briefing in person from Georgio. Excellent work, indeed! Any updates?"

"Other than Georgio, I haven't heard from any of the mountain cave team since they were dropped."

"Were you expecting to hear from them by now?"

"Negative. Their instructions are to contact Georgio if it is a situation requiring immediate evac, or to contact me if it involves the treasure."

"You're saying if they find El Dorado, they will call you. Otherwise they will try until they run out of resources and require extraction, then will call Georgio."

"Basically, yes. But I have also asked Georgio to bring our standby team, now in Bogota, as am I, to the site where we found Hunt's team. I personally will be accompanying the team to the site to ensure things go as smoothly as possible. I understand the great importance of this project to you and our company."

Daedalus stroked the stubble on his chin for a moment while he watched the orange glow of the setting sun color the harbor water. "When is Georgio leaving to pick you up?"

"Tonight. He said he would refuel on the way to Bogota and then should be able to drop us at the site before dawn."

"Tell Georgio that I will be going with him and you and the drop-team to the site." Daedalus glanced over to the helipad and saw that the *Helicoptera* was still there, engine off.

"You...you're..."

"I'm what?" Daedalus snapped. Yes, he thought, I've stayed out of the field for too long.

"Nothing," Phillipo said defensively. "It's just that you don't usually—"

Daedalus cut him off. "Well this time I am. Contact Georgio and tell him I'm going. I'll be packing my field bag. I'll gear up with you and the team when I get to Bogota."

He ended the call and grabbed one of the oysters Moscow chilled on ice as he rose to go pack. A smile of anticipation crossed his face as he looked out across the harbor at the now golden sunset.

El Dorado awaits!

CHAPTER 25

Jayden felt like he was falling for too long. The waterfall hadn't seemed this high....and then he was splashing into a pool. He tensed for impact, and it came, but only after a fall through about three feet of water. Enough to break his fall the way he landed, but barely so. He winced with the pain as he hit on his side, including his head. He was grateful he still wore the climbing helmet. The ex-SEAL tumbled about in the shallow pool as the waterfall dumped down on him. He kicked and dogpaddled with his arms, glad that he didn't seem to have broken anything, until his head cleared the surface of the water.

He took a deep breath and immediately looked up. He could see cones of light stabbing out through the air, the dust particles suspended in the cave making them visible. But his hunters weren't quite to the edge yet. He didn't want to turn on a light, but it was almost pitch dark down here and he needed to find cover before the intruders were able to take another shot at him.

He switched on his flashlight—awfully glad now that he had selected an actual dive light for this purpose—and kept it underwater to keep the light from reflecting up to the top of the waterfall. He could see now that he was in a narrow chamber where the waterfall landed in the pool. From there the stream flowed into another narrow channel which dropped out of sight not that far ahead. The sides of the pool featured narrow rock shelves, at least for part of the length of the chamber. Jayden couldn't be certain while relying on a flashlight held underwater, but he was confident enough that he could get himself up and out of the water, where he felt like the proverbial fish in a barrel.

While the lights approached the edge of the waterfall, Jayden switched off his own illumination and swam a quiet breaststroke, not easy while wearing his frame backpack, to the left edge of the chamber while facing the waterfall. There he had to temporarily turn his light on again while he slipped off the pack and pushed it up onto the rocky shelf. After that, Jayden flipped off his light and hauled himself up and out of the water in the dark, knocking and scraping a knee badly in the process but paying it no mind. He was setting up to drag his pack as far back into the recesses of the rocky shoreline as possible when a better idea lit up his brain.

He kept a small red LED light clipped to the outside of his backpack for locating it easily at night, usually at a campsite. This allowed him to set it down and walk away from it without fear of not being able to find it easily. Also, in situations where stealth was not required, it let other members of his team see where he was. But now he had an altogether different purpose for it. Jayden looked up at the waterfall and saw the light beams close to the edge now. He heard voices. He switched on his little pack light. Even though the red LED glow was not that bright, in the near total darkness it stood out like a lighthouse on a foggy night.

Now that the LED was on, Jayden knew he had mere seconds in which to take up his position. He left his pack on the rocky shelf and executed a shallow dive into the water. He held the form of the dive, hands together out in front of him, as he allowed his momentum to carry him underwater to the other side of the aquatic chamber. Once there, he had a moment of panic when he couldn't find a spot to climb up to the shelf on that side. It was too steep and high up. But, sliding his hands along the side, he came across a cutaway in the rock. He pulled himself up to the rocky shelf.

As soon as he climbed out of the water he saw the two human figures reach the edge of the waterfall. Both immediately doused their search beams upon seeing his red decoy light. Jayden unsnapped his holster and took out his pistol. He would have liked to reload it since it had been submerged, but there was no time for that and he knew it would probably work anyway. He'd done it more than a few times before.

Jayden assumed a one-knee shooting stance and took aim at the taller of the two interlopers. He knew that once he fired, the muzzle blast in the dark would pinpoint his position to his opponents, so he had to be ready to move after his opening shot. His goal was to eliminate one of the two, not to try and take out both.

As expected, both of his foes fired at his lighted backpack. The ex-SEAL targeted the muzzle flash he saw and double-tapped two rounds into where he thought the shooter's chest would be based on the flash from a standing position. Jayden backed away from his shooting position as soon as he had fired, in case the second opponent returned fire. He saw one of his pursuers fall unmoving off the top of the waterfall and splash into the pool not far from Jayden's position on the rock shelf.

He also saw the other man back away from the top of the waterfall so that he was out of Jayden's line of fire. Knowing that he had beat them back for now, Jayden once again dove into the pool. He could escape downstream right now with his life, but only if he wanted to negotiate the cave system with what was on his back, which would likely amount to a long and slow death sentence. He needed his backpack if he were to survive. So he risked the swim across the pond to the opposite ledge, keeping an eye on the top of the waterfall as he stroked, where there was now only darkness. He was also mindful of potentially swimming into the fallen gunmen he had shot, and of the possibility that mercenary may still be alive, though he doubted it. Once at the ledge, he watched for a few seconds to see if the remaining shooter was waiting for him to turn his back to the pond before firing on him. But he saw no indication of human presence up there. He may have fled back up into the cave system to make his way out, Jayden speculated.

He climbed up onto the smooth shelf and turned the red pack light off. Without stopping, he dragged the pack away from its position and then picked it up and slung it across his back. He ran as fast as he dared down the narrow shelf until it became too skinny to walk forward along. He found he was able to hug the wall and sidestep a ways further. By the time he got to the end of the shelf, he paused to monitor the shooter situation up top.

Satisfied there was no one there, Jayden stepped back into the water, activated his dive light again and allowed himself to float in the stream through the natural arch into the next passageway. He was taken down a sharp but short slope, like a roller coaster ride, that soon levelled off again. Satisfied he was now out of sight of the gunman, he smiled to himself.

One down, one to go.

Then he raised his dive light out of the water and examined his new environs.

CHAPTER 26

Even beneath the thick tree canopy, the rain still found them. Hunt and Maddy pulled on ponchos, the plastic hoods keeping their heads dry as they forced themselves through the unruly plant life on the jungle floor. Hunt put out another radio message for Graham now that line-of-sight-transmission should be possible. Nothing came back at first, so he continued to follow the reverse compass course Graham said he would be taking.

The rain came down even harder, pelting their poncho hoods, hammering loudly next to their eardrums. Maddy put her wide-brimmed straw hat on over the hood to mute the sound effect. She couldn't help but shriek as a foot-long millipede crawled into view on a palm frond inches from her face. Hunt brushed the creature aside and put a finger to his lips, reminding her of the need for stealth. He was thankful for the noise cover of the rain, but aware at the same time that it worked both ways. Their adversaries would be that much harder to hear as well.

They had just started to pick their way through the dense foliage again when Hunt's walkie-talkie bleated a call-tone. He put a hand on Maddy, telling her to stop while he did the same and looked all around while he transmitted.

"Copy, copy. Do you read?"

A few seconds later the strained voice of an American male came through over the radio. "Carter, it's me. Where are you? I need help, bad."

Hunt checked his compass before replying. "We're down here in the jungle now. Are you still following the compass course? Over."

"Negative. Everything went to hell and I had run off course. Carter, there's guys with guns down here. I—"

"Okay, hold it together. Can you follow this course now?" Hunt read him a number based on his own compass heading. Graham copied it back to him and said he would follow it.

"We're moving out now. From the strength of our transmission, I'd say we're not too far away from each other. We'll see you soon. Over and out."

Hunt and Maddy resumed trekking through the plants as the rain forest lived up to its name, the downpour continuing unabated. "I'd hate to be here during the rainy season," Maddy joked. Hunt travelled with his pistol drawn and his machete in his left hand, leading the way with Maddy following close behind him. When they stopped at a wall of trees spaced close together, Maddy pointed out a spot of yellow higher up on a branch. Two black eyes peered down on them. Then the animal hopped away out of sight.

"Frog," Hunt said, waving her off to the left where they could get around the stand of trees. Hunt eyeballed his compass and pointed in a specific direction. Then tried his radio again for Graham, who answered immediately. The transmission was crystal clear with zero static.

"We're close," Hunt said. "Keep following the course, over." Soon they came to an overflowing stream winding its way away from the mountain across the valley floor.

"Where do you think this goes?" Maddy asked.

Hunt looked back toward the mountain, where the uppermost of the green cliffs were barely visible through snatches of gaps in the canopy trees. "Probably drains out of the mountain and runs across and out of the valley at the end where the field is we took off from. Or it's possible it doesn't go anywhere, that it dead-ends in a pool somewhere on the valley floor."

"Wherever it goes, it looks like we need to get across it." Maddy frowned at the roiling water while Hunt glanced up and then downstream. He pointed some distance off to their left. "I think I see some boulders down there we might be able to use as steppingstones for at least part of the way. Let's check it out."

They picked their way along the banks of the swollen stream until they reached the boulders Hunt had seen. "This is better," Hunt said. The stream was shallow here, with a cobblestone bottom visible beneath shallow rushing water, punctuated here and there with large boulders. "We should be able to get across here without too much trouble."

They picked their way over, stepping onto the boulders where possible, Hunt noting the cool temperature of the water. Maddy slipped once as the weight of her backpack dragged her backwards after leaping from one boulder to the next, but Hunt was able to steady her in time. "It was the hat that saved you," he joked, staring into her eyes through the curtain of water that dripped from the straw brim of her hat. She smiled at him ever so briefly before turning him in the direction of the opposite stream bank. "Let's get to semi-dry ground, shall we?"

Hunt led Maddy the rest of the way across the bulging stream without incident, and then he took another compass bearing. He pointed off into a dense copse of trees, and they trekked into it, the rain still pouring down. They had just reached a point where the trees became more spaced apart when they heard a voice.

"Over here!"

Mentally chiding himself that he had been seen first, Hunt turned toward the voice and saw Graham standing off to the left, leaning on a tree trunk, holding a rifle Hunt knew he didn't have before.

"Graham!" Maddy ran to him and Hunt followed, looking around with his pistol at the ready. "Are you safe?" he asked Graham when he got to him.

Graham shot him a serious look and nodded. "I think so." He stared at him from one ex-military man to another with eyes that said, *I killed people.* He gripped Hunt's arm while he spoke. "There were two of them. I took one out."

"The other is still active?" Hunt looked up into the canopy as if a sniper could be lying in wait in the trees. But Graham shook his head.

"A tribal guy took out the other one." He recounted how he had witnessed one of the shooters kill the indigenous man, and how that man's partner had taken revenge.

"And you saw only those two operators?" Hunt said, using the term that suggested a paid professional. Because he now had no doubt they were dealing with Treasure, Inc.

Graham nodded, looking pretty queasy, Hunt thought. He tried to cheer him up. "Good work, Graham. If you saw two and two are down, it doesn't get much better than that."

But Graham shook his head. "I'd be dead if it weren't for that tribal dude. I know that!"

He looked to be on the verge of tears and Hunt put a hand on his shoulder. "Did you happen to see how many people were in the helo when they were shooting you down?"

Graham made a disappointed face. "No, I tried to remember that, too, but I only remember seeing the pilot and the guy shooting out the door. And then on the ground two guys. No way to know if one of them was the same one who shot me in the helo dogfight, but it's possible since this rifle would do the job." He hefted his new long gun.

Hunt nodded to it. "Loaded?"

Graham nodded. "I didn't get the extra magazines, but it's got one standard thirty round mag that's almost full in the chamber. And I've still got this with two extra mags," he finished, patting his pistol in the holster on his side.

Hunt noted he was having a difficult time seeing any kind of detail here under the canopy with the sun going down. Soon it would be almost as dark as in the caves. "I think we should find a spot where we can hunker down for the night; build a small shelter and conceal it."

Graham and Maddy nodded their agreement, but Maddy asked, "What about Jayden?"

Hunt grabbed his radio and spoke into it: "J-man, J-man, do you copy, I repeat, do you copy, over?" Then he let go of the transmitter button and let the walkie-talkie dangle once again from his pack. "I'll be monitoring all channels for any radio channel activity as we hike. Let's move out."

The trio fanned out to cover more area and began looking for a place to shelter. They combed high and low, not discounting the possibility that an arboreal platform could be constructed. Whatever it was going to be, it would have to be simple. Hunt knew that a campfire was out, even if they would be able to start one after the rain stopped, since they couldn't afford to give their position away. Daylight was nearly gone, so they didn't have a lot of time to set up, and with thick rain forest all around, there wouldn't be a lot of open ground space.

"Check this out!" Graham called. Hunt and Maddy joined him at a grouping of large rocks. They were spaced at intervals such that plants grew up between them, but still Graham saw potential. "We can clear some of these out, then lay down a ground cover between the rocks…"

"….and maybe place a tarp over the top to stop the rain, Hunt said, from inside his tightly tied poncho hood. The three set to work setting up the shelter. The rain did not let up, but all they wanted was the most basic place to rest. Maddy lay down the ground covers while Graham and Hunt collected a few tree branches and erected a framework over the boulders to support a camo tarp, which Graham augmented by covering the entire camp with his camo net that he had used to conceal the chopper.

The end result was an inconspicuous lean-to that offered simple shelter from the hard downpour. Hunt would have preferred to be elevated in the trees to avoid nocturnal jungle predators, but given the rain, this would have to do. They settled in between the big rocks. With the camo cover pulled all the way down to the ground, they were camouflaged but could still see out. They arranged their packs around the edges of the shelter where they were out of the way but still out of the rain. Hunt also considered that they would provide cover from bullets should a round get through the rocks. Hunt apologized for not being able to have a fire, but he did have a small butane hot plate that heated without an open flame, so they were able to brew up some instant coffee and make a simple meal of rice, beans and tortillas.

After they ate, Hunt tried for Jayden on the radio again, but once again he received no reply in return. Talk turned to their plans, and Graham muttered something about how his included sleep. Hunt suggested they keep someone on watch all night, and rotate sleep schedules. Graham volunteered for first sleep shift, crept between two boulders with his sleeping bag and promptly started snoring.

To his surprise, Maddy asked Hunt if she could take a another look at the map. "We haven't found El Dorado in there yet, so it can't hurt to revisit it."

"You think we're looking in the wrong place. Should have gone to Lake Guatavita?" Hunt asked, referring to the famous body of water north of Bogota that was also a hotspot for El Dorado treasure seekers.

"I don't know, but there's not much else to do right now, so let me have a look." Hunt brought up the map image on his phone and handed it to her. She settled in on top of her sleeping bag while Hunt tidied up the cookware. The rain continued to slam down and Hunt was glad to see that they had a little bit of elevation such that pooled water on the ground ran away from their little camp. By the time he turned back to Maddy she was fully engrossed in the map.

"You're curled up with that thing like you had a steamy romance novel in front of a fire," he said.

"I wish." But she didn't look up from the map. Hunt watched as she drew her fingers over the screen, pinching and zooming to bring different areas into greater detail.

"We're in the right area, right? I mean, it has to be the mountains south of Pasca, doesn't it? What else could it be?"

"Hold on, let me think…." She kept looking at the phone, turning it this way and that in her hands, pinching and zooming. "It superficially looks like the northern part of South America, yes."

"Superficially?"

"I say 'superficially' because I don't think it was actually called that back when Sir Walter Raleigh went there. It was just another part of the New

World."

"The southern part."

"If they even thought of it like that, yes."

Hunt lapsed back into silence. He was glad that Maddy was able to concentrate on anything other than the fact they were in the middle of a torrential downpour in a barely adequate lean-to in the middle of the Colombian high-altitude rain forest. A lot of people, even those who enjoyed "camping," which typically meant transporting the majority of the comforts of home to a designated RV hookup in a state park, would never be able to tolerate this situation. And here was Maddy, studying a map. He had to admire that.

Hunt left her to her work and lifted the cover of the camo tarp to duck his head outside on watch. The only good thing about this rain was that it was so heavy it kept all the flying insects down. But then later after it died, he knew they would rise up with a vengeance. He stared out into the dark rain forest in all directions around the shelter. Listening for potential threats wasn't much use because of the rainfall.

"Carter?"

"Coming, dear…" He ducked back inside the shelter and crawled over to where Maddy lay in her sleeping bag. "What's up?"

She held his phone with the map displayed on it out for him to see. "I thought of something."

"Uh-oh. Do tell." He was pleased to see her point to part of the map.

"What if this map isn't actually a traditional map of South America, but instead it's a close-up of the cave system itself?"

Hunt stared at her for a second to see how serious she was being, but her expression was earnest. He switched his gaze from her face to the image on the phone. He spoke slowly, testing out her theory in his mind as he said the words. "A map of the cave system itself…."

She nodded. "Yeah. You see the cross-hatching?"

"Yes. I thought it was just indicating that this is the region of interest out of this part of the continent."

"Right, and the incredible thing is that it does seem to work like that, as well. But on another level, I think that shading, the cross-hatching, means something else."

"Such as?" Hunt leaned in closer to the electronic image held in Maddy's hand.

"At first I thought it might be directional, where the cross-hatches are like tiny arrows pointing a certain way. Because they do zig and zag in different directions, she said, momentarily turning the screen her way before holding it back out again. "But now I'm thinking it means something else entirely."

Outside, a thunderclap boomed ominously, the rain unabated.

"What's that?"

"I think each style of cross-hatching represents a different level of the subterranean cave system." She pointed to a part of the small screen. "Not just a cavern, but an entire level of passageways and chambers. And according to this, there are at least three of those."

"And if this is a representation of the cave system," Hunt asked, "where is El Dorado itself?"

She stabbed her finger into a central portion of the map, where the shading was darkest. "Right here. I'm fairly sure it's actually *under* the mountain. So we were too high up."

"But we did find some artifacts." Hunt reminded her.

She shrugged. "Sure, but not *El* freaking *Dorado*, Carter. Those are just trinkets hinting at what's inside, like the display in the entrance hall of a museum when you first walk in. The real good stuff has its own dedicated room."

Hunt took a longer look at the map, eyeing it anew with Maddy's interpretation. He had to admit that it could be possible. It was another way the map could have been designed. He looked up from the screen and into Maddy's eyes.

"So we need to get lower into the cave system."

She nodded as she handed him his phone back and pulled him onto her sleeping bag. "Deeper down."

CHAPTER 27

Jayden knew he wouldn't be able to tread water while holding up his backpack for that much longer. He aimed his dive light around what appeared to be a narrow chamber with high ceilings as he drifted with the current toward the opposite end. He couldn't yet see what awaited. Unlike the last chamber, there did not seem to be a dry shelf on either side of this one, only water between two sheer walls of rock.

He needed to do something about his pack, so he swam to one side of the water-filled chamber, hoping that maybe he had overlooked some crevice that he could use to get out of the water. He didn't find anything like that, but when he got near to the side, he was pleased to see the smooth rock bottom, and found that it was shallow enough here for him to stand. That was something. There were items in his pack he might have a use for, or want to ensure they were as protected as well as possible, such as his radio. To work with his pack like that, he needed something solid to support him.

The radio had gotten wet, but was supposedly able to withstand submersion in water for a limited depth and time. Hopefully, he hadn't exceeded that. He tried transmitting with the radio in case he might be ablt to get a signal out, but no reply to his message came. He thought it not worth the risk of getting it wet and knocked around and so he opened his pack to put it inside, rather than leaving it clipped to the outside. That's when he saw a piece of orange rubber peeking back at him from deep inside his backpack.

The raft!

He couldn't believe he hadn't thought of it earlier. He shook his head now, recalling how he had briefly argued with Carter about who would carry it in their pack. Overjoyed that he had lost that argument, Jayden ripped the inflatable boat free and set to inflating it. Fortunately, it came with a battery powered auto-inflator that made the job much easier, and in a few minutes he had a five-foot by three foot raft, complete with plastic oar, at his disposal.

He tossed his backpack into it and then climbed in himself. Taking up position with the paddle, he flipped his headlamp on and pocketed his dive light. After a last check to be certain he hadn't dropped anything in the water, Jayden rowed out to the center of the chamber and began to float downstream.

He covered his headlamp with a hand and looked back at the waterfall he had jumped over, checking to see if the surviving attacker was still there, but he didn't see anyone. Satisfied he had eluded his foe for now, Jayden turned around and uncovered his headlamp.

He only needed to use the oar for steering, since the current carried him downstream through the chamber. He noted that the walls were chock full of gold and emeralds. Even the submerged floor glittered with them in places. He floated through the cavern, wondering where it would lead next but knowing he had no choice. He couldn't get back they way he had come, so he had to go wherever it was taking him downstream. He started to shiver from being wet in the cool cave air, and realized he had the luxury of changing clothes. He did that while he drifted onward, shedding his wet garments and putting on fresh jeans and long-sleeved shirt, and wool socks from his pack. His boots he could do nothing about, but he knew he needed to keep them on to be prepared for the unknown, and with the dry socks they weren't bad.

As he neared the end of the chamber he could hear rushing water and rowed to one side, prepared to stop himself if necessary. He didn't want to fly over a fifty-foot drop or even a ten-foot drop onto dry rocks or anything like that. The current was slow enough that he was able to hold himself to the sides of the tunnel. He crept forward in a controlled fashion, stopping himself when he was close enough to the end of the chamber to see that it ended in what looked like an eight-foot drop. He'd gone over worse on whitewater rafting trips for fun, so wasn't scared of it, but at the same time he knew the stakes were much higher now. He was completely alone in here and a mistake had a high chance of costing him his life.

Jayden saw no other choice but to take the plunge. Going over in the raft seemed to offer the best case for survival. He didn't see rocks at the bottom of the plunge, only water, so it was a chance he would have to take. He clipped his backpack to the grab line that ran around the perimeter of the boat, so that in case the raft flipped his pack would not fall to the bottom of the stream.

Jayden pushed out into the middle of the stream and pointed the nose of his craft so that it was oriented in line with the stream. He was committed to the drop now. He centered himself low in the raft, his backpack in front of him so that it wouldn't fall on him when he went vertical. Then the bow of his boat passed over the edge of the waterfall and the boat began to tip. Forgetting the need for stealth for the moment, Jayden let out a whoop of joy as he went over the falls.

He leaned back to transfer his weight so that the raft wouldn't bury its nose in the water when it landed. He had a scare when he began to tip sideways, to the left, but when the nose of the inflatable boat hit the water, the boat was bounced back onto its keel as it should be, but not before water flooded into the little boat. Jostled violently, Jayden gripped the grab line to steady himself, his other hand clutching the oar so that it wouldn't be lost overboard. Gradually the raft became steadier in the water, and the underground river itself became less turbulent.

Jayden pulled a camping cook pot from his pack and used it to bail out the water that had flooded his raft. That done, he aimed his flashlight around at this new part of the cave system. As the noise of splashing water receded into the distance, Jayden cocked an ear to see if another waterfall waited for him up ahead, but there was something different about this chamber. As he played his flashlight beam around the walls, it became clear to him that he was no longer in a flowing stream or river, but more like a lake or pond.

He paddled around the roughly circular body of water, marveling at the chamber in which he found himself. The pond itself was large but the chamber ceiling was low—most of it was not as high as the level of the waterfall in the tunnel he had just dropped from. Water continued to pour in from above as he paddled around the chamber in counterclockwise fashion, looking for passages or side-chambers. But by the time he had circumnavigated the pond, he had found no outlets of any kind. Concerned, he looked back at the small waterfall to gauge whether he might be able to somehow get back up it—if retracing his route was even a possibility. He shook his head to himself. It sure didn't look like it. Climb eight feet against a torrent of falling water?

The waterfall itself seemed to be increasing in volume; whitewater cascaded from the tunnel down to the pond with steadily increasing fury. And then he looked to the right, at a large fissure of gold—a vein that streaked its way across the cave wall—and noticed that the water level of the pond was now nearly covering it. He was certain that before he had started paddling around the pond it had been a couple of feet lower.

Could the water level in the pond be rising or was his mind playing tricks on him?

He sure hoped his mind was playing tricks on him, that was for sure. Because if it wasn't, and the water level really was rising in this place, he had no idea what he was going to do if it filled up to the ceiling. With no other outlets off this chamber and the tunnel above out of reach, what could he do? He paddled around the pond again, this time looking even more carefully for a way out. But again, by the time he had completed his circumnavigation, no exits had been located.

He looked back to the gold fissure on the wall. Couldn't even see it. It had been submerged. Still the waterfall burst forth with a never-ending avalanche of whitewater, filling the subterranean pond. Jayden rose with it on his little raft. He considered what might lay below him, underwater. But even if there was a passage there, it must be flooded, so he didn't give much credence to the idea of looking for a way out there. But that's how trapped he felt, trying to think outside the box for any hope of an escape. He even transmitted an S.O.S. message into his radio, but of course it went unanswered, entombed as he was within inestimable tons of rock.

He yelled curse words to the cave, no longer caring who heard. It dawned on Jayden that it must be raining outside. If the chamber were always full of water, it would not have been partially empty now, so he reasoned that when it rained a lot outside….He studied the cave ceiling while he thought.

…that it flooded up to the ceiling here, then slowly drained back out when the rain subsided. But that could take days, long after he would drown. Jayden looked up at the ceiling, knowing he was rising toward it with each passing minute. He rowed the raft around, unable to sit and do nothing while the water level inexorably rose. He looked all around the chamber again, but still saw no breaks in the rock walls of any kind. He looked up to check how close he was to the ceiling. It would only be a few more minutes until he was pressed up against it.

He studied the ceiling itself, since it looked to be the last piece of Earth he would see and touch before he met his untimely demise. *So many glittering jewels and gold veins!* Even in the face of death, he was dazzled by the beauty of it. The entire expanse of cave ceiling seemed to be covered with precious gems and veins of precious metal ores. He paddled around the pond, an expenditure of nervous energy, while staring at that marvelous ceiling. It's not going to be a good way to die, Jayden thought, but it is a beautiful place in which to die.

Were he able to stand in the unstable raft, his head would now be hitting the ceiling? He glanced over to the waterfall to see if maybe by some stroke of luck the rain had stopped outside and so stem the flow, but no such luck. If anything, it appeared stronger and faster than before. Jayden paddled the raft some more and then looked up at the ceiling again. A patch of exposed emerald crystals made for a sharp and jagged place to be pressed into when the water level rose, so he paddled away from it. Drowning was bad enough, he didn't also need to be cut to ribbons while it happened.

As he paddled, the ceiling became closer and closer to his head. He looked up and saw that he was underneath a patch that was free of jagged crystals, with only flat, smooth rock. But somehow that, too, looked different to Jayden than the rest of the cave rock. The color was off, and the texture was different, too. He shone his flashlight on the area of ceiling and paddled his boat directly underneath it. A couple more feet of water and his boat would be pressed into the ceiling. Then behind him he heard the sound of large chunks of rock falling. Probably the massive waterfall swollen with additional rainwater breaking away part of the chute through which it travelled, but the possibility of so much rushing water causing a cave-in was not outside the realm of possibility, either.

Suddenly Jayden had no more time.

This was it, he realized as he heard the rubber of his raft scrape up against the ceiling. Still the water rushed into the chamber and still the water level rose. What had been an air chamber with a pond was now a totally flooded cave. The raft was jammed up into the ceiling and Jayden lay inside of it so that he was not instantly crushed by the weight of all that water pressing into unyielding stone.

Entombed inside the raft, he occupied an air bubble as the buoyancy of the air-filled boat kept it pressed tightly against the ceiling with the rising water. So he would hang on for a few more minutes, he thought. Either until the raft burst from too much pressure on it, or the seal against the roof was broken, or until he breathed all of the oxygen in the small air space he had left.

He pushed his hands against the ceiling to try and alleviate some of the pressure pushing against the raft. He was surprised to feel a soft, spongy surface rather than the smooth, firm rock of the rest of the cave. That was the only real thought he had time for before the popping noise that signaled one of the raft's air tubes bursting. Cold water invaded the inside the raft.

Jayden took his oar and jammed the blade into the spongy part of the ceiling. He felt it give before the blade was stopped about halfway in. He withdrew it and rammed it into the ceiling again, this time penetrating a little further. But the water was now usurping the last air space in the raft. Jayden hyperventilated—taking three rapid breaths in a row before taking a final deep one and holding it, saturating his lungs with the last available oxygen. Then he jabbed at the ceiling with the oar again, and this time he felt the oar pass through the ceiling and into some resistance-free space above.

He kept his eyes open underwater as he wiggled the oar to pull it back down. As he did, he saw a patch of the ceiling come free and plant matter drift into the water, where it swirled around in the ruined raft—particles of dirt and leaves and twigs.

What's going on?

He thought that maybe he was hallucinating about breaking into a fresh air space, the way lost desert travelers did about seeing an oasis of fresh water to drink. But he thrust up with his oar again—holding his flashlight against the tubular shaft so he could work the oar with both hands. More ceiling material came loose and this time he was able to knock the oar back and forth for a good couple of feet. Jayden pushed off the bottom of the raft and clawed at the soft ceiling with his hands.

He was flabbergasted, as if in a vivid dream, to feel his head break into a cool air space. Suddenly he could see clearly again, his eyes no longer underwater. It was still dark here, wherever he was, but his headlamp somehow still worked even after being submersed, and his dive light was still on.

Still the water rose, but now it was helping him, pushing him up and into this new air space. It occurred to him that it could be a cruelly false hope, that this new space would simply flood all the way to the top as well. But then he saw a rocky shelf to his right, maybe a couple of feet up, and he pulled himself over to it, grabbing hold of a vine.

Jayden took in another series of deep breaths, not trusting that the air supply would last. Then he pulled on the woody vine while kicking off of the deck of the ruined raft. He hauled himself up through the pond chamber ceiling onto the floor of a new space in the cave.

He felt the water still rising up from below, covering his lower half. He pulled himself further up onto the rocky floor. Then he stood and aimed his light at the rocky ledge a few feet away. He ran to it on unsteady legs, then jumped and pulled himself up onto the shelf like a seal launching itself out of the water.

He was overtaken by an intense moment of panic as he realized his backpack was still in the raft. But when he looked down from the ledge he was on, he saw that the entire platform on which he'd hauled himself out was now underwater. He could not even see his raft anymore, which meant he was now without his backpack. The soaking wet clothes on his back, his helmet headlamp and the dive light in his hand were now his only possessions in this unknown part of the cave system.

Jayden allowed himself to lay on the rocky shelf and rest for a minute, every fiber of his being absolutely exhausted. Then the unknown variables that now defined his continuing existence forced him to his feet. Was the water level still rising? What was the new place was in? He had no backpack of supplies—no radio—would he be able to get out of here?

He forced himself to his feet and looked back down at the water. It sluiced around down near the hole in the floor that was also the ceiling of the pond chamber below. It didn't seem to be rising further. Then aiming his light around this new space, he saw that it was exceptionally large and soared much higher than where he currently stood, the ceilings vaulted and the floor flat and wide. Strange mosses and lichens proliferated in here; some of them had an iridescent glow to them. But the relief that he should have felt upon seeing he was free from the immediate danger of drowning was overshadowed by something else, a sight so incredulous, that it pushed all other thoughts from his weary mind.

His mouth dropped open in utter disbelief as he gazed upon the rich details of this splendid new chamber.

CHAPTER 28

Hunt awoke to Graham's rough voice saying, "Rise and shine sleepyheads. School day today!" He and Maddy were entwined in her sleeping bag, and for a few moments Hunt had forgotten all about the dangerous expedition they were now on, like they were on a weekend camping trip in a national park.

"Coffee's on!" Graham lifted the hanging edge of the camouflage tarp to let the breaking dawn light into their lean-to among the boulders. Hunt and Maddy got up and the three of them had a quick camp breakfast. They noted that while it still rained steadily, it was no longer the deluge it had been mere hours ago. Hunt picked up his radio and put out calls for Jayden, but nothing was returned but silence.

"I'm worried about him," Maddy said.

Hunt nodded to Graham. "We found our pilot, now we just have to find Jayden. We'll make our way back to the cliff and then work our way back up. Hopefully, we make radio contact soon. After spending the night in there, he has to know that we're extremely concerned and will be doing everything he can himself to meet up with us."

They dismantled their camp, careful to leave no trace of their presence. After taking a compass bearing, they donned their backpacks and set out into the dripping wet forest toward the cliffside caves. The ground was soggy in places which made it slow going to pick their way from one solid patch of ground to the next, while hacking their way through the exuberant plant life. Bug spray was passed around to combat the clouds of gnats, mosquitos and other unknown flying pests that rose from the recent rains to assault their skin. It remained nearly dark on the ground with the sun obscured by clouds and what little daylight there was so far heavily filtered by the thick rain forest canopy.

They pushed on, elated to find a small game trail that cut a path through the foliage. They followed this for some distance until Hunt alerted them that it was taking them off course and that they would have to forge their own way through the uncut jungle again. Many times each of them stumbled over a tree root, and many times they helped one another back to their feet. All three of them had rips in the knees of their pants and the elbows of their shirts or ponchos. The environment was as unforgiving as the lure of El Dorado was strong, and for the first time, Hunt began to question if it was worth it. Yet at the same time he knew he had no choice but to keep going now, at the very least to find Jayden and make sure that all three of the people he had brought here with him to this green hell got out of it safely.

The explosion of chlorophyll all around them was so unending that Hunt felt as swallowed up by it as he did the ocean when diving in a submersible craft, like he was invading another world. They came to a stream overflowing its banks and stopped to figure out how to negotiate it. Ferns, palms, and even tall canopy trees grew almost right up to the edge on either side of the waterway. Hunt noted that it ran away from the cliffs, in the opposite direction from where they wanted to go. Graham pointed out a fallen log nearby and they dragged it into place across the stream to use as a bridge.

Hunt held it steady while Graham crossed first. When he made it to the other side, Maddy walked easily across, and then then Graham held the log for him while he walked on it. He was almost to the other side when a large animal, sort of like a beaver in appearance, burst out of the jungle and waded into the stream. An arrow protruded from its hindquarters, and as soon as it reached the opposite side of the stream, near where Maddy and Graham stood, it flopped over on the bank.

"Capybara." Hunt stood in place on the middle of the log bridge, looking around for the archer who brought down the beast. He didn't have to wait long. A tribal man with a bow and arrow at the ready emerged from the trees on the edge of the stream. He saw the three Caucasians and immediately lowered his bow, but remained tense. Graham already had his hand on his sheathed pistol.

"Don't raise your weapon," Hunt cautioned in what he hoped was a low and steady voice.

"I won't if he won't."

As a show of good faith, Hunt nodded at the indigenous man and held his hands in the air. Hunt nodded at the fallen capybara, then at the tribal man, who nodded in return.

"Back up a little, you two," Hunt said to Graham and Maddy, who stood only a few feet away from the hunted prey. They moved some distance away until the tribal hunter felt safe enough to approach his kill. He stood over the giant rodent and looked over at the humans. Hunt walked slowly, keeping his hands in the air, which he found also helped with his balance, until he stepped off onto the other side of the stream and stood next to Graham and Maddy.

The hunter eyed them all carefully for a time but said nothing and then knelt to his kill without taking his gaze off them. He removed a small blade of some type, but Hunt saw that it was actual metal not a tribal bone implement, and delivered a death blow to the huge rodent. That done, he glanced up at the humans, who still stood there mutely watching, and began to skin his kill. Hunt would have thought the tribespeople would use every single part of the animal, but then realized that, since this man seemed to be alone, that he would probably dress it here so that it was manageable in size to carry back to his village or camp.

As the hunter was about to bring the knife to the capybara's hide, he paused and made eye contact with Graham, who returned his stare without saying anything. Then he bent to his kill and set to work while the three outsiders watched. Hunt eased out of his backpack and set it on the ground, hoping that the move wouldn't be taken as a threat. The hunter looked up from the carcass and eyed the group as well as the pack on the ground, but then returned his attention to his task.

Hunt opened an outer compartment of his pack and took out a Bic lighter. He flicked the spark wheel and saw the tribal man snap his head to look. Hunt held out the yellow lighter toward the native, an offering. "For you," Hunt said, then again in Spanish, "*Para ti.*" The indigenous man eyed the object and held up his hand as if to say, *Toss it to me.* Hunt did, and he caught it. Holding it out, he flicked the wheel and smiled at the little flame.

Maddy and Graham laughed. "He knows," Graham said.

"Still a useful item."

The tribal man, though not quite smiling, nodded to Hunt and took his lighter back over to the capybara.

"What else can we give him?" Graham asked. "I want this guy to like us, since I've seen firsthand what he's capable of."

"The *aguardiente*," Carter said. He went back to his pack and pulled out the flask of Colombian hard liquor. He tossed it over to the hunter, who grabbed the bottle, looked at it, dropped it on the ground and nodded his thanks before turning back to his work.

He separated the hide from the animal with a practiced efficiency that suggested he had done it many times before. Then he made cuts to the red meat and put those on the hide, along with a couple of the organs, and rolled the hide up around them. He held out a cut of meat to Hunt, Maddy and Graham but they shook their heads and the hunter simply added it to his own hide. The rest of the animal's innards he left where they lay on the bank of the stream.

When the hunter was ready to leave, he opened a small leather pouch, probably made from the hide of some animal like the one he had just taken, and dropped in the two items Hunt had given him. Before he could close it again, though, something yellow jumped out of the bag. Maddy pointed to it and said it's one of the golden frogs they had seen earlier. It jumped toward Hunt, but the tribesman took two steps toward it and easily scooped it up using a broad leaf. He was about to drop it back into his bag when Hunt pointed to it and held his hands up in a universal gesture that meant, *What for?*

The hunter pulled an arrow from the quiver on his back, mimicked licking his finger then putting it on the toad, then rubbed his fingers on the arrow tip. Finally, he pointed to what was left of the capybara. Hunt nodded. "I think he's saying that the frog secretes a poison in its skin that he rubs on the arrowheads…"

"…and the poison knocks the prey out that much faster so that he doesn't have to chase the wounded prey as far."

Then the tribal hunter was walking up to Hunt, one hand curled in a fist, which Hunt knew was because he still held the frog inside a leaf to protect his own skin form the poison. The hunter held his hand out to Hunt, offering him the golden poison frog. Hunt held a finger up to the man, which appeared to confuse him until Hunt reached down and pulled a small plastic Tupperware container he used for his "camping kitchen." He quickly used his pen knife to poke a couple of holes in the lid. "Like being a little kid again," said, before placing the golden frog in the container and closing the lid. He secured it in a pocket of his backpack.

"Not sure we'll ever need it," Hunt told the others, "but it's probably best not to refuse a gift, or a trade, if he thinks of it that way."

The hunter completed the task of wrapping up his kill and collecting his belongings. Hunt had an idea and took out his cell-phone.

"You want a selfie with him?" Graham asked.

"No, I want to see if he recognizes the caves up there." He rapidly scrolled through the few photos he'd taken in the caves. He showed the one of the tribal figurine artifact taken in the chamber with the beehive. The tribal man leaned in toward the screen, then held his hand out for Hunt to give him the phone, which he did. His eyes went wide when he saw the image of the cave and he shook his head rapidly before handing Hunt his phone back. "*Zipa!*"

The hunter pointed over at the cliff, part of which was visible from here, and shook his whole body in a way that conveyed something negative.

"Zipa is the Muisca name for the chieftain depicted in the golden raft ceremony," Maddy explained. "I don't think he likes us going in there."

"I wish we could find out why, exactly," Hunt said.

The tribal hunter only made a sour face at them before crossing the stream using the same log they had laid down. Then, without looking back, he disappeared into the dense foliage with his capybara meat and hide.

"We should get moving, too," Hunt said. "We need to find Jayden."

They took another compass bearing and moved off toward the cliffs. "That guy obviously didn't think we should be messing around in there," Graham said.

"If he's a Muisca descendent," Maddy said, "then he would hold any artifacts related to El Dorado—the *zipa* he referred to—to be sacred. It wasn't the gold they valued. They were not materialistic. To them the metal was used mostly for spiritual and ritualistic purposes. It was their god to whom it was offered."

"There's no curse, is there?" Graham wanted to know. "Does El Dorado have a curse, like King Tut's tomb?"

"It's more like the most spectacular treasure *never* found. Not really cursed," Maddy said, "unless you count the hundreds of explorers who have died looking for it over the centuries."

"To which I was nearly added to the list yesterday," Graham said with a sarcastic laugh.

It began to weigh on Hunt's mind that they could be doing all this work for nothing—that El Dorado really could be nothing more than a myth. He was putting people's lives at very real risk.

"Maybe we should get out of here as soon as we find Jayden." He slashed at a cluster of hanging vines with his machete. It was a thick tangle of woody cords that required a lot of hacking to break through and made a lot of racket.

"Wait, hold up a sec, you hear that?" Graham craned his neck to look up at what little he could see of the sky through the jungle canopy. Hunt ceased slashing and listened.

His blood ran cold as he processed the unnatural sound: The rhythmic thrum of a helicopter beating over the valley.

CHAPTER 29

Jayden closed his eyes to clear the awesome sight his eyes had just registered but that his mind insisted couldn't be real. He kept them closed for a few seconds while he pictured other things--surfing big waves, diving crystal clear reefs in the South Pacific, beautiful women, anything different than what he had seen. But when he opened his eyes again....

...it was all still here. He tried adjusting the angle at which his headlamp and flashlight were held, but it made no difference. Any way he held the light the room was no less spectacular, though without the lights on at all, it was pitch black. He took a deep breath and allowed himself to accept that what he was seeing was real, that it was not some hallucination due to being physically stressed, nor was it some trick of the subterranean light.

The sound of Jayden's heavy breathing, of water dripping from his body and clothes onto the cave floor, and that of the pond water from below sloshing around in the open floor pit were not the only noises in the room. Water also poured from the center of the chamber, where the undeniable cynosure of the room had been not simply placed, but *installed*, was the word Jayden thought of. For so imposing was its sheer size, the complexity of its presentation, the meticulous planning it must have taken to implement it was nothing short of mind-boggling.

Jayden estimated the largest statue—he guessed that was the right word for it--was about twenty feet high and seven or eight feet wide. Around that one were several smaller statues, though even some of these were up to ten feet high and four wide. All were made of gold or a gold alloy. Some of the figures on the perimeter around the central one carried sticks of some type—but Jayden knew by looking at the entire sculptural scene that they were not sticks, but oars.

He was staring at an outsized, massively scaled-up version of the Muisca Raft, complete with the raft itself, which in this chamber translated to a massive expanse of pure gold flooring in the shape of a boat. Around the boat, like a natural slip or dock, was the cave rock walls, as if cut out on purpose to be a garage for this mythical vessel.

As with the other Muisca rafts—the one in the Bogota museum and the one Carter Hunt had won at auction and then had stolen from him—this one also featured the tribal figures surrounding the chieftain, or *zipa*, carrying various items. Musical instruments and animals were well represented, as were staff-like weapons, and all figures were decorated with various "bling" as Jayden thought of it, from feathers and crowns to necklaces, earrings, and bracelets.

He scratched his wet head in wonder as he took it all in. A giant, larger-than-life version of the Muisca raft! But that wasn't even the most spectacular thing about it, for the *zipa* figure was positioned such that it received the flow of a small waterfall that drained out of a hole in the ceiling far above. Not just any water, though, Jayden noticed, but water containing millions of gold specks. Gold dust, he reasoned, resulting in a shimmering cascade of gold-infused water that rained down on the effigy as it must have for centuries, a hidden subterranean chamber where the golden one stands indefinitely through the sands of time, perpetually bathed in gold.

The trickle of water was small, Jayden noticed, staring far up at the ceiling from where it issued. Somehow, the chamber up there must be chock full of gold dust, with a water supply running through it, Jayden reasoned. He didn't know whether it always flowed, or only after a heavy rain. Either way, it was the most astounding thing he'd ever seen, and as a

Navy SEAL deployed around the globe, he'd seen some astounding things, in both good and bad ways.

He couldn't believe it. He had to tell Carter. Then he remembered he no longer had his radio or even his backpack. That stark reality got him to think about his survival situation despite the grand majesty on display before him. He tried to take in details of the entire chamber, not only the golden wonder that was at its center, but he found he just couldn't do it. His eyes were drawn to all that gleaming metal. The entire floor of the chamber—that is, the deck of the raft—was pure gold, and not unprocessed gold ore, either, but flat, smooth polished gold that had obviously been worked with to produce the sheets and ropes that made up this mega-Muisca raft, as Jayden now thought of it.

He walked to the edge of the natural rock ledge and eyeballed the golden depiction. To really explore the room, he would have to step foot on it. He was oriented such that he viewed the raft from the side, looking at the starboard side of the raft. Its bow was close to the solid rock wall of the cave to Jayden's right, the stern almost touching the opposite wall. He couldn't see any obvious exits or side-chambers from here, but the raft itself took up most of the entire chamber, so to explore it he would have to step onto the gold boat itself.

Absolutely amazing, he thought as he took the first step out onto the golden platform. He tested his weight on one foot first before committing himself, but it felt solid—like gold—and so he swung his other foot onto the raft and stood on its edge. He remained still for a time, like one of the figures themselves, paying homage to their gods while supporting their anointed one on the boat.

He started walking, gingerly at first but then taking confident steps after feeling how solid the structure was. He went to the nearest of the human figures, one of the smaller ones, which was about his same height. It had what looked like spiky hair or a headdress of sorts, and carried a long golden shaft with a flared blade on one end—an oar to row the raft with. The eyes were open and stared ahead at the cave wall as they had for who-knows-how-long this construction had been here.

He couldn't help himself and reached out and touched the statue, placing the tips of his fingers on a golden shoulder. Nothing dramatic happened, he simply felt the smooth, cool surface of manipulated gold. He knew that the Muisca tribe—one of the major four civilizations of pre-Columbian North, Central and South America besides the Incas, Mayans, and Aztecs—were metallurgical masters when it came to working with gold. Early on they had developed the techniques of utilizing molds and melting down solid metal to cast specific shapes with desired lusters.

Jayden continued to walk around the raft, marveling at the intricate details wrought from the precious metal. He'd never seen anything like it in his life and, although for the time being he had no idea how much longer that life was going to last if he couldn't find a way out of here, he was enthralled all the same by the out-scale work of art, and felt inspired and lucky to have seen it.

After passing between a couple of other supporting figures, he came to a stop in front of the *zipa*. Gazing up at it, the massive headdress extended far out to either side of where Jayden stood, and about fifteen feet above him. He took another couple of steps forward and put a hand out to feel the water that rained down on the *zipa*. Cool to the touch and flecked with gold, he shone his light on his palm Which came away looking like he had found a bag of glitter. Following the course of the water downward, he saw that it drained out into a shallow conduit that carried it off of the raft, where it funneled down into the cave rock itself. That must be what kept this chamber from filling with the gold-water that came down from above, Jayden thought.

But what of the rest of this chamber? He walked about the raft, seeing it now more as a platform from which to look for potential exits rather than the ancient wonder it was. He walked to the front of the craft where the square line of the bow nearly abutted with the cave wall. He passed by the front line of tribal figures, one of them holding an oar, and stood on the bow, staring at the rock. Leaning forward, he could reach out and touch its dry, smooth surface, studded with football-sized chunks of naturally occurring gold ore. The ceiling, far above, also seemed to be pockmarked with both gold ore and emeralds. But as wondrous as it was, it offered no way out.

Jayden continued walking around the raft, now moving to the port side, which, like the starboard side, was a foot away from a rock ledge that itself abutted the cave wall. The wall was unbroken, though studded with gems and ore, all the way up to the ceiling. The roof of the cave appeared to have no openings other than the central aperture through which the gold-flecked water poured, and it had to be at least fifty feet high and therefore unreachable. Jayden reminded himself that he no longer had his climbing gear.

He walked around the perimeter of the raft again, which due to its size and the careful inspection he made of its surroundings looking for an exit, took the better part of half-an-hour. But at the end of his tour, he had come no closer to finding a way out. Dejected, depressed, and noticing that his flashlight beam was getting weaker, Jayden flipped it off and sat down. Then he also turned off his headlamp to conserve its power, too. He sat there in the dark, looking all around to see if he might spot a pinpoint of light anywhere, some indication that there was an opening.

But the absence of light reigned, and so he sat there on the raft of gold in the dark listening to the pitter-patter of water raining down on the *zipa*. He thought about his predicament, about where he was and the frightening extent of his isolation. To get to this splendid chamber that now threatened to become Jayden's tomb, one had to first reach the underground river by dropping down the hole in the tunnel where he had left his note. He thought that much was at least possible. But then, they had to raft down the underground river.....He stopped himself right there because he knew Hunt and Maddy didn't have the raft. So unless they improvised one or swam down, they wouldn't even be able to reach the pond chamber. And the pond chamber at the moment was one hundred percent flooded. How long would it take for it to drain back down to the level it had been when he first saw it? Days? Weeks? Would the rain even let up?

Jayden changed from a sitting position to laying down flat on his back. He imagined this room a hundred years from now, the golden raft with its golden chieftain and crew, bathed in the waterfall of gold….and one white set of bones laying in the middle of it. He was exhausted and knew it wouldn't take much for him to fall asleep right here. He thought about whether that would be a mistake—he could miss something, like his team shouting for him from down below—but on the other hand he would get some much needed rest and wake up feeling refreshed and more able to figure a way out of here.

After a while he dozed, but the rest was fitful, interrupted by strange dreams and the tossing and turning that resulted from trying to sleep on a hard metal surface. Gold, Jayden thought as he rubbed the sleep from his eyes, it was pretty to look at but sure made for a crappy bed.

He sat up and decided to call out to the darkness in case he had missed anyone trying to yell for him. "Hey, can anybody hear me!" His voice boomed and echoed throughout the chamber, aided by the metal surfaces to bounce off of. But no one returned his call. He thought of the surviving gunman who he hadn't eliminated, and that now even finding him would be preferable to this stark and utter seclusion. It was almost a form of sensory deprivation, Jayden thought, especially with the lights off. He decided he better get up and do something that might add to his survival chances instead of laying here, so he rose to a sitting position and then activated his headlamp.

He was greeted with the sight of the golden tribespeople once again. The figure above him held out an oar, which he sat directly beneath. Groaning while getting to his feet, Jayden reached up and grabbed the shaft of the oar with one hand to help pull himself up. To his great surprise, the force of his hand on the oar pulled the shaft down, lowering it all the way to Jayden's knees until he felt something *click* into place.

Jiggling the oar shaft, he found that it was now immovable and fixed in position. Fearing how he was going to explain this damage to Hunt and Maddy and basically the entire archaeological community at large--but at the same time hoping that he would have to since it would mean he survived-- Jayden pulled himself to his feet just as he heard and felt a deep rumbling.

CHAPTER 30

Hunt addressed Maddy and Graham. "We have to assume that chopper is Treasure, Inc. bringing in reinforcements to try and finish what they started before."

Graham hefted his new rifle. "They probably want this back, but you know what they'll have to do. Cold dead hands, baby. Cold dead hands!" He gripped the rifle and shook it in the air.

Maddy's lower lip trembled as she looked at Hunt. "What are we going to do?"

"You have your pistol, right?"

She gave him a *Come on now* look and pointed to the not visible sky through the jungle canopy. "Yeah, but Carter, from what I've been hearing, if they've gone through all the trouble to come back here, I think they're going have more than a couple of pea-shooters with them."

"Darn tootin'," Graham agreed.

Hunt pointed to the caves. "I think our best bet is to get back to the cliffs and make our way inside to the tunnels. At some point we'll hook up with Jayden and that will add to our numbers."

Hunt could see from the expressions of Maddy and Graham that he hadn't given much of a pep talk. At the same time, the helicopter noise grew louder by the second, announcing its impending presence. He looked up at where it should be based on the sound, even though they couldn't see it through the canopy. "There's nowhere for them to actually land down here, so they'll probably fast-rope down like we did up on the cliffs."

"Question is, where?" Graham asked.

"Seems like they're coming in closer to the valley floor rather than up on the cliffs," Maddy pointed out as the chopper noise intensified.

Hunt took a compass bearing and pointed to the cliffs. "Let's move out."

But sadly, "moving out" consisted of slowly slashing down one tenacious vine or branch or unknown cluster of leaves after another, because they couldn't simply troop away down a trail. They still had to pick their way painstakingly through this living force that thoroughly constricted them. But it also concealed them. Hunt knew that they were invisible to the eyes in the chopper above. He knew there was exotic technology such as thermal imaging goggles used by specialized military units or law enforcement groups to show a heat signature given off by a human, but he doubted that even Treasure, Inc. would be utilizing such niche technology. He sure hoped not, anyway, as he ducked beneath a thorny vine and stepped his right foot into a puddle of water.

The rain had let up somewhat but still came down, judging by the din of drops landing on the canopy above. Down here on the rain forest floor, they didn't get much direct rainfall. The bugs were out again and in spite of worse dangers like helicopter gunmen, they paused to pass around a can of bug spray. After course correcting a couple of times to negotiate obstacles such as flooded or overly soggy ground, or piles of fallen trees and other plants, the team made its way to the edge of the forest, where the mountainside loomed before them.

The chopper continued to zoom low over the canopy, sometimes passing almost directly overhead, scaring them into thinking they had been spotted, but then they would fly out more into the middle of the rain forested valley.

"They're looking for us," Graham speculated, and they all knew that was likely the truth. Hunt told them he was going to leave the cover of the foliage until he could get a clear look at the mountainside. He needed to pick out a route for them to take to the nearest cavern or tunnel that led into the cave system. He tasked Graham with watching their backs, and Maddy with keeping an eye out to either side.

Dropping to his belly, Hunt low-crawled through the tall wet grass until his head poked out into the thin strip of ground that was nearly free of vegetation between the rain forest and the bottom of the cliff. He brought his binoculars to his eyes and scoured parts of the mountainside, looking for people--either Jayden or Treasure, Inc. operatives. He saw none. By the time he had put away the optics, the helicopter was flying back their way, still extremely low over the canopy.

"Do they see us?" Graham asked. Hunt noted that he had to nearly shout to be heard, such was the chopper noise. It was incoming, and suddenly Hunt *saw* the aircraft, its white paint job in stark contrast to the surrounding greenery. Hunt saw the craft slow into a controlled hover, facing him. He tensed, hand travelling to his pistol holster, but the helo executed a 180 spin. It cruised at the same low altitude for some distance away over the thin tract of land that separated the jungle from the mountain. This time, as Hunt raised the binoculars to his eyes again, the helicopter began to lower itself to the ground.

He ducked back into the bushes and called to Maddy and Graham, who still dutifully carried out their assigned patrols. "Looks like they're trying to land a little to our left, in front of the mountain." He turned back around, knowing they would want to know what they were going to do, but Hunt himself had no answer for that yet. He stared through the binoculars again, patiently bringing them into focus as the aircraft descended all the way to the ground.

His anxiety level rose as he saw that they had managed to find a landing zone. He doubted most pilots would have attempted to shoehorn their craft into that tiny space, with jungle trees on one side and mountain rock on the other, but Treasure, Inc. no doubt incentivized its employees and contractors to the point where bad judgement was sometimes encouraged. *There was that lure of El Dorado again*, Hunt mused darkly. Still getting people to lay their lives on the line for some hunks of yellow metal, well into the 21st century.

As he watched, two paramilitary-style operators jumped out of the open door onto the ground, rifles slung on their backs, handguns drawn and ready. He shook his head, not liking the odds as he counted four more men still in the chopper—five counting the pilot.

He turned his head and yelled back to his people. "They landed! Two on the ground here! Five more still in the chopper!"

He heard Graham spitting out a thesaurus' worth of curse words while he trained his binoculars on the inside of the craft again. The helicopter started to ascend, slowly, and Hunt got a look at the faces of the men inside. He was stunned to recognize two of them: Daedalus himself and that of his brother, Phillipo. Hunt felt sick to his stomach. He knew Daedalus didn't have much of a reputation for going into the field, though he would sometimes do it. He must think this site is worth making the trip for, Hunt thought. He didn't know if that meant he had some new information, or if he was simply following him, but either way, it wasn't good. He watched the helo rise straight up until it was out of his view, then he slinked back into the jungle and ran to Graham and Maddy.

"Heads up: two armed operatives on the ground in our vicinity."

"Where's the chopper going with the other four guys?" Graham asked, knowing four individuals not counting the pilot had yet to be dropped.

"Up, was all I could see," Hunt answered.

"So we have a two-on-three down here," Graham said, checking the action on his rifle. "Check your weapons—safeties off, rounds in the chamber. No excuses." He switched to his pistol and opened the chamber while Maddy and Hunt reluctantly did the same.

"If you have extra mags or ammo," Graham said, put 'em somewhere it's good for easy access on the fly."

Hunt gave Maddy a few of his rounds and when they had everything distributed, Hunt began talking strategy. "I've got an idea. We climb up a tree—each of us in a separate one near each other, and then we create a distraction to draw them near."

"What kind of distraction?" Graham asked.

"A gunshot fired from our location at the trees. They come running to check it out, looking for us on the ground, and we blast them from up high."

Neither Maddy nor Graham looked entirely convinced, but since they did not have any better ideas, it became the plan by default.

"Let's find some trees," Hunt said, waving them deeper into the forest.

"Did you say trees, plural?" Maddy asked.

"That's right," Hunt hacked his way past an unruly cluster of prehistoric-looking plants. "Each of us should climb our own tree, but nearby each other."

Graham nodded, knocking his hat off is head on a low-hanging branch in the process. "We don't want them to be able to take out all three of us at once," he summed up. They spread out and began looking for a good area to ascend into the canopy, knowing they didn't have too much time before the two deployed gunmen found them.

It took longer than they all would have liked before they found the first cluster of three trees that might work. But after examining them closely, they decided that one of the trees would be prohibitively difficult to climb and that all three were a little too close together, meaning that if one were found, all three would be found. They kept walking, pausing to listen frequently for signs of their adversaries.

"This one here would be okay by me." Maddy pointed to a canopy tree with branches that appeared scalable. Graham and Hunt found trees that would suffice not too far away from each other, but with other trees in between.

"This is about as good as we can hope for," Hunt said. Then he put his fingers to his lips and they listened. Graham pointed into the dense bush where they could hear a machete hacking away. Then he pointed up his tree, and Maddy moved to hers, with Hunt right behind her.

"Let me give you a boost." He pushed her up to the first branch and waited until she pulled herself up. "Safety rope!" he reminded her, before darting over to the tree he needed to climb.

He was pleased to see Graham already moving up his tree. Hunt reached his trunk and tossed a climbing rope up and over the first stout branch, almost fifteen feet up. It took the second try, but he got his rope up and over the limb, then was able to use it to "walk" up the trunk with one hand gripping each side of the rope. It didn't take him long before he was perched on that first branch, yanking up his rope. From there it was a simple matter of climbing up branches ladder-style without needing a rope.

As discussed, he used his walkie-talkie with an earbud to communicate with the others so there would be no voices carrying across the forest, but they had to be able to communicate to coordinate their plan. Hunt didn't want to be so high up in the tree that he couldn't see the ground. He wanted a clear shot at the Treasure, Inc. hunters when they came to investigate. Also, he didn't want to be visible from the air, and so halfway up the tree was good enough. He found a good perch on a stout limb with a comfortable Y-crook, and set up his sniper's nest.

He heard a scuffle—rustling leaves and a small branch snapping from over in Graham's direction. He inquired on the radio. "Sorry, lost my footing there for a minute. Crappy sleep last night, I'll blame it on that. Got it under control now, won't happen again, over."

Maddy checked in to say she was situated and the three of them settled in to wait. The rain came down a little harder, dousing them more intensely being higher up toward the canopy, but they held their positions and maintained radio silence unless absolutely necessary.

A few minutes later they heard the snap of a twig. Hunt eyed the ground below and didn't see anyone, but kept his gaze fixed on the area. He was beginning to think it must be only a small forest animal when he heard what sounded like the crunching of leaf litter under boots. *Someone's coming.* Hunt gave a hand signal to Maddy, whom he could actually see in her perch, though he couldn't see Graham. He froze in place while watching the ground below.

Presently a single paramilitary-like figure came into view, stepping carefully, head on a swivel as he looked around 360 degrees while he moved through the forest. He even looked up now and then, too, Hunt noticed, which caused him to aim his pistol. But the operator did not happen to see them up in the dense tree cover.

Hunt saw the heavy weapons they carried and knew they didn't have much chance against them in a prolonged firefight. He wondered if Daedalus' orders to them were to take Hunt prisoner in order to extract information about where the treasure lie, or if they had instructions to shoot to kill. Either way, Hunt supposed, if the operator feared for his life out here, he would shoot first and explain it away later.

The gunman walked to a spot almost directly beneath Hunt's tree and gave a hand signal to his associate, out of sight, that meant to *come here*. Hunt watched as the other man approached, similarly watchful and wary. Hunt tried to think of a non-lethal way to neutralize the operators. He didn't want to kill anyone, but at the same time he knew that these men were charged with killing him and his friends. He didn't see any other alternative. He looked over at Maddy, who was already eyeballing him, waiting for his reaction.

Hunt now noticed that the gunmen wore earpieces, no doubt connected to their radios so that the unit itself couldn't be heard by others. The gunman directly beneath Hunt seemed to be receiving a transmission, because his fingers went to his ear, where they adjusted the earpiece, and he turned and looked toward the mountain cliff, which was not visible to him down on the forest floor.

And then Hunt, too, was looking toward the cliff, because he heard a low rumbling and grinding noise coming from that direction. From his lofty perch, he could see part of the cliff. At first he thought his eyes were playing tricks on him, that the leaves blowing in the wind were creating some kind of motion effect.

But as he watched, the mountain face itself started to shake, sending loose rock tumbling down its side.

CHAPTER 31

Feeling as though the rumbling emanated from deep within the cave rock itself, Jayden flipped his flashlight on and began to look around the chamber. He glanced down at the lever disguised as an oar and saw that it remained fixed in the "down" position. Fearing he triggered some kind of trap, he stepped away from the oarsman statue and looked all around the chamber.

Chunks of rock fell from the ceiling, making him grateful for the helmet he wore. Slabs of rock also fell from the walls, but the one in front of the raft's bow shook especially hard. He wasn't sure how it was happening, but the entire rocky wall in front of the raft was falling away. Beneath his feet, the raft began to feel wobbly. This is it, he thought. *I'm going to die in a cave collapse.*

He glanced around all parts of the cave looking for any place that would afford shelter from falling rock. But he could find no such refuge. He thought that maybe the portion of the chamber not taken up by the raft might consist of more solid substrate, but as he watched, the ledge he had climbed out of the pond on became inundated with water. He wondered if that meant this entire chamber was also going to flood, but he didn't have time to worry about that because it wasn't really a chamber anymore. As he watched, the cave began to fall apart, starting with the wall in front of the raft. It began crumbling away, slowly at first but with larger and larger sections disintegrating, and soon Jayden could see daylight.

What was happening?

As more of the cave wall fell, the raft itself became increasingly unsteady. He had to keep shifting his legs in order to maintain his balance, sort of like surfing a wave, he thought. He could still feel via vibrations in his feet the shifting and grinding occurring somewhere below the raft, as if seismic processes were occurring. Rock continued to cleave in front of the raft, and soon Jayden had an actual view of the outside, and a surprising one at that.

He hadn't realized how deep into the mountain he'd travelled, but looking through the broken wall now he found that he could see the forest. Not from high up, either, but from just above the tree canopy. He watched a flock of birds pass from left to right over the trees and considered whether it was safe enough to try and jump through the broken wall to the outside. It was certainly not safe in here, he thought, as dangerously sizable pieces of rock fell from the ceiling, and water continued to rise from the pond room below.

Jayden tried to walk to the front of the raft, but was knocked down after a couple of steps by the erratic movement of the entire platform as it rocked and rolled from below. He felt and heard an impact as a baseball-sized chunk of rock struck his helmet. Consider that a warning, Jayden thought. He knew he had better get out of here before something hit him that even the helmet wouldn't protect him from. But as he neared the front of the raft, grabbing onto one of the golden figures for support, his decision was made for him.

Suddenly the raft was pitched upward and then sharply forward. Jayden assumed a wide stance in order to stay in one place as the entire raft was moved from its long-standing position in the cave chamber. Jayden glanced back and was horrified to see the water level even with that of the raft and still flooding in from below. At the same time, a large gap in the ceiling fell free, releasing tons of gold dust that poured into the room from above. A glittering spectacle meant to be slowly released over the centuries, now it was suddenly loosed at once. It would have covered the entire raft like sand dumped into a plastic kiddie pool from a truck, but the raft was already set in motion—floating, it seemed to Jayden on the water that entered the chamber from above *and* below.

Then Jayden was pitched sharply forward. Had he not been holding onto the golden statue he would have fallen off the front of the gigantic raft and then been run over by it. But he held on and saw he was in for a roller-coaster ride as the entire golden boat began to slide down the remaining lower portion of the mountain slope. Jayden didn't know how it was possible for so much gold to float, but the raft began to rise on all of the water converging into the collapsing chamber.

Then it began to slide downhill. Jayden took one quick look back—and up—to see tons and tons of rock caving in from the chamber ceiling. The golden raft picked up speed down the mountain, and he turned around to face forward. He liked to see where he was going even if he had no control over the wayward vessel. Massive amounts of rock, dirt, even entire trees were tossed about in his path as the massive avalanche unfurled, with Jayden surfing it down the mountain on a golden raft.

He clung to the golden tribesman like life itself, knowing that were he to be tossed over the side of the raft, he'd never be seen again. And then his peripheral vision registered something that really had nothing to do with his immediate predicament, but was interesting enough to take notice: a helicopter. Above and to his right. Different color than the one Graham had. And that was all he had time to process, because then he was dodging a small tree that threatened to hang up in the statues of the raft, but he kicked it to nudge it free and it fell by the wayside while the gold raft screamed on down the mountainside.

It picked up speed as it descended, leading the way ahead of an onslaught of falling material. As Jayden watched, the rain forest canopy trees drew nearer. The raft plummeted toward the forest, and Jayden wondered what was going to happen when he reached the bottom of the mountain. Would it slam into the ground nose first, like a head-on car accident? He didn't think he could survive that, at least not without extremely serious injury. But on looking right and left, ditching the craft sure didn't seem like a way to increase his chances of survival, either. He'd be drowned or crushed by the avalanche, or perhaps even by the golden raft itself. He preferred to avoid such an ironic death, a treasure hunter being run over by a symbol of the very treasure he sought.

He stayed with the raft, wishing now that he weren't so close to the front. He didn't dare let go of the tribal statue he clung to and attempt to make his way further to the rear of the boat, for to go toward the stern now meant to go almost straight up, vertically. So he stayed put, waiting for it all to be over, one way or another.

Torrents of whitewater and debris washed *over* his head on the way down the mountain, drenching the massive raft platform as it plummeted toward the jungle. Jayden did a double-take as he saw something recognizable fly past him before coming to terms with the fact that it was a human body, one of the shooters from back in the tunnels. He watched the body float past, somehow the man's rifle still slung over his shoulder. He barely had time to register the beret cap the shooter wore, which marked him as the one he had not shot. The shooter he'd killed had not been wearing a cap. He barely had time to register that those two shooters were now no longer a threat to him or anyone. They must have been caught in the flooding that happened when Jayden accidentally pulled that lever.

And then he had to dodge out of the way of a tall tree. He wasn't sure if the raft would sail right over it or hit it head on. It rammed over the top half of the tree, bending it down while the raft passed right over it without slowing whatsoever.

As he neared the bottom of the mountain, the slope became less steep. Whitewater splashed all around as it washed down what had been a near vertical path before abruptly transitioning to a more gradual slope. And below that, Jayden could see, was the narrow tract of land that was home to scrubby vegetation but no mature trees. He knew something was going to happen when the colossal sled reached that ground, but whether that meant coming to a dead stop or flipping over or something else, he had no idea.

He looked back up at the mountain and was dismayed to see massive slabs of it sliding out of place. It looked like the whole thing was coming down, and suddenly Jayden didn't want the raft to stop moving. The farther away he got from the crumbling cliff, the better. He steeled himself for impact as his golden chariot reached the bottom of the slope. Water was already pooling there and when the nose stuck into the ground, Jayden was doused in a massive plume of muddy water before being knocked onto his back. The entire craft rocked over onto its side and Jayden started to slide down the deck. A single golden tribal figure stood between him and falling off the edge of the platform into the roiling maelstrom that was now the base of the jungle mountain.

He wrapped the crook of his elbow around one of the legs and wrenched himself into position, disregarding the pain as he had been trained to do as a SEAL. To Jayden everything was a kaleidoscopic blur of white, brown, green, and of course, gold, as water, earth, trees, and the raft itself all collided. He clung to the statue as his legs slid out from under him, pointing down. He was jostled wildly about as the entire raft experienced gyrations from hitting the ground, as well as its besiegement by water and mud on all sides.

After a scary moment where he thought the raft was going to flip end over end, Jayden shook his head as the raft spun around backwards and levelled out, still careening toward the forest. This orientation gave Jayden a good look at the mountain, and his first understanding of how bad it really was. Anyone inside up there would have perished by now. That much was plain to see. The entire mountain on that side was coming down into the valley, while the other three sides bordering the valley remained unchanged. He flashed on pulling the oarsman lever and knew that he had inadvertently triggered this reaction, this trap, this curse, whatever it was meant to be by the Muisca designers so long ago.

He pulled himself up on one knee, as stable an upright position as he could muster while the raft continued to be carried away like a matchstick down a rain gutter. He saw trees that were still rooted on either side of him now, with the raft gliding over the top of them. So he was in the jungle proper now, on the valley floor, and all that resistance meant that the raft was starting to lose its forward momentum.

He found that the rocking motion had subsided enough that he was able to stand upright, though still gripping the tribal statue for support. Leaves and branches now littered the floor of the golden boat, and the tribal chieftain now wore a garland of green branches that had become stuck in his neck and chest. Still the errant raft continued on its raging course off the mountain, forging ahead into the rain forest. Most of the water had abated and Jayden could see the actual gold decking again. Water still sloshed about beneath the raft, but up ahead he could see normal rain forest floor.

Looking up, he found he could see the sky because he was riding atop the trees on the raft, the atmosphere a dull brown color due to the dust expelled from the crumbling mountain. Then the immense weight of the gold raft began to push it down through the trees. Jayden knew the that the forces propelling it this far must be incomprehensible. At last they were subsiding. The raft began to sink through the canopy at a downward tilt. Jayden still held onto one of the golden tribesman, standing directly behind it so that it shielded him from the blow of branches that whipped past them as the raft was hurtled along.

As he passed down through the canopy, he did a double-take as he looked to his right and thought he saw something in one of the trees. Something that didn't belong. But he was past it in a blur as he dropped rapidly toward the jungle floor, the raft's frenetic pace finally slowing as the energy that had propelled it dissipated.

Jayden braced himself for that inevitable moment when the raft hit the ground or otherwise came to a sudden stop against a stout enough stand of trees. He gripped the golden figure, hiding behind its metal lines. When the impact came, the raft tipped up on its nose, the stern raising a few feet off the ground before plopping back down. Jayden had the odd sensation of being in the dense jungle, but with a wide swath cleared behind him where the raft and river of debris had trampled the entire forest from canopy to understory all the way back to the base of the mountain.

Gazing back, he could see the mountain itself, the avalanche still in progress, threatening to overtake the jungle where he had come to rest.

Jayden let go of the golden figure and slid to the edge of the raft. From there he jumped down to the forest floor. Looking back up at the raft, he noticed the set of robust logs attached beneath the structure that had allowed the entire craft to float. Ingenious, he thought, marveling at the planning and craftsmanship that had gone into ensuring the heavy gold raft would be able to ride on top of water.

Eyeing the still-crumbling cliffs, he could only hope that he would have as much ingenuity when it came to escaping this jungle in one piece.

CHAPTER 32

Carter Hunt saw the oncoming avalanche of rock and water and immediately abandoned all sense of stealth. What was coming at them was much worse than the Treasure, Inc. gunmen. It could not be negotiated with, outsmarted, or shot down. Nothing more—or less—than tons and tons of fluid earth threatening to overrun them and the very trees in which they perched.

He yelled over to Graham and Maddy. "Rockslide, it's coming all the way down!" He heard Maddy's tense voice carry across the forest air between the canopy trees. "Stay up here or get down?"

But Hunt didn't reply, because what happened next was so otherworldly, so surreal and outlandish, that it effectively hijacked the speaking part of his brain, leaving him to say nothing while he watched the spectacle unfold. Because at the leading edge of the wave of avalanche debris rolling toward the rain forest floor, was a massive yellow object. Like a sled, Hunt thought at first, with some weird poles sticking up from it. But as it drew closer, he saw what it was and the realization stunned him even further into a non-verbal state. Not yellow, he could see now, but *gold!*

"Is that...." He distantly heard Maddy's voice calling out from a few trees away, as if in a dream. "....is that a giant Muisca raft?"

"Yes!" he yelled back to her. "With Jayden riding on it!"

"Whoa!" This from Graham, who rarely seemed to be impressed by much. "I hope he can steer that thing. Looks like it might hit us!"

"Should we get down?" Maddy asked.

Hunt yelled, "No, stay put!" It was difficult to tell where exactly the raft was going to end up. It still moved fast but Hunt could see it starting to slow, the pile of watery sludge it rode on diminishing. Even so, it still launched itself over the canopy trees, and they could now hear the destruction being wrought by its gravity-fed passage down to the rain forest.

As Hunt watched, the entire raft canted up on one side. He saw Jayden go down and then reappear in a kneeling position as the structure semi-righted itself, but now veering more to the right. Good, Hunt thought, the course change spared them from being in the direct path. It would still be close, though.

"We're not out of the woods yet!" Graham yelled, cackling like a hyena. "Get it?"

"Hold it together, Graham," Hunt replied, watching the raft like a hawk. It seemed to soar over the canopy trees on the edge of the forest, and then began to sink into the trees, crushing them as it plowed into the rain forest. He could hear tree trunks bending and snapping as the rocketing raft came closer.

"Stay put, stay put!" he reminded his team. As long as they didn't sustain a direct hit, they should be safer with some elevation than being down on the forest floor and subject to the toppled trees and crashing raft itself, not to mention the shooters.

He saw the flashes of gold through the foliage as the metallic boat lurched by their tree stands. It moved slow now, and he had time to see Jayden looking over at them, clinging onto the golden tribal figure on the raft. Graham had his pistol drawn and followed the progress of the raft with the barrel, not knowing what to expect.

"I only see Jayden, don't shoot!" Hunt told him.

"Copy that, no shot," Graham said, lowering his weapon.

Hunt turned away from Jayden's Muisca spectacle to look at the mountain. The avalanche was still coming down. His mind reeled with attempts to explain what had happened, but he knew there was no time for that now. He turned back and saw the raft slowing and dropping all the way to the forest floor. The golden projectile had missed them but now the mountain sliding apart threatened to overtake them all. It still fell, not only the caverns from where Jayden had emerged on the raft, but the entire mountain, top to bottom, was crumbling down and then slowly but steadily rolling toward the jungle like an earthen wave.

"Everybody down! Let's get to Jayden." Hunt rapidly dropped to the next set of tree branches and from there, bear-hugged the trunk and slid firehouse pole style to the wet ground. Graham and Maddy were still making their arboreal descents while Hunt moved toward where the raft had come to rest in the jungle.

He was surprised to hear Jayden's voice before he reached the golden curiosity. "I thought I saw a couple of monkeys hanging out in the trees when I surfed on by! Glad you guys are okay!"

Hunt eyed Jayden, who looked as though he'd just lost a mudwrestling contest, but still seemed to be able-bodied. The two men bear-hugged, each saying something about how they weren't sure if they'd ever see them alive again. Graham and Maddy caught up with them, and the sentiments were repeated anew. When the reunions were done, Jayden pointed to the raft. "You've got to see this, come on."

They made their way across to the swath of destruction the raft had carved in the jungle, and followed the newly created road right to the raft, which was still in one piece, including the detailed sculptural work on the deck. Jayden pointed out something in front of the craft and said, "Wow, these three rocks stopped me. Look at this." All of them gathered at the bow of the raft and saw that it had come to rest lined up perfectly with three large boulders.

"It almost looks like they're meant to fit," Hunt observed. "Like these notches at the front of the raft were made to receive them."

Graham guffawed loudly. "Oh, come on! Some kind of docking system that still works centuries later?"

But the others appeared less skeptical. "It does look like an engineered fit," Maddy observed.

Graham let out a low whistle. "Regardless of how it came to rest, that is a *lot* of gold! That's solid gold, right?"

Jayden nodded. "The deck, the tribal statues, all of it except for the logs on the bottom that allow it to float."

Hunt and Maddy walked up to the raft and gazed in wonder at the majesty before them. "Incredible…" was all Maddy could muster before trailing off into her own thoughts. "It's a scaled-up replica of the known Muisca rafts," she managed after a restless silence. Even though her cell-phone had no service, she used it to snap some photos of the awe-inspiring relic.

"How do we know this one isn't the original and the little ones are the replicas?" Hunt asked.

Maddy shrugged while clicking away. "I guess we don't, but usually people make a small version of something that's complex before they scale it up." The flash of her camera phone gleamed off the golden spires of the wonderous construct.

"You're probably right." Hunt turned to Jayden. "So where was this thing? How did we miss it?" Hunt was aware of the rumble of mountain rock as soon as he finished talking.

Jayden was also attuned to the danger. "Probably best if I give you the details later. It's still coming down." He pointed toward the green wall, now partly visible through the flattened forest. Through it he could see the tumbling rocks, dirt, trees, and slushy water that threatened to flatten them all.

Maddy turned her head toward the gold raft. "As awe-inspiring and astonishing as it is, I don't want to die over it. So can we please do something that gets us the heck out of here, Carter, please? Wait, just let me see that map image again."

It was the closest thing he'd heard to her being mad at him in a long time. Knowing there was no time for personal differences, Hunt brought up the most concrete plan he could think of.

"We run."

"What?" It came from Maddy while the others eyed Hunt.

But he didn't hesitate. "Run!"

"Run where?" Graham asked.

"What?" Hunt wasn't sure what he had said. He was dimly aware of another noise, far way, not a voice, but a noise. "You hear that?"

"I don't—" Maddy started.

"Oh, crap!" Graham's head was tipped skyward. "I hear it!"

And then they all did, the whirring grind of a helicopter's engine. "You're kidding me," Maddy said.

"Afraid not," graham said. "That's an Airbus ACH145 if I've ever heard one. And I've heard one. And I know for a fact that they're typically used on super-yachts."

"Before we run, let me grab one thing." Jayden jumped back on the raft and ran to one of the golden figures that held up an elaborate golden mask and headdress. "I noticed that this thing looks detachable. I remember I was going to grab it back up there and decided it might not hold. So if it is detachable, there's no reason to leave it for those goons. If we take it, it will prove that we found the mega-Muisca raft first. Otherwise, Treasure, Inc. will say they found it."

"Be quick about it, Jayden. They're coming in for a landing."

Jayden was already in motion toward the massive golden raft. He reached it running and jumped up onto the deck without breaking his stride.

"Yeah, I used to be able to do that," Graham muttered.

"I believe you," Hunt said, one eye on the descending chopper up above. "Hurry up, Jayden, they might have binoculars."

On the golden deck, still slick with water, Jayden ran to the figure holding up the mask. He felt a knot form in his stomach as he examined it. It *was* detachable, right? He was going to feel silly if it wasn't. Even if it were not actually designed to be detached, he started to think, if he could rip it off, it would prevent Treasure, Inc. from getting it and be concrete evidence that Omega Team was here first.

The tribal figure's fingers of his left hand were curled around a headband in the shape of an inverted U that was the main structural surface for the feathers that stuck up and the mask portion of the ensemble that hung down from it. Jayden gripped the upper part of the mask and pulled up. It did not give. The helicopter noise became louder.

"Come on, Jayden, they're going to see you soon," Hunt warned.

Jayden plucked up one of the individual fingers of the tribal man and was surprised to feel it click up into an extended position, so that it was no longer curled around the mask. He repeated the process with the three other fingers until only the thumb was holding the mask. He grabbed the mask with his own left hand, then using his other hand he released the thumb's grip. The large mask—about three feet wide and two high, came loose into Jayden's hands.

Suddenly, a discernable click was heard, followed by a low grinding noise. The entire raft began to sink into the Earth.

CHAPTER 33

Sitting in the co-pilot's seat of the helicopter, Daedalus turned around to scowl at Phillipo. "We still have heard nothing from our first extraction team. That's four men lost."

In the back of the custom outfitted chopper, sitting on a jump seat, Phillipo shrugged. "We still have two operators, and ourselves." Phillipo patted his own snub-nosed machine gun. Reading his brother's unease, he added, "They probably got trapped in the mountain collapse or avalanche."

"Or they were killed by Hunt's team," Daedalus spat.

"I highly doubt it was due to superior fighting power," Phillipo countered.

"And yet you continue to underestimate this....this Omega Team which you said I had nothing to worry about. Maybe it's you I need to worry about."

"Where do you want me to put down?" Georgio asked, fully aware of the rising tension in the small, enclosed space.

"As close as you can to the giant gold object," Daedalus said.

"Watch for resistance," Phillipo cautioned. "I never said Hunt's team was helpless."

The pilot nodded. "If we get shot at, I'll evade. But our gunners can also provide cover fire." In the back, two fully-outfitted warriors, one with a sniper rifle at the ready, the other with an automatic weapon, gave a hand signal to acknowledge the pilot.

"The entire mountain is still falling apart," Daedalus noted, looking with trepidation at the avalanche of Earth moving out his window.

"We have time to drop down and check out whatever this thing is, the pilot said.

"Whatever it is, "Phillipo said. "It's all there is left to find. Any treasure inside that mountain is buried forever now."

Daedalus stared down at the golden object below. He knew it must be very large to be so visible from this high up. As the chopper descended, more detail became apparent. Earlier he'd seen it slide down the mountain and thought it looked like....No, he thought, shaking his head to himself. It couldn't be....But as he stared at it again now, he knew it was true. It was a gigantic Muisca raft. A smile spread over his features as the helicopter lowered down to the toppled and flattened trees the sledding raft had left in its wake.

Incredible. The find of the century!

* * *

"I triggered something!" Jayden yelled. "The whole raft is dropping underground!"

He couldn't see anything below him, since he stood on the raft, and in front of him was only a wall of dirt and rock. But he saw the jungle floor disappearing slowly above him. He heard the crunch of running footsteps and then saw the faces of Hunt, Graham and Maddy peering down at him from above. The approaching helicopter's undercarriage was also visible above their heads.

"You coming with me, or what?" Jayden beckoned them.

He saw Hunt wave an arm and then Graham jumped first, landing on the deck of the raft behind Jayden with a thud and an *oomph*. Jayden looked back at him. "We get back to the states, buddy, I've got a workout program for you. Feel the burn!"

Graham gave him a *Who, me?* Look as he got to his feet. The raft was not at an incline, making the jump easier. Hunt and Maddy went next, hand in hand. They landed smoothly onto the golden surface. Hunt watched as Graham swung his acquired rifle up at the descending chopper.

"Don't fire unless they fire on us," Hunt said.

"Copy, that, no fire unless fired upon," Graham acknowledged. Meanwhile, Hunt unclipped a climbing rope from his pack and readied it as he rode down into the Earth on the golden platform.

"Don't see any call buttons on this elevator," Jayden said, removing his Glock from his holster.

Maddy took her phone out and stared at the screen intently. "You checking your email, or getting a weather report or what?" Jayden kidded.

Maddy smiled while shaking her head. "I'm taking another look at the map…"

"This must have been carefully planned out," Hunt said, admiring the precision with which the raft platform lowered into the ground.

"It stopped right against those three rocks, as if it was meant to do that," Jayden said.

Then the earthen wall in front of them suddenly disappeared and they were facing forward into a massive subterranean space.

"We landed in water!" Graham noted. Indeed, the entire raft now floated on its foundation of logs, and they began to drift along the flowing subterranean river.

"Where do you think this leads?" Hunt asked.

"Away from Daedalus and his Fun Corp, that's all I care about," Jayden said. But no sooner had he completed his sentence than they heard the frenzied whine of a helicopter engine, closer than ever. "You've got to be kidding me!"

Jayden faced toward the rear of the raft and watched the bottom of the giant hole in the Earth into which they had just dropped down. The surface of the water there was whipped into a boil, while the helicopter noise grew increasingly deafening.

"They're flying down here!" Hunt said.

And then the chopper came into view, nose facing their way.

"Will it fit under the overhang?" Jayden wondered aloud. But the answer was clear as the pilot skillfully lowered his craft almost to the waterline and then nudged it forward into the vast, open subterranean space. The helicopter then moved to the bank of the waterway, made of solid gold ore. After hovering tentatively, the aircraft set down on the metallic ground, such that the golden raft would soon have to float past it.

A voice issued from the aircraft's loud-hailer, deafening in the enclosed space, even over the engine noise.

"Don't shoot, we're coming out, peacefully. I have a simple message for you."

On the raft, Hunt told the others not to shoot. "It's Daedalus. He could pepper us with automatic rifle fire if he wanted." Two gunmen, clad in jungle camo fatigues and holding automatic rifles over their heads to show they were not going to use them, jumped out of the craft. They walked down to the edge of the river, a little ahead of where the raft was. Then Phillipo exited the helicopter, and lastly Daedalus stepped down, carrying a small box, while the pilot remained in the aircraft. They walked down to the edge of the river and stood next to their armed mercenaries.

"This place is amazing!" Daedalus shouted to them through cupped hands. "Thank you for discovering it!" He waved an arm at the underground realm. "Gold ore as far as the eye can see. Congratulations, I do believe you have found El Dorado, or at least the source of the myth!" He clapped his hand together a few times while the box rested in the crook of his elbow.

"What do you want, Daedalus?" Hunt asked. The massive gold raft continued to float slowly down river.

"I want nothing. My curiosity got the better of me and I decided to see what was down here after we watched your giant Muisca raft lower slowly into the Earth. It is a most astounding craft." The pilot was already gesturing to Daedalus' group, urging them to return to the chopper. "Too bad it is about to buried forever under tons of mountain rubble."

"What's in the box?" Jayden asked.

"Oh, this?" Daedalus held out the box. "Why, this belongs to Mr. Hunt. It's his auction winning." He opened the box and pulled out the miniature Muisca raft. "Trade me for the big one?" He and Phillipo laughed hollowly.

"Bet you wish you had this!" Jayden picked up the large mask that had been the key to unlocking the golden underground. He held it up to his face, wearing it. "I'm the golden one!"

Daedalus extended a hand as the large raft drew near. It took up almost the entire width of the river and so would be possible to walk onto it from shore once it reached them.

"I'll trade you the little raft for it." He held it out, an offering.

Hunt was indignant. "Oh, how nice of you! Trading me my own item back in return for something else that is already mine! So magnanimous!"

Daedalus shrugged. "You might change your mind." He tossed the little Muisca raft onto the giant raft, at Hunt's feet. "For me, this is El Dorado, and it's all about to be buried under a massive landslide. You see, you forgot one thing when you rode down here on your golden raft. How are you going to get back out? Because the entrance…." He pointed back to the chopper, where the pilot still gesticulated for them to hurry up, and the vertical shaft that led to the above-ground world. "…is about to be buried under tons of collapsing mountain. We have a ride out of here. You don't."

On the raft, Hunt walked over to Jayden and took the mask. Jayden gave him a quizzical look, but said nothing. Hunt reached into the pouch tied to his belt and picked up the golden frog by wrapping it in a leaf to protect his skin, knowing how deadly the toxin was, even to touch. Hunt knew that museums used to spray antiquities with pesticides in order to preserve them. But he had heard of a few cases where American Indian tribal objects were repatriated, causing severe illness after items such as clothing and masks were worn without being decontaminated.

Hunt rubbed the frog over the surfaces of the mask that would come into contact with the wearer's face. He knew what he was doing, but he also knew that Daedalus had already tried to kill him, and may even shoot them all now, if he thought that leaving them for dead wasn't good enough. Or if he simply became angry enough.

He held the mask out towards Daedalus, who was now only a few yards away. "You want it? You can have it. Just leave us alone, okay?"

Daedalus tapped his brother on the shoulder, meaning that he should take the mask, then nodded to his two goons. Instantly they raised their weapons while Phillipo walked to the very edge of the river and held his hand out to receive the mask. Hunt held it by the one spot he had not rubbed the poison on. He extended it at arm's reach until Phillipo took it from him with a smug smile before retreating back to his group. The golden raft continued on its way down the river, where ahead lie darkness and the complete unknown. Hunt wondered if there was another way out or if the only entrance was about to be sealed forever by the avalanche. The latter seemed more likely.

Daedalus waved to those on the raft. He took the mask from his brother, and, as Hunt had hoped, raised it to his face. "Goodbye, Mr. Hunt and friends! The Golden One wishes you well on your final journey!"

With that, he lowered the mask and handed it to his brother before turning and striding for the helicopter, where the pilot sat motioning wildly for them to hurry up. Phillipo followed Daedalus, turning his back on the raft and Hunt's group, but the two mercenaries, knowing Omega Team was armed, walked backwards with their guns aimed at the raft. Daedalus and Phillipo had nearly reached the chopper when a commotion ensued.

Phillipo suddenly doubled over in pain and stopped walking. Daedalus turned to him and asked, "What's wrong—" before he, too, experienced similar symptoms. Daedalus dropped to his knees and clenched his stomach while making retching noises. Phillipo gripped his shoulder but soon succumbed to his own symptoms. The two mercenaries, distracted by their boss' sudden collapse, ran to Daedalus and Phillipo. Each soldier began to pull one of them to their feet.

In that moment, Hunt, Jayden, and Graham all raised their weapons. "Don't shoot!" Hunt yelled. Daedalus and Phillipo were non-responsive due to their rapidly declining conditions. One of the mercenaries complied, dropping his weapon and raising his hands in the air. But the other operator whirled around and dropped into a roll, raising his automatic rifle. He got a shot off that went high over the raft, and was then cut down by a hail of bullets from the three Omega team members.

Hunt waved Maddy onto shore, and then all four of them walked toward the helicopter. The pilot, on seeing the threat, started to lift off, but with a last gasp of energy, Daedalus waved him down. "Don't...leave us!" He squawked into a walkie-talkie. The pilot leaned out the window and yelled to them.

"We can't take this many people!"

Hunt knelt and felt for the pulse of the dead shooter before shaking his head. "He's not going. It'll just be eight of us including you," he said to Georgio.

"And we only need to get above ground!" Maddy shouted.

Hunt made it clear to the pilot. "We're all getting in long enough to get above ground, or this chopper's getting shot to pieces with you in it."

In response, the pilot frantically waved them on. "It's almost here, come on!"

By this time, the effects of the poison had advanced and both Dedalus and Phillipo were unable to move. Hunt and Jayden dragged Daedalus to the open chopper door, while Graham and the surviving mercenary took Phillipo.

"Nice gun," Graham said after they shoved the body inside. He hefted the automatic rifle he'd taken from the man who died in the jungle. "You can have it back." He forcefully shoved the weapon into the man's hands, knowing that with Daedalus and Phillipo incapacitated, and the other soldier dead, that this mercenary was now on the lower end of the force scale and him having one more gun wouldn't make a difference.

"Go, go!" Hunt told the pilot the second all persons were inside the door frame. Daedalus was seizing and vomiting and Jayden turned him over on his side so that he would not choke. The chopper pilot wasted no time in raising the craft off of the solid gold ore it rested on. The helicopter rose vertically through the shaft they had rode down on the raft. Just before they passed up into the four-walled section of the shaft, Hunt glanced back down on the underground river, where he saw the ancient golden raft sailing downstream, manned only by its golden crew.

He wondered where it would end up and if it would ever be seen by human eyes again. And then, as the chopper neared the top exit of the shaft, brown dirt and rocks began to fall past the window. Hunt's face was sprayed with mud, and he pulled the door shut.

"Faster, up, up, up!" Jayden implored the pilot, who for his part, had already been rising as fast as possible in a controlled fashion. But he kept it up, and though they heard terrifying impact sounds of rocks hitting the sides of the chopper, somehow the craft stayed airborne. They lifted out of the underground realm into the jungle.

Or what remained of it.

"Whoa!" Graham yelled in fear. In front of them was a tremendous wall of avalanche-born rock, rolling at them like a wave. Georgio banked the craft hard left, pointing them away from the wall to where the jungle was still green. They wouldn't be able to rise over it in time, but they could run from it. Hunt saw the co-pilot's window crack as it was nailed by airborne rocks. The door windows soon spiderwebbed into a maze of cracks. The pilot accelerated the aircraft's engine to the breaking point, eliciting a whine of protest from the overworked engine. Looking below, Hunt saw trees blanketed by mud and rock, the green forest disappearing. They watched in horror as the shaft leading to the golden realm was solidly filled in and then covered over with a hill of displaced mountain rock.

The pilot continued racing in front of the avalanche, beginning to outpace it now that the chopper was in open space and the engine fully running. He gained altitude, and Hunt watched as the brown wave of rock continued to spread across more of the green rain forest. He shook his head to himself. So much destruction and death, he thought, and over what? A shiny metal that even the people who had recognized its usefulness as a tool and item of trade had not considered worth anything in and of itself. The Muiscas did not value gold for gold's sake, he knew. Its worth to them was only as an offering to their deities, so that they might be allowed to continue their humble existence in peace. And now, so many centuries later, after innumerable attempts at pilfering the physical symbols of those beliefs, it seemed to Hunt like the ancient tribal people would finally have peace again.

He thought of the golden raft, at this very moment plying the waters of the underground river, controlled by forces only the Muisca's creators could have conceived of. And he smiled. He smiled as pointed his pistol at the pilot.

"Land us in that field over there on the north end of the valley. We're getting out there, and then I suggest you get these two to the hospital in Bogota, STAT."

He indicated Daedalus and Phillipo, who were now unconscious on the deck of the helicopter. Both of their hands and faces had swollen grotesquely from the effects of the fast-acting poison. Phillipo's legs twitched uncontrollably as if in a never-ending seizure.

"Yes, sir. Don't shoot, I'm going!" Georgio said. Now higher than the avalanche, he turned the nose of the craft toward the field. Hunt looked down on the entrance to the underground realm and saw only a pile of rock that now blanketed much of the valley's rain forest.

CHAPTER 34

Anyone watching would have called it a rushed, hasty landing. Georgio set the chopper down in the same field Graham had landed in the previous day. The impact when they hit the ground was harder than it should be, but he was in a rush to offload the oddball team who had just hijacked his aircraft beneath the jungle and poisoned his boss. He knew he needed to seek medical attention for Daedalus and Phillipo, who had both lapsed into near coma states.

The second the skids kissed the dirt, Hunt ushered Maddy, Graham and Jayden out of the already-open door. Then he turned to the pilot and handed him a Styrofoam cup he'd found in the back of the helicopter with the golden frog in it.

"Here. This is the exact same animal that poisoned them. Do not let it come into contact with your skin." He nodded to Daedalus and Phillipo by way of example. "Take them to the hospital in Bogota and make sure you give them the frog so that they know what antidote to give. Good luck."

With that, Hunt turned and jumped out of the doorway onto the ground. He and his team ducked the rotors until they were clear, and then jogged away from the aircraft which had already started to lift off again. Hunt watched the chopper veer north toward the capital city and its lifesaving hospitals.

Graham put a hand on Hunt's shoulder. "Sorry again about the helo you rented. I know that's gonna be a big bill."

Hunt looked at him and smiled. "No need to apologize. It's all part of the risk in this business. Thanks for being there for us. If you want it, I'd like to offer you a full-time job flying for Omega Team, helping to keep cultural artifacts like El Dorado out of the private hands of scumbags like Treasure, Inc."

Graham appeared incredulous. "You would offer me a job after I got your 'copter shot down?"

Hunt levelled his gaze directly at his eyes. "You did what you had to do. And we found El Dorado. I call that a successful mission."

Graham looked like he might be about to shed tears of joy. "I, I don't know what to say!"

Hunt shrugged. "Say you accept the offer."

"I accept!"

Jayden and Maddy applauded. "Welcome aboard, Graham!" Jayden said, clapping him on the back.

Hunt pointed toward the road, where people had already gathered to observe the destroyed mountain and rain forest covered with its rocks. "We better start the hike back into town where we can hopefully find Graham another bird to fly us back to El Dorado International."

After a last look down on the transformed valley, noting how different the view looked with one side of the valley now open to a flat, forested area pockmarked with agricultural fields, the four of them walked across the field and up onto the single road leading in and out of Pasca.

Many people lined the side of the road now, alone and in groups, gawking at the spectacle far below. The four of them began to walk down the hill to town, blending in with the farmers, vendors and merchants carrying various goods, either strapped to the back of scooters, pickup trucks, bicycles, or on their heads. Jayden offered to carry Maddy's pack for her since he no longer had one, and she was more than happy to let him do it.

While they walked, Maddy pulled out her phone and stared at something on the screen intently.

"No service yet," Graham pointed out.

"I know, I just can't stop thinking about this map." She showed him the image that Hunt had sent her of Raleigh's old treasure map. "It wasn't making sense to me before but now that I look at this shading, I think…" She stopped walking and peered down at the valley below, and its new covering of dirt that had spilled about one-third across its expanse due to the crumbled mountain. The others stopped also and waited for her to complete her thought. She brought the phone over to them and pointed to the darkest shaded area.

"You remember how I was saying that the map actually represented the cave system and not the wider country or continent of South America?" The others nodded and she continued. "Well, looking down at it now, I think the shaded portion represents the valley *after* the golden raft was set free. They were trying to tell us, the raft is here, the gold ore underground is down here, but if you find it by setting the raft free in the caves, it is all going to be covered over in a giant landslide."

A dubious smile took hold on Jayden's face. "Gee, I don't know why I never saw that!"

Hunt nodded. "Your 16th century cartographic interpretation skills are a bit rusty, I guess."

"16th century *crypto*-cartography," Maddy corrected.

"Yeah," Jayden laughed, starting to walk again, "I'll have to work on that."

"Crypto-cartography," Hunt said, rolling the term off his tongue as if considering something. "*Crypto*…."

"What?" Maddy asked, falling into step beside him.

He shrugged it off. "Nothing. I guess what I was thinking of is crypto-currency, like Bitcoin."

"That's totally different."

"I know. Just one of those things where a word that sounds a certain way triggers something in the memory." He told her about the mini-Muisca raft he'd won at auction, and how the reason for it being auctioned was to repay the deceased CEO's creditors after he died leaving an encrypted laptop loaded with cryptocurrency funds.

"So no one could access those funds until his laptop is decoded?"

"Right, and some of the top computer experts have so far been unable to do it. Which is how I got the Muisca raft. Hold on...." He took it out of his pack and showed it to her, pointing out the hole in the base where the zipa figure had snapped off. "That's where the map was."

"Whoa, maybe don't flash it too much around here," she said, noting the hoards of passerby intermingling to look at the valley below, heading both into and out of town.

"Right. Just want to show you really quick. So obviously, CEO Tyler Harding was very into El Dorado. His laptop also supposedly contains gold ETFs, or Exchange Traded Funds."

"That's where you don't own the physical gold but just trade shares of it like stocks as the underlying spot price of an ounce of gold rises and falls?"

He gave her an admiring stare. "Exactly. So Tyler Harding supposedly has millions of dollars worth of those, as well as the bitcoin, on his encrypted laptop that nobody knows how to access after his sudden death in a hang gliding accident. But the point being, he was really into the El Dorado myth."

Maddy tapped him on the shoulder and pointed down to the newly terraformed valley, where a cloud of dust still hovered over the rain forest. "Myth?"

Hunt smiled. "Right, well at that time El Dorado was the same for him as everyone else—an unfound treasure that might be nothing more than a myth. And he was really into it. Obviously, he liked gold, he had a whole lot of those ETFs. And he had an entire collection of pre-Columbian treasures from the Muisca, Aztecs, Maya and Incas. I think he just felt it connected him more deeply to the myth. And then he acquired *this* from whoever stole it out of the caves." He tilted the little Muisca raft in her direction before shielding it from view with his hands.

Up ahead, Graham and Jayden were discussing the finer points of different automatic weapon functions and which they preferred. Hunt fell into a contemplative silence, staring at the Muisca raft while walking, but Maddy knew he had checked out of the conversation for now and didn't interrupt his thoughts. She looked over at him every now and then to see him pointing his finger repeatedly at the various golden spires atop the tribal figures, as if counting them, but she didn't inquire as to what he was doing.

A few miles later an open bed work truck slowed for a bend in the road. An elderly Colombian man sat behind the wheel, with two younger local men next to him in the cab. "Sorry, friends, no room in back or we'd give you a ride to Pasca," he said in accented English.

Jayden eyed the stack of chicken coops in the back and had an idea. He held up a finger and took off his pack. The driver watched him closely while he ripped through it and pulled something out. Jayden held up the chunk of emerald he'd found in the cave system.

"What if I gave you this, and in return you leave the chickens here on the road." He waved at the other vehicles and foot traffic. "Other people will take them and put them to good use, I'm sure."

The old man lifted a pair of reading glasses on a retainer cord around his neck to his eyes and beckoned for Jayden to show him the stone. Jayden dropped it right into his hand. The old man inspected it for all of two seconds before turning to his companions and telling them to unload the chickens. They exited the cab and climbed into the truck bed, where they proceeded to hand the crates down to Hunt, Graham and Jayden, who placed them on the side of the road. They waved to passerby, telling them in Spanish and English that the chickens were free. By the time all of the crates were unloaded and Omega Team had hopped into the truck bed, people were pulling over to pick up the first crates or simply walking away with one.

The driver's companions smiled at Jayden and got back into the cab, and the driver pulled back out onto the road. They bounced along the dirt road towards the village, and after a while settled into a quiet state, reclining on their backpacks and bedrolls. Even here, Hunt stared at the Muisca raft, refusing to put it away.

"You okay?" Maddy asked him when they got closer to town. "You thinking abut the big version of it that we left down there?"

Hunt looked up from the artwork and smiled at her. "Not really, no. I'm thinking about this one right here, because this is the same exact one that Harding had access to. I mean, he had it in his possession, could hold it and look at it whenever he wanted, so this is the one that represented El Dorado to him."

"And now to you, since it's yours."

"Actually, like you said, the big one down there is the one that will always symbolize it for me. But Harding never saw that one. So this is the one he would have connected most strongly with the legend."

She gazed at him for a moment, eyes expressing concern. "Why is it you care about how he would have connected to the legend? Wasn't he one of those wealthy private collectors you're trying to keep these types of artifacts away from?"

The truck lurched in and out of a pothole, causing Hunt to fumble the statue in his hands He put the Muisca raft back into his pack. "I feel like gold is the key with this guy. Gives me an idea." Hunt rummaged through his pack until he found his satellite phone. He powered on the device and placed a call.

"Kelsey? Hey, glad to reach you. The noise? Oh, squeaky truck wheels bouncing on a dirt road. Long story. Yes, we're safe. Still in country but on the way back to the States now. Listen up, I've got an idea, kind of a longshot, but something I want you to work on until we get back…."

As they rode along toward town and Hunt continued his conversation with Omega's new technology specialist, Maddy couldn't help but be drawn to the conversation, watching Hunt as his fingers traced different parts of the Muisca raft while he spoke. By the time the old truck had jostled its way into the outskirts of town, where rows of shacks lined the dirt roads and numerous vendors offered various street food for sale, her mouth had dropped wide open, and not due to the scenery.

EPILOGUE

Hidden Hills, California
One week later

Carter Hunt flipped a couple of steaks on his grill and added more seasoning. He'd been entertaining Dr. Madison Chambers in his backyard, doing nothing but relaxing and not talking about work. The sun would set soon, and it was a warm, dry evening in Southern California. The stream bed in his backyard, which only sometimes ran with water, was currently dry. A red-tailed hawk wheeled over the property, taking advantage of the dying light to begin its hunt.

The days following their return home to the States were surreal, spent watching the news reports of the "seismic event" that triggered a landslide of a mountain in Colombia. No specific mention of El Dorado was made, only that the region was known for its pristine, old growth rain forest and that it remains a "region of long-standing cultural significance."

Hunt monitored a bevy of sources, both local to the Pasca region as well as among the worldwide archaeological community, and he heard no reports of stunning Muisca relics or massive underground gold ore deposits. It occurred to him that Daedalus wouldn't want to mention it for fear of drawing attention to the spot, which could bring authorities. He probably had designs on visiting the area later to see if any of what they saw might be recovered later. Hunt laughed to himself at that thought, at the tons and tons of rock now covering the underground golden lair. As a result, Hunt was satisfied that, for now at least, the legendary El Dorado was safely buried, literally and figuratively.

The Omega founder had learned through a combination of local news reports and hospital inquiries that Daedalus and Phillipo had been discharged a couple of days earlier after they were administered an antidote for the golden frog poison. Both were told they were lucky to have survived the experience and cautioned about entering the rain forest without a local guide. He didn't think for a second that their near-death experience would give them pause when it came to plucking sacred artifacts from their resting places in order to sell them for their own gain. But it might make them think when it came to directly interfering with Omega Team again. Time will tell, Hunt thought, while he watched Maddy across the yard as she checked her work emails on her phone.

He had asked her to join Omega full-time before, and she had turned him down then. He didn't think her answer would be any different now should he ask her again. Her academic career was too important to her. He admired that she went along on his adventures whenever she could, primarily to learn about whatever culture they were investigating, to gain new perspectives that she might be able to incorporate into her professional arsenal, not for the sake of treasure hunting itself. Or maybe because she just wants to spend time with me, he thought, looking over at her across the yard.

Overall, Hunt was pleased with the mission to Colombia. Yes, it had been expensive. He'd already paid the aviation company for the loss of their helicopter. It had been a tense moment, with them threatening to have him detained by *policia,* his passport confiscated until he paid up, but Hunt had taken care of it immediately with a wire transfer, and the same company actually rented him another chopper the next day, which Graham had used to fly them to El Dorado International where they'd caught a commercial flight back to the States. Hunt, Maddy, and Jayden had flown to Los

Angeles, while Graham returned home to New York. Thanks to his new job working for Omega, he was able to take care of his own debt and free his airplane from hock the legal way. He told Hunt he'd be flying a crop-duster until he needed him, and that he hoped that day would be sooner rather than later.

Hunt was just about to flip the steaks again when his cell-phone chimed. Glancing at the screen he saw it was Kelsey Pawar, his new technology hire. She had done as requested of her thus far, but not being part of the field team, he had not been able to establish a real working bond with her yet, which he regretted. Hunt hastily flipped the steaks again and turned the heat down on the grill. Then he answered the call.

"Carter, I've got two things. One, and this is minor, but you did ask me to have the map analyzed by your lab, so I did that."

"Okay, and?"

"Nothing earth-shattering, but the paper was carbon dated to be about 3,000 years old, putting it in the ballpark for something the Muisca people could have used. Also, the type of tree used to make the scroll itself was DNA tested and confirmed to be that of the mahogany tree, which is found in the Colombian high-altitude rain forests where you were exploring."

Carter nodded to himself, mentally picturing the one he had climbed to find a sniper perch on the mountain. "Okay. Good to know, thank you for doing that. And the other thing?"

He heard her let loose a sort of sigh, and he thought she might be about to tell him she had to quit OMEGA already to pursue other things. "I've got it! I'm in! I can't believe it, but it worked!"

Even though she wasn't on speaker, her voice was so loud and exuberant that even Maddy turned her head from across the yard.

"Wait, you're in what?"

"Tyler Harding's laptop!"

It was Carter's turn to produce a confused noise out of his mouth. "Wait, they already gave you his actual laptop?"

"No, it's a mirror, like a simulation that if it works, will also work on the real deal. Just to let people work with it. And I've been playing with it and finally got it!"

"You mean, you decrypted Tyler Harding's laptop?"

"I have to tell them I did it, and like I said, this is a simulation, not the actual laptop, but it should work. I broke the encryption, which is supposed to be identical. All I did was use a text to hex converter on the characteristics of the Muisca raft. I tried hundreds of variations, but when you said there were nine figures on the raft, I decided to work with that and ultimately I came up with: 'Muisca9Zipa', in hexadecimal format which is a long string…."

Carter saw a text message flash up on his phone screen with the characters:

4d7569736361397a697061

"You're saying this is the string that is the decryption key for Tyler Harding's infamous laptop that has all his Bitcoin on it?"

"Yes! The same one that they offered a ten million dollar reward for anyone who could crack it. We did it, Carter, we did it!"

Hunt could smell the steaks starting to burn but his feet were frozen to the ground. In his mind's eye he pictured the massive golden figures of the giant raft, probably still floating down the underground river even now, nine golden figures including the Zipa, following a course set for them over three thousand years ago. And now it would seem that they've unlocked a modern day treasure. It was enough to make his head spin.

"Carter?" The voice was not Kelsey's but Maddy, who had walked over to the grill. "Everything all right?"

He nodded to her and said, "It's Kelsey, our new technical person. She says she was able to decrypt Harding's laptop using hex code based on information about the Muisca raft."

"That's remarkable!"

"Carter?" This time it was Kelsey's voice, from the phone.

"Sorry, Kelsey. I'm just…a little stunned, is all. Honestly, I didn't think it would really work."

"Oh it worked all right. I've already sent the solution to Harding's estate. Carter, you're going to get ten million dollars! I know it's not El Dorado, but…"

"I knew I made the right choice in hiring you," Hunt said, now eyeing the grill and Maddy. "Kelsey, I'm going to let you go and follow up on this. I'll check in on the matter first thing in the morning. Congratulations, and we thank you for all your hard work. Start making a wish list of your dream equipment, because One: you're getting a raise, and Two: going forward I want you to have whatever you think you might need in order to further our cause and keep us all safe and secure. El Dorado may be under control, but cultural treasures are still being plundered around the world as we speak. Let's use this windfall for good."

"Thank you, Mr. Hunt. I will make a list of that equipment, but I want you to know that I'm doing this for the same reason you are. You remember the mosque rom my hometown in India I told you about?"

"I do."

"It keeps me fighting the good fight." Kelsey then went on to thank him profusely and assured him she would stay in contact with Harding's estate before ending the call. Hunt pocketed his phone and turned to Maddy, putting his arms around her waist.

"Ten million dollars."

She smiled and shook her head slowly. "You are amazing, Carter Hunt."

"No, you're the real treasure, Dr. Chambers."

The two kissed while embracing and then watched the sun sink low over the California hills, bathing them in a fiery golden light.

THE END

Sign up for Rick Chesler's mailing list to be informed of new releases: **www.rickchesler.com/contact**

If you enjoyed GOLDEN ONE, you might also enjoy the following novels by **Rick Chesler:**

ATLANTIS GOLD (Omega Files Book 1)

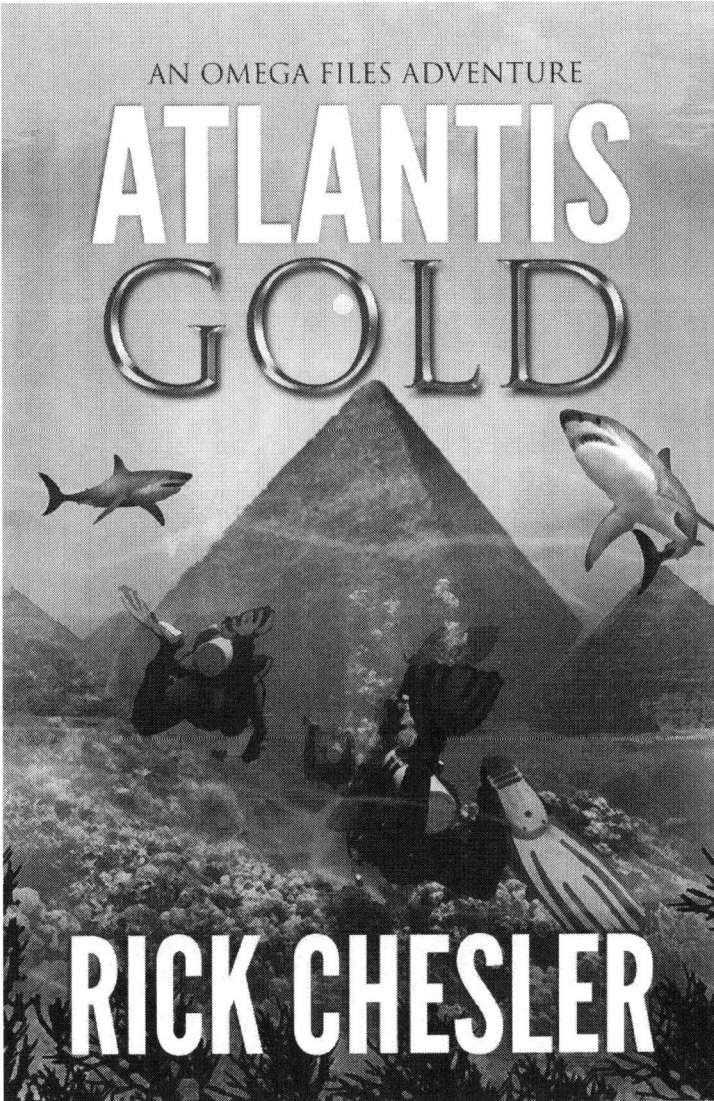

AN OMEGA FILES ADVENTURE

ATLANTIS GOLD

RICK CHESLER

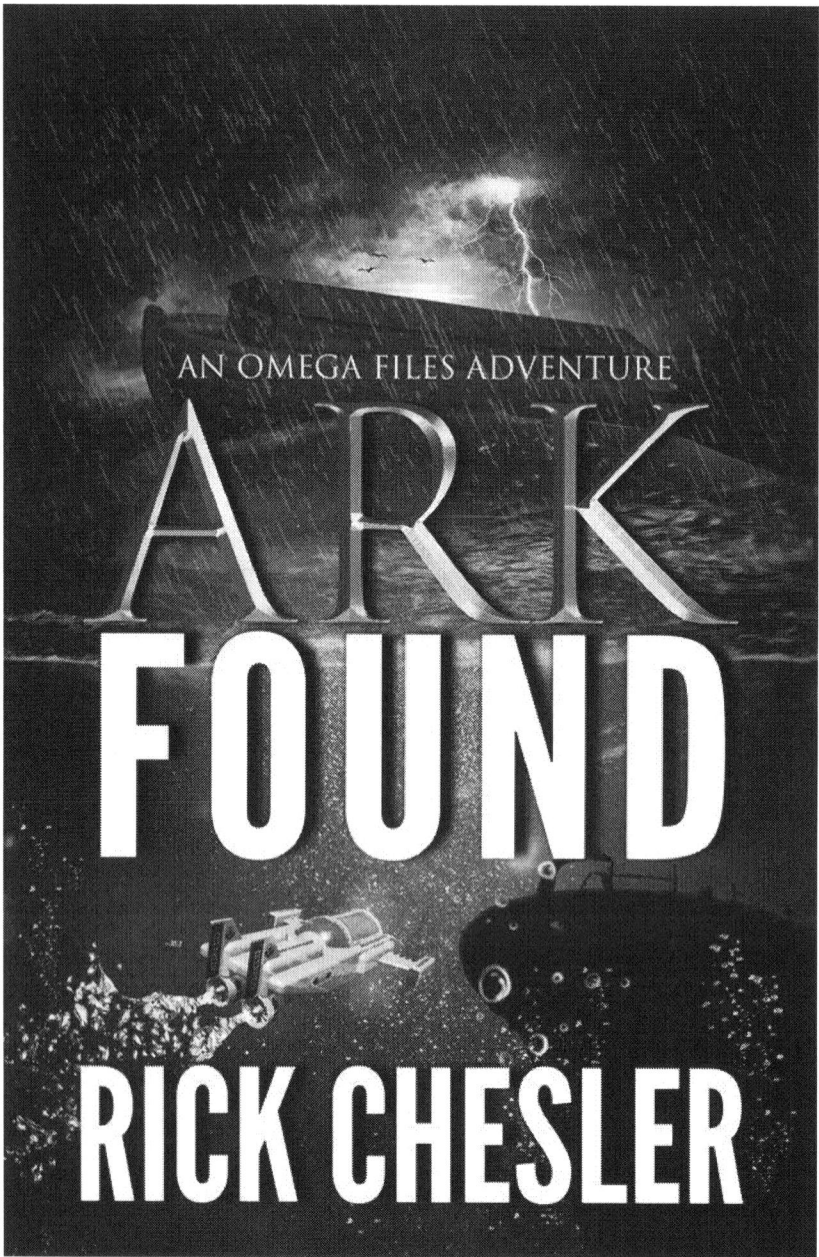

AN OMEGA FILES ADVENTURE

ARK FOUND

RICK CHESLER

UNCONTACTED

**TWO PRIMITIVE TRIBES LIVING HALF A WORLD APART.
ONE GUARDED REVELATION THAT WAS NEVER
MEANT TO BE SEEN.
AND A CALAMITY ABOUT TO BE UNLEASHED.**

In the jungle cities of the Amazon, thousands of tribal descendants suddenly drop dead at the exact same moment for no apparent reason. Strange truths start to emerge that lead respected ecologist, Antonio Medina, into the deepest reaches of the rain forest, to a tribe that has seen virtually zero contact with the outside world.

MANUSCRIPT 512

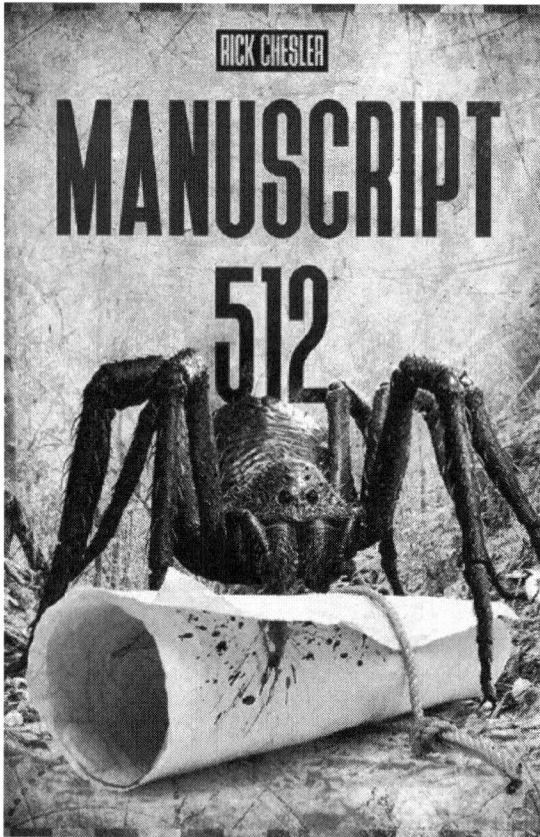

For centuries, would-be explorers have examined a document written in 1753 rumored to hold the key to locating the so-called Lost City of Z, a fortified settlement containing many treasures and built entirely of gold. Thought to be buried somewhere within the Mato Grosso region of the Amazon rainforest, the lure of the vanished riches has long proven deadly to treasure-seekers who brave the forbidding wilderness and mysterious creatures in search of it.

OUTCAST Ops: The Poseidon Initiative

During a terrifying break-in at a marine laboratory, a European-North African terror group makes off with a large quantity of deadly nerve agent. Demands are made and large-scale attacks are launched in the United States from coast to coast. Enter OUTCAST (Operational Undertaking To Counteract Active Stateside Threats)--six ex-operatives from six of America's most powerful organizations. When the President of the United States becomes a target of the terror group while hosting a party on his yacht, OUTCAST is hell-bent on showing America that their way isn't the best way--it's the only way.

Manufactured by Amazon.ca
Bolton, ON